Why start something that's only going to be temporary?

Beatrice's earlier remark about having an affair unwittingly penetrated his thoughts, and he realized he wasn't all that surprised by her attitude on the subject. Sure, she'd admitted that she'd been a bit boy-focused since her kindergarten days and she'd had plenty of boyfriends over the years. Yet it was plain to Kipp that "friends" was all the young men had meant to her. He figured most of the men she'd dated had never gotten past kissing her. And the others? Well, he didn't much want to picture her having sex with any man. But oddly enough, it was easy for him to picture himself undressing her, laying her back on a soft bed and kissing every inch of her body before he claimed her.

Damn, Kipp. Before you climbed into this truck early this morning, you were a man with a fair amount of common sense. Being cooped up with Beatrice for a few hundred miles has warped your brain. Sex with this honey-blonde beauty is out of the question for you. Tonight, tomorrow or ever!

"You did promise to take care of me on this trip. So, I trust you."

Her voice interrupted the mocking words of warning going off in his head, and he took his eyes off the road just long enough to glance at her face. The impish expression had him wishing he could safely stop the truck on the side of the highway and pull her into his arms.

Dear Reader,

When Kipp Starr goes to Stone Creek Ranch to visit his sister Clementine, he isn't expecting to be corralled into making a three-day road trip with Beatrice Hollister. How can he survive being cooped up with the chatty blonde for hours on end? Especially when her smiles make him forget the ten-year age gap between them, the fact that she's a ranching heiress and he's nothing but a cowhand. Even if he was in the market for romance, the two of them together would never work.

Beatrice is thrilled when she learns she's going to be traveling with Kipp to meet her estranged grandmother. The hunky cowboy is everything she wants in a man. Unfortunately, he's not interested in having a woman in his life on a permanent basis. Still, she tells herself a lot can happen between Beaver, Utah, and Burley, Idaho. Especially with a snowstorm growing worse with each passing mile. Given a little extra time with the man, she might just convince him that they're destined to be together.

I hope you get as much pleasure reading about Beatrice and Kipp's journey to finding love as I did in writing it.

God bless the trails you ride,

Stella

The Cowboy's Road Trip

—

STELLA BAGWELL

HARLEQUIN
SPECIAL
EDITION

HARLEQUIN®
SPECIAL EDITION™

Recycling programs for this product may not exist in your area.

ISBN-13: 978-1-335-59454-9

The Cowboy's Road Trip

Copyright © 2024 by Stella Bagwell

For questions and comments about the quality of this book, please contact us at CustomerService@Harlequin.com.

Harlequin Enterprises ULC
22 Adelaide St. West, 41st Floor
Toronto, Ontario M5H 4E3, Canada
www.Harlequin.com

Printed in U.S.A.

After writing more than one hundred books for Harlequin, **Stella Bagwell** still finds writing about two people discovering everlasting love very rewarding. She loves all things Western and has been married to her own real cowboy for fifty-one years. Living on the south Texas coast, she also enjoys being outdoors and helping her husband care for the animals on the small ranch they call home. The couple has one son, who teaches high school mathematics and coaches football and powerlifting.

Books by Stella Bagwell

Harlequin Special Edition

Men of the West

Her Kind of Doctor
The Arizona Lawman
Her Man on Three Rivers Ranch
A Ranger for Christmas
His Texas Runaway
Home to Blue Stallion Ranch
The Rancher's Best Gift
Her Man Behind the Badge
His Forever Texas Rose
The Baby That Binds Them
Sleigh Ride with the Rancher
The Wrangler Rides Again
The Other Hollister Man
Rancher to the Rescue
The Cowboy's Road Trip

Montana Mavericks: Lassoing Love

The Maverick's Sweetest Choice

Visit the Author Profile page
at Harlequin.com for more titles.

To all the road trips I've taken with my family
and the memories we made together.

Chapter One

"Dad, are you serious? You want me to make the trip to Idaho?"

Beatrice Hollister stared in astonishment at her father. Hadley was the family patriarch and owner of Stone Creek Ranch, the only home she'd known for the entire twenty-six years of her life. Now as he sat behind the wide cherrywood desk, eyeing her with an indulgent look, she had to wonder, what had come over him? Out of his eight children, he'd never chosen Beatrice to deal with a family matter, especially one that would require her to travel hundreds of miles away from home!

"I don't understand why you're so surprised, Bea," he said. "Ever since your brother Jack made the trip down to Arizona to meet our distant relatives, you've been complaining how you never get to go anywhere or help tend to family business. I thought you'd be jumping for joy over the idea of traveling up to Coeur d'Alene. Do you not want to go?"

His eyes narrowed as he asked the question and Beatrice fought the urge to squirm in her seat. Hadley had always been a loving father, but no one in the family would deny that the tall, burly man could be intimidating at times. Especially if his patience was tested. This was one time Beatrice didn't want to test it.

"Of course I want to go, Dad! You've taken me by surprise, that's all. I never expected you to trust me with this important meeting with Scarlett. After all, she might be the key to finding the missing branches of the Hollister family tree."

Even as she said the words, her mind was whirling. If everything went as planned, she was going to see her grandmother. A woman she'd never met and had only seen in one grainy black-and-white photo taken sixty years ago. Beatrice hadn't yet had time to consider how she felt about coming face-to-face with a relative who'd been estranged from the family for more than fifty years. She'd worry about that detail later. At the moment, all that mattered was the trip itself and the fact that her father had chosen her for the important task. Usually, he turned this sort of assignment over to her older brothers.

His expression wry, he said, "Just because you're not a bookworm like your twin sister hardly means your mother and I think of you as an airhead."

Her father's description caused her to chuckle. "I'm relieved to hear my parents don't think I'm empty-headed. But in the smarts department, Bonnie is a hard act to follow. Between the two of us, she got most of the brains. But I hardly feel bad about that. She has the most brains than any of your eight kids."

He shook his head. "You got plenty of brains, too, Bea. Your problem is that you don't use them to their full extent."

Beatrice didn't have to wonder what her father's remark meant. Both her parents believed she was wasting her college degree in fashion design by working as a clerk in a women's boutique in Beaver, Utah, a town with a population of less than four thousand and only a thirty-minute drive from the family ranch. Neither her mother nor her father really understood that she wasn't ready to take on a more demanding job. She made a decent salary at Canyon Corral and she loved her job. For now, she was perfectly content.

His broad shoulders settled back against the leather executive chair. "I imagine you've been wondering why I'm not going to make the trip to Idaho myself. After all, Scarlett is the woman who gave birth to me and my two brothers."

The notion had crossed Beatrice's mind. But considering the circumstances, she wasn't surprised her father had declined to face the mother who'd chosen to desert him and his siblings when they were very small boys.

"To be honest, Dad, I'm glad you're not making the trip to Coeur d'Alene."

He made a sound that was somewhere between a snort and a laugh. "Why? So you can make it for me?"

She gave him a sheepish smile. "Okay, I am excited about going. But I'd hate for you to be—well, hurt. Seeing Scarlett wouldn't be easy for you."

His expression solemn, he absently tapped his fingers on the desktop. "That's kind of you, sweetheart, to consider my feelings. But I think you and your siblings understand that I've never thought of Scarlett as my mother. To me, she's only a shadowy image of a woman who clearly made my father miserable. Or maybe he made her life unbearable—none of us really know why their marriage imploded. I'd be lying, though, if I said I haven't wondered about her and why she left Lionel.

After all, they made three sons together. There had to have been something between them."

Obviously. Something like lust, Beatrice thought. The physical attraction between her grandparents must have run mighty hot for a while.

Curious at her father's choice of words, she said, "You just implied that she's the one who left Grandfather. I've never heard you say that before. Is that the way things actually happened? Scarlett divorced Lionel? Or was it the other way around?"

Shaking his head, Hadley shrugged. "I don't really know the truth about who initiated their divorce. You know how your grandfather was about his past. What little he ever mentioned about Scarlett was always bitter. But he never explained why the split between them occurred or why she basically disappeared afterward."

And since Lionel had passed away several years ago, they'd never get the truth of the matter from him, Beatrice thought sadly. "Well, let's just hope Scarlett is willing to talk about her late ex-husband. Otherwise, you're going to be wasting your money sending me all the way to northern Idaho."

He swatted the air with one big hand. "No matter what Scarlett agrees to say, the trip will be worth it, Bea. Learning that she's still living and locating her is bound to lead us closer to information we need about my father—your grandfather."

For nearly two years, the family had been trying to uncover background information about Lionel Hollister. Particularly, evidence of his birth taking place in Utah. But so far they'd had no luck. Reaching out to Lionel's ex-wife seemed like a long shot to Beatrice. But if her father was willing to take the chance, she wasn't about to be the one to dampen his hopes.

She shot him an optimistic smile. "I hope you're right, Dad."

"You couldn't hope it any more than I do, honey," he said, then added, "Now, I imagine you're wondering about the details. How you're going to get there and that sort of thing."

Nodding eagerly, she said, "I am. Will I be driving? I hope so. It'll give me a chance to see the countryside."

He chuckled. "And do some shopping along the way? Well, don't worry. You're going to be driving. That is, if I can persuade someone to be your traveling companion."

Beatrice instantly scooted to the edge of her chair. "Traveling companion? Dad, I don't want—"

Her words broke off as a knock sounded on the closed door of her father's small office.

"Hopefully that's him right now. So try to be on your best behavior, Bea," Hadley said to her. Then, in a louder voice, he called to the person at the door. "Come in."

Beatrice looked over her shoulder and her mouth promptly fell open as she recognized the rugged cowboy walking into the room.

Kipp Starr!

Her father wanted *him* to be her traveling companion? Surely not! She'd only met the man a few days ago!

He took a few steps into the room, then pushed back the cuff of his denim shirt to glance at his watch. "Oh. You have company. Am I early? You did say one?"

Smiling, Hadley was quick to assure him. "You're right on time, Kipp. Come in and have a seat, and I'll explain what I wanted to speak with you about."

Beatrice watched the Idaho rancher lift off his black Stetson and, holding it in one hand, ease his lanky frame into the wooden chair sitting at an angle to her right. From the first moment she laid eyes on the man, she'd dubbed him as one hot stud. Tall, with long legs and broad shoulders, he was every inch a man. And when you added the muscular body to his chiseled features that were dominated by a pair of warm brown eyes and a layer of three-day-old whiskers, he made the perfect image of a saddle tramp riding straight out of the 1880s. Tough, rough and oh, so sexy.

Kipp had come to Stone Creek Ranch a few days ago to visit his sister, Clementine, who'd just gotten engaged to Beatrice's brother Quint. And because he'd arrived so near to Christmas and had no family or parents of his own, her parents had convinced him to stay on through the holiday. Beatrice couldn't deny she was drawn to Kipp. But this was one time in her life she'd not openly expressed her attraction for a man. Mainly because she had the horrible suspicion that if Kipp knew she was darn close to developing a crush on him, he'd laugh right in her face.

Hadley said to Kipp, "I know you and Quint are going out to look at some of the pregnant ewes this afternoon, so I'll get right to the point and not keep you long. When were you planning on going back home to Idaho?"

Beatrice felt her cheeks grow warm as Kipp glanced uncertainly at her, then back to Hadley.

"Monday morning," he answered. "That is, if the weather is permitting flights out of Cedar City. I'm hearing a winter storm might be bringing snow. Hopefully I'll be back at the ranch before it hits."

Hadley thoughtfully stroked his chin. "Have you purchased your plane ticket yet?"

He shook his head. "Bonnie offered to do it for me, but I haven't yet told her what day to make the flight for."

"Good. That will save her having to cancel the ticket."

"Cancel?" Kipp repeated the word with a blank look. "I don't understand, Hadley. I—uh, I've enjoyed my time here on Stone Creek, but I promised the foreman I'd be back to the Rising Starr this coming week."

"I realize you have obligations," Hadley told him. "And as much as we'd love for you to stay, we understand that you need to get back. But I'm suggesting a different mode of transportation. That is, if you'd be willing to put up with Beatrice for two days or so."

Kipp slowly turned his head to look directly at her and Beatrice was shocked to feel her cheeks growing hot. What was wrong with her, anyway? She'd always felt comfortable around men. Even sexy hunks like Kipp Starr. In fact, her family often called her man crazy. So why was she suddenly feeling tongue-tied in front of this cowboy?

"Are you going to Idaho?" Kipp asked her.

She forced herself to breathe. "Dad is sending me up to Coeur d'Alene."

A faint frown pulled his dark brows together. "Oh. That's in the northern part of the state. I live in the southern area."

"Yes, Clementine has told us that the Rising Starr Ranch is located near Burley," Hadley said quickly. "So I do understand Coeur d'Alene is a good distance out of your way. But I don't want Beatrice traveling alone. And since you're headed back to Idaho, I thought you might be willing to accompany her up to Coeur d'Alene. She could drop you back by your ranch when she heads back home. That way she'd only have to make the drive from Burley back here to Stone Creek Ranch by herself."

"Which I can certainly do." Beatrice spoke up firmly. "In fact, Dad, I honestly don't know why you think I need anyone with me on this trip. I'm perfectly capable of handling the drive by myself."

Hadley leveled a look at her that said if she didn't quiet down, he'd gently usher her out of the room.

"You have two choices, Bea," Hadley said flatly. "Travel with Kipp or stay here."

Beatrice argued, "But Kipp might not want to make such a huge, unnecessary loop of driving around the state."

Hadley turned his attention to Kipp. "Don't hesitate to tell me if you're not up to this, Kipp. I won't hold it against you. Nor will Bea's mother, Claire. But just so you know, we don't expect you to do this out of the goodness of your heart. I intend to pay you a nice sum for your time and effort."

Beatrice wished she could slink off and never have to face Kipp Starr again. If it took money to persuade the man to join her on a three-day trip, then she'd rather not go at all, she thought.

Liar. Liar. Just the thought of spending three whole days in Kipp's company has you feeling like you could fly over the moon. No matter if your dad has to coerce him into making the trip.

The taunting voice going off in her head very nearly drowned out Kipp's reply.

"I'd never accept your money, Hadley. You and Claire have been such gracious hosts while I've been staying here. If accompanying Beatrice will help you out, then I'm more than glad to make the trip with her." He shrugged one shoulder. "Besides, I have to get back to Idaho one way or the other. And I've never been fond of plane rides."

Hadley gave him a grateful smile, while a strange mixture of joy and relief washed through Beatrice. Kipp would be making the trip with her! She wanted to jump to her feet and do a joyous jig. But she'd reserve that happy reaction for when she raced upstairs to give her twin sister the fabulous news.

Glad to make the trip with her.

Hell, when did he get so good at lying? The last thing Kipp wanted was to be cooped up in a vehicle with a chatty blonde ten years his junior.

Not that he didn't like Beatrice. He did like her. What little time he'd spent around her, he'd found her friendly and sweet and oftentimes funny. But a man could take just so much sweetness. And so much temptation, he thought grimly. Whether he wanted to admit it or not, there was something very provocative about Beatrice Hollister. Something that pulled at him every time he was near her.

"You've made me one happy father," Hadley said to him. "I won't worry knowing that Beatrice is in your capable hands."

The man's trust in him made Kipp feel like a heel. If Hadley were to guess some of the carnal thoughts that ran through Kipp's head whenever he looked at Beatrice, he would've already sent him packing. He certainly wouldn't ask him to chaperone her on a long driving trip.

He cleared his throat and refrained from glancing

in Beatrice's direction. Not that he needed a second glance to remind him just how fresh and pretty she looked sitting in the wooden chair. With her long hair flowing down her back in a cascade of golden waves, her blue eyes smudged with just enough smoky color to give them a smoldering look, and her full lips the color of pink cotton candy, even the briefest look at her was more than enough to play on a man's senses. Not to mention his libido.

"I'll do my best to see that she gets to Coeur d'Alene safely, Hadley," Kipp said to the rancher, then asked, "When did you plan for Beatrice to be leaving? Does she have to be in Coeur d'Alene on a certain day or time?"

"That's the easy part of the situation, Kipp. Doesn't matter exactly when Bea gets there. She has a two-week vacation coming that she hasn't yet started. So she can follow any timetable that suits you. If you're aiming to be back on your ranch on Monday, then you might need to leave a day or two earlier to make up for more traveling time."

"Right." He glanced over at Beatrice to see she was looking directly at him. A faint smile curved the corners of her lips and he found himself focusing on the soft, plump curves and wondering how it might feel to kiss them. Damn it.

"Can you be ready to leave in the morning? Or is that too soon?" Kipp asked her.

Her eyes widened a fraction. "Certainly. I'll pack tonight."

"Then it's all set," Hadley said with approval. "I'll have one of the hands make sure Bea's truck is ready to travel. And I'll leave it up to you, Kipp, to route the drive. I'm sure Bea will do her best to persuade you to stop at every fashion boutique you pass. But don't pay her any mind. Just remind her that the two of you aren't on a shopping trip."

Beatrice groaned. "Oh, Dad, you're going to have Kipp thinking all I do is spend money on frivolous things."

Hadley chuckled. "Don't you?"

"No! For your information, my savings account is growing!"

"How can that be? Only a few weeks ago you were asking to have your bedroom closet enlarged."

Her father was clearly teasing her, but Kipp could hear a flash of annoyance in the tone of her voice. Apparently she didn't appreciate Hadley painting her as superficial.

"Dad, you know very well that Bonnie and I share a bedroom, a closet and most of our clothes."

"Yes, and just about everything else," he said with an impish grin at his daughter. "Except boyfriends."

"Thank goodness. I'd be bored out of my mind if I went out with a man of Bonnie's choosing!" she exclaimed, then suddenly seeming to remember Kipp was present, she looked over at him. "Sorry, Kipp. All of this nonsense has to be boring you. Just rest assured that I won't be asking you to stop for any shopping sprees. I'll do all my shopping after I leave you at Rising Starr Ranch."

Since Kipp had arrived on Stone Creek Ranch, he'd spent most of the time out with the men doing ranching chores with the Hollister brothers and the ranch hands. But even in the little time he'd passed in the house with the family, he'd quickly learned that Beatrice and her twin sister, Bonnie, were practically identical in looks, but far different in personalities. Bonnie, the elder of the two, was quiet and reserved in manner and dress, while Beatrice was outgoing and a bit flamboyant. Yet even with their differences, it was easy to see the two sisters were extremely close.

"I'm not worried, Bea." At least, Kipp's worries weren't about her wanting to stop and spend her daddy's money. No, he was more concerned about keeping his hands off her.

Hell, Kipp, what's the matter with you? You're not in the market for romance. Especially with a woman like Beatrice. Her head is filled with visions of love and happy-ever-after. She's not old enough to know how ugly things can get between a man and a woman. And you don't want to be the one to show her.

She gave him a cheery smile. "Thank you, Kipp. I promise to be on my best behavior."

Hadley let out a grunt of amusement. "When she says that, Kipp, you better watch her."

Kipp was wondering how to reply to Hadley's comment when the landline on the rancher's desk rang.

While he excused himself to answer the call, Kipp looked at Beatrice. "Considering how close you and Bonnie are, I would've thought she'd be joining you on this journey."

She shook her head. "Dad could never manage all the ranch's paperwork and phone calls without Bonnie handling things. And anyway, she's not keen on meeting new people. It makes her uncomfortable."

"I'm new and she doesn't appear uncomfortable around me," he reasoned.

"Yes. But you're—our kind. Dad is sending me up to Coeur d'Alene to meet Scarlett Hollister Wilson—

and she is considered a dragon lady by our family," she said with a frown.

Her explanation only planted more questions in his mind but he didn't voice them out loud. He figured the less he knew about the Hollisters' personal family matters, the better off he'd be. He had his own family dragon lady to worry about.

The click of the telephone receiver landing back in its cradle had Kipp glancing around to see Hadley had ended the call and was rising from his chair.

"You two will have to excuse me. Jack needs me over at the cattle barn," he explained. "If you have any more questions about the trip, Kipp, we can go over them tonight."

Kipp quickly rose to his feet. "At the moment, I can't think of anything. But if I do, I'll let you know," he told Hadley. "Uh, can I be of help over at the barn?" he offered.

"Thanks, Kipp. Nice of you to offer, but this isn't a manual job. Jack is dealing with a cattle buyer. The man wants the best for the least. You know how it is. I've got to go over there and be the ringmaster."

Yes, at one time Kipp had helped his father deal with cattle and sheep buyers. But those days were long gone. His father was dead and Kipp had no authority over any of the sales or purchases of livestock on the Rising Starr. It was a fact he tried not to dwell on, but most days the situation pushed itself into his thoughts anyway.

"Sure, Hadley. I'll catch you later."

He watched Hadley leave the room before he glanced over at Beatrice. "Well, I need to head on over to the ranch yard. Quint's probably waiting for me."

Smiling, she rose from the chair, and as she walked

over to him, he couldn't help but notice how her brown
suede skirt outlined the shape of her hips, while the
hem swirled at the top of her black knee-high boots. He
figured if the weather was warm, she'd be bare legged
with her feet encased in a pair of strappy sandals. But
with it being the middle of winter, he doubted he'd get
a glimpse of her legs, or for that matter, any bare skin.

She said, "Before you go, Kipp, I want to thank you.
I'm sure traveling hundreds of miles out of your way is
not necessarily what you want to do. But if you hadn't
agreed to make the trip, Dad would've made other plans.
And they wouldn't have included me."

"I wouldn't say that. I'm sure he could have found
someone to make the drive with you."

Strangely, the idea of Beatrice traveling with some
other guy didn't appeal to him, at all.

She shook her head. "Not likely. Maybe it's because
Bonnie and I are his youngest, but Dad is very protective
of us. Even though we're twenty-six, there are times he
still seems to think of us as teenagers. I think if you'd
refused to go, he would've probably gotten one of my
brothers to make the journey."

She smelled like wind and a rain-soaked flower garden,
and he found the scent as tempting as the upturned corners
of her lips.

"All your brothers are very busy men. I can't imagine
him sending any of them away," Kipp told her. "Unless
this trip to Idaho is super important to him."

One of her slender shoulders made a negligible shrug.
"Well, it's not a make-or-break thing for the ranch or
the family, but it is important to him. He's searching
for back history about his father and there's a woman

in Coeur d'Alene who might be able to provide it. I'm going to meet with her."

Frowning, he asked, "Can't he speak with her on the phone and save you all this traveling?"

She turned her gaze away from him to focus on a window at the opposite end of the room. The view exposed a portion of the backyard where a low rock wall was bordered with some sort of shrubs. Presently the plants were covered with gray tarps to protect them against the winter weather. Kipp figured the yard would look splendid in the warm summer months, but for now everything was dormant.

"Dad was told that for some reason, she won't take phone calls. She's elderly, you see, so maybe her hearing isn't good. Anyway, she does receive visitors. So here I am, headed to Idaho." She flashed him a smile. "With you."

With him. The two of them together. For miles and miles. He couldn't think of anything more torturous or tempting. "Sorry. I shouldn't have questioned the reason for the trip. It's really none of my business. Besides, I've been around Hadley long enough to see he doesn't do things on a whim. He has to have a reason."

She let out a soft little laugh and Kipp wished he could feel just a fraction of the humor and joy that Beatrice radiated. She was basically a happy person. He could see it in her eyes and the flash of her smile. If she'd ever experienced a broken heart or a huge disappointment, she'd obviously made a complete recovery.

"Dad thinks everything through," she told him. "Which tells me he feels comfortable with you being my—companion."

Resisting the urge to clear his throat, he said, "I'll do my best to get you up to Coeur d'Alene safely."

She stepped closer and surprised him by placing a hand on his forearm. The contact reminded him of a time he'd accidentally burned his arm on a branding iron. The scorching heat had shot all the way up to his shoulder. Beatrice's touch was equally fiery.

"Thank you, Kipp. And I'll do my best not to be a pest."

He could think of plenty of things she might be, but a pest wasn't one of them. "I'm sure you'll be a model traveler, Beatrice."

She said, "You've been here on the ranch for a few days now. Don't you think it's time you started calling me Bea?"

Her gaze met his, and as Kipp found himself looking into the blue depths of her eyes, he realized it was high time he made a quick exit from Hadley's office.

"Okay. Bea it is." Turning, he walked to the door. Then, with his hand on the knob, he glanced back at her. "See you later."

Smiling, she gave him a little wave, and Kipp hurried off with his mind spinning. He didn't know what he'd just gotten himself into. But he had a feeling nothing about the next two or three days was going to be easy.

Chapter Two

Once Kipp was out of sight, Beatrice raced down the hallway, then up the long staircase to where her sister's little office was located.

Bursting into the room, she then rushed over to the desk where Bonnie was just hanging up the phone.

"Sissy! Something incredible has just happened! You're not going to believe it!"

Bonnie calmly looked up at her. "Let me guess," she said in a bored tone. "Nick has asked you for a New Year's Eve date. And don't tell me—he probably has tickets to a rock concert."

Laughing, Beatrice bounced on her toes. "No! No! Nothing that predictable or boring! Besides, I've already put Nick in my rearview mirror. He's too stuck on himself," she explained, then gave her sister a wicked grin. "This is much better! This is stupendous!"

Leaning back in the desk chair, Bonnie eyed her with faint curiosity. "Okay. So why don't you tell me what *this* stupendous thing is?"

Holding her skirt to one side, Beatrice began to hum and waltz around the open area of the room. "I'm going on a trip to Idaho. And guess who's going with me?"

Clearly surprised, Bonnie stared at her. "Dad is sending you to Idaho to see Scarlett? Really?"

Beatrice halted her little dance and hurried back to her sister's desk. "Yes! Really! I just finished discussing the whole thing with Dad a few minutes ago. We'll be leaving in the morning. Isn't it wonderful?"

"Well, yes. I'm happy for you. You said *we*, so I'm assuming Mom is going with you. I can't think of anyone else available. Our brothers are weighed down with work obligations. Our sister is too busy doctoring half of Beaver County. And our sisters-in-law are tied up with their own jobs, with Van teaching at the high school and Maggie nursing at the hospital. That only leaves me, and I have to keep Dad's business dealings and the ranch's books in order."

Beatrice's grin turned smug. "You're right on all counts except one. Mom isn't going with me. I'm going to be traveling with Kipp Starr."

Bonnie wasn't easily surprised, but at this, her jaw dropped.

"Kipp? Is this one of your jokes?" she asked.

With a breathless little laugh, Beatrice plopped onto the edge of the chair in front of her sister's desk.

"I admit it does sound like one of my jokes, but this time I'm serious." She quickly explained how their father insisted she needed a traveling companion and then how Kipp had walked into the room. "I tell you, Bonnie, when Kipp agreed to join me on the drive, I nearly fell off my chair. To be honest, I'm still in a daze. I mean, he's soooo cute!"

"Cute? He looks dangerous to me. Like a cowboy who spends all his time hanging around either the branding fire or a bar on the rough side of town."

Beatrice sighed. "Exactly. That's what makes him so appealing."

Bonnie rolled her eyes and groaned. "Bea, would you quit swooning for a minute and think? Kipp lives hundreds of miles away from here. It would be senseless of you to fall for the guy."

Frowning, Beatrice shook her head. "Who said anything about falling for the man? My only plan is to enjoy his company until I drop him off on the Rising Starr Ranch."

Rolling her eyes for a second time, Bonnie said, "I'm sure that is your plan. But—well, Kipp isn't the sort of man you can play around with. He's much older than you. And obviously more experienced. I imagine he's left plenty of women crying into their pillows."

Beatrice groaned. "Oh, Bonnie, you sound like Mom trying to warn me off David Thompson. She was so afraid I would be silly enough to let him break my heart. I knew all along he was a cheater and no good."

With a shake of her head, Bonnie asked wryly, "If you knew he was no good, then why bother going out with him?"

Beatrice chuckled. "Because the guy was entertaining. All I ever expected from him was a few laughs."

"All I can say is that I hope you're not expecting anything like that from Kipp. He's clearly not the laughing sort. Or the falling-in-love sort."

Irritated by her sister's negative attitude, Beatrice frowned at her. "Why are you trying to rain on my parade, Bonnie? For the first time in my life, Dad has trusted me with a responsible task. I thought you'd be happy for me. Not give me a lecture on men! Especially when you're hardly an authority on them!"

Sighing, Bonnie rose from her chair and walked around

to stand in front of Beatrice. "In spite of what you're thinking, I'm happy that Dad is sending you on this mission to meet with Scarlett. And I'm sorry for lecturing you. It's just that I don't want you to get hurt."

Ashamed she'd made such a cutting remark to her sister, Beatrice closed her eyes and shook her head. After years of hiding in a shy shell, Bonnie had recently begun to blossom and become more sociable. More than anything, Beatrice wanted her sister to have a full, rounded life. She could only hope her dig wouldn't make Bonnie retreat back into herself. "Forgive me, sissy. I shouldn't have made that remark—it was a mean thing for me to say. I didn't really mean it. The little green envy guy was coming out in me."

Bonnie grunted with amusement. "You? Envious of me? Come on, Bea. You can do better than that."

Opening her eyes, Beatrice frowned at her sister's skeptical expression. "I'm serious. It was a stupid thing for me to say. You do know more about men than me."

Laughing now, Bonnie asked, "How could that be? You're the one who dates all the time. I'm the one who stays at home and watches the grass grow."

"It's winter," Beatrice drolly reminded her. "The grass is dead right now."

"You know what I mean."

Beatrice watched her sister walk over to a wide window with a northerly view. From this angle, one could see a portion of the old barn and corrals. A couple of miles beyond the old ranch yard stood a ridge of tall mountains covered with a mixture of evergreens and hardwood trees.

"I've not forgotten you're mostly a homebody, sis. But I think—you study people and can immediately see important characteristics about them that I don't notice.

Not until it's too late. That's why you have quality dates, whereas mine are a large quantity, that's all."

Her expression wry, Bonnie glanced at her. "Quality? You don't have to be nice about it, Bea. We both know that the most I can say about my dates is that I get home from them safely."

Beatrice couldn't help but chuckle. "I'm glad you're not angry. I wouldn't have wanted to leave in the morning thinking you were upset with me."

Leaving the window, Bonnie walked over to where Beatrice was still perched on the edge of the chair.

"Upset? Don't be silly. We've always said what we think to each other without worrying about one or both of us getting angry. That's never going to change with us. At least, it won't ever change with me." She curled her arm around Beatrice's shoulders and gave them a slight squeeze. "And I apologize, sissy, for raining on your parade. I admit I'd be much better off if I could be more like you and not analyze or worry over every little thing. And would you like to know what I really think about Kipp?"

"I'd love to know," Beatrice told her.

"Okay. I think that beneath all those tough good looks, Kipp is a nice guy."

Beatrice was a bit surprised by Bonnie's admission. Her sister didn't hand out "nice guy" compliments very often. She had to ask, "You honestly think so?"

Nodding, Bonnie said, "I do. But that hardly means he's incapable of breaking your heart."

"I hope I'm smart enough not to let that happen with Kipp or any man." She gave her sister a wry smile. "You know, I think I can safely say that neither of us has ever had our heart broken. At least, not from loving and losing a man."

Bonnie shook her head. "Not really. You and I have been disappointed a few times. But we've never been hurt like our sister, Grace, or brother Hunter."

"No. Or like our grandparents."

Stepping back, Bonnie studied her with a pensive frown. "Mom's parents had a long, loving marriage until they passed away. You must be talking about our paternal grandparents."

"I am. I was thinking about them earlier when Dad was talking to me about the trip to meet Scarlett. The way I see things, she must have been wildly in love with Grandfather to have given him three sons."

"I'm not seeing it. A woman doesn't have to be wildly in love with a man to give him children."

"Okay, maybe she wasn't crazy in love with Lionel, but she surely felt something to have married and had sex with him. And then something went terribly wrong between them and their marriage was over. Don't you imagine her heart was broken?"

"No. If she loved our grandfather that much, and their children were a reminder of that love, then she would've wanted to be with the sons they had together. Instead, she left and never came back or tried to contact anyone in the family."

"You're probably right, sissy. But it's so hard for me to believe any woman could be so heartless. Especially a woman who gave birth to our father," Beatrice said.

Bonnie shook her head. "Perhaps. But what about Grandfather? Don't you think he must've been heartbroken over the divorce?"

Beatrice rolled her eyes. "Grandfather? I'm not sure he had a heart. If he did, it was like a rock."

"Bea! That's a terrible thing to say! Yes, Lionel was gruff and strict, but I think he loved his family very much. He just had a hard time showing his soft side. And after Scarlett, that might have been his way of protecting his heart."

"Hmm. Well, I didn't realize just how very little we know about Lionel's personal life until this family relative thing with the Arizona Hollisters came up." Shaking her head, she said, "Not having any verification of his birth date is just a small part of the problem. Dad has no idea why his parents divorced or why his father refused to ever say his ex-wife's name, much less talk about her."

With a grim nod, Bonnie said, "It's sad, isn't it? Dad had to steal a photo of his mother from personal items Lionel believed he'd locked away from his little sons."

"It's worse than sad. Dad said if Lionel had ever discovered he had the photo, he would've probably taken a belt to his backside. Does that sound like a man who'd once loved a woman?"

"It sounds like a man full of bitterness to me," Bonnie said grimly. Then, struck by another thought, she looked at her sister. "Are you worried about meeting with Scarlett? To be honest, Bea, I'd be dreading the moment."

Shaking her head, Beatrice said, "All of that happened some fifty-five or more years ago. Hopefully, she's not still harboring ill feelings toward us Hollisters."

"Hmmp. I wouldn't count on it. Otherwise, she would've contacted her sons."

Beatrice eased up from the chair. "You're probably right," she admitted, then gave her sister a bright smile.

"But I'm not stressing over meeting the woman. At least, not now. The only thing I'm worried about is what am I going to wear tomorrow and what kind of clothes am I going to put in my suitcase for the rest of the trip."

Laughing, Bonnie looped an arm through hers. "Warm clothes. That's what you're going to take with you."

"Warm? How can I catch Kipp's attention if I'm dressed like I'm going to the Arctic Circle?"

Tugging on her arm, Bonnie said, "Come on. I'm not very busy right now. I'll help you choose some things."

"To make me look matronly?" Beatrice joked.

Bonnie laughed. "That would be impossible."

He had to relax, Kipp thought, as he steered the truck north on the busy interstate. He had to get his mind on the landscape whizzing by the windshield. He needed to concentrate on the weather, or the music coming from the radio—anything but the woman sitting next to him. Otherwise, he was going to have a meltdown before they made it to the Idaho state line, much less all the way up to Coeur d'Alene.

But how was a man supposed to ignore a sexy little minx sitting only an arm's length away? One that smelled like flowers and with a smile that sent an anxious dread crawling up his spine? From the moment she'd joined him in the kitchen early this morning, Kipp had realized he was in for a day of agony.

She was dressed in a pair of tight black jeans and a white sweater that clung to her pert little breasts. The clothing perfectly accentuated her petite curves and reminded him of just how long it had been since he'd held a woman like her in his arms.

Hell, who was he kidding? He'd never made love to

a woman like Beatrice. At one time he'd believed Evie was special. But she'd not had Beatrice's class or morals. She'd not had much of a heart, either, he thought grimly.

"…the weather app on my phone this morning. The forecast for this part of Utah said sunny. I think they got it wrong."

Beatrice's voice managed to break through his thoughts and he glanced over to see she was gazing intently out the windshield at the overhead sky. For the past several miles, high gray clouds had grown thick enough to blot out the early morning sun.

"Bad winter weather is on its way. But meteorologists are saying it shouldn't reach Idaho for a couple of days," he commented. "Let's hope they're right. I'm not a fan of driving on icy roads."

"When we get deep snow, Dad has the hands put chains on the truck so I can drive safely into work. But I hate driving with those things. They make traveling slow going. Besides making lots of noise."

"Slow and noisy is better than being stranded," he reasoned.

From the corner of his eye, he saw her gaze turn away from the windshield and land on him.

She said, "You sound like Dad. Always cautious."

Her remark had him wondering if he seemed like an old man to her. Probably, Kipp thought. Ten years was a substantial gap between their ages. Maybe if he kept reminding himself of the fact, he wouldn't be tempted to look at her as a desirable woman. But with her eyes reminding him of blue flames and her plush lips stained to the color of dark berries, all he could think about was tasting her smooth skin, pressing his mouth to hers.

He cleared his throat and focused on the high desert

landscape stretching away from the highway. "It pays to be careful."

"Yes. Careful about more than just driving," she murmured.

Was she talking about men now or life in general? he wondered. With her head turned toward the passenger window, it was impossible to see the expression on her face. Not that it would answer his questions. When he'd first met Beatrice, he'd thought she was an open book. Her cheerful demeanor didn't appear to hide anything. She had a zest for life and nothing seemed to worry her or dampen her mood. But the farther the two of them had driven away from Stone Creek Ranch and the more they'd talked, the more he was beginning to see there was another side of her. A thoughtful, perceptive side that, frankly, was far more dangerous than her tempting smiles.

He said, "It's a fairly long drive from Stone Creek Ranch to Beaver. Do you ever have to miss work because of snowy roads?"

She shook her head and his gaze was drawn to her hair. She'd pinned the top part of the golden waves back with a pair of sparkly white pins, while the bottom section rested loosely against her back. The strands were soft and shiny and he didn't have to ask if the color was natural. The infinite shades of pale corn silk graduating to the dark gold of an aspen leaf could never be produced at a beauty salon.

"About three years ago we were having blizzard conditions and the owner of the boutique closed for a couple of days," she told him. "Other than those days, I've never missed work. I love my job."

"Clem told me she visited Canyon Corral once. That

was the day she was waiting for Quint to decide whether he wanted to hire her or not. I think she was just killing time around town. You've probably already figured out that my sister isn't much of a shopper. But she did say she enjoyed the boutique. Quaint and unique is how she described it."

A wide smile tilted her lips. "I'll have to tell my boss. She'll love hearing Clem's comments. That's exactly what we strive for. Being unique."

"How long have you worked there?"

She looked at him. "About five years. Ever since I finished college in St. George and returned home to the ranch."

It didn't surprise Kipp that Beatrice had gone to college. Claire and Hadley were the type of parents who wouldn't necessarily demand that their children get a higher education, but he figured the couple would encourage each child to expand their learning so they'd have more opportunities for their careers.

"What did you study in college?"

She let out a low chuckle and Kipp wondered how the soft little laugh could be so provocative. It was the sound of wicked fun. Something he'd not experienced in years.

"The question always amuses me," she replied, "because Bonnie says my major was having fun. Which is sorta true. I did enjoy myself in college. But to answer your question, I graduated with a degree in fashion design."

He arched an inquisitive brow at her and she pulled an impish face at him. "Go ahead and groan if you'd like," she told him. "I realize it sounds ridiculous. Me, living way out in the country on a cattle-and-sheep ranch.

The town where I work has a population of maybe four thousand, and that's if you stretch it. You have to be wondering how I ever expect to put my degree to use. Well, you're not alone. My parents have also wondered about it. Especially since they footed the tuition bill."

He kept his eyes on the highway and the northbound traffic. "The only thing I'm wondering is what does a fashion designer do. Or maybe I should rephrase that and ask what you want to do as a fashion designer."

"Well, basically a fashion designer sketches designs of clothing and accessories like shoes or purses and things of that sort. Then picks out fabrics and materials to make everything and instructs the seamstress or company on exactly how they want everything constructed."

"Hmm. Sounds like you'd need to go to the city for a job of that type," he said.

"Right. I mean, I can sketch at home. And I have been working on a few designs in my spare time. But to really make a good living at such a job, then yes, I'd have to move away from Stone Creek Ranch, and I'm just not ready to do that—yet. I love living on the ranch with my family. And being with my twin—oh Lord, I can't imagine not being with Bonnie. We went through college together. We've never been separated for any length of time. She's like my right arm and I'm like her left."

Yes, these past few days Kipp had spent with the Hollisters, he'd noticed how very tight the twins were. Which was hardly a surprise. He'd gone to high school with a pair of male twins and they'd been virtually inseparable. After graduation one of them had entered the air force and the other had followed.

"I'm sure you're saying to yourself that I sound like

a juvenile. Well, I suppose I do still have some growing up to do," she said with a thoughtful tilt to her head. "And I probably need to move away from my twin to become more independent. Because, frankly, Bonnie is my leader. In case you couldn't tell, she's the eldest by eight minutes and the dominant twin. In size and intellect. She tries to make me think and I try to make her laugh. So we balance each other pretty well."

"To be honest, Bea, I can't see you moving away from Stone Creek for any reason. Unless you find a man that you want to marry and then your father will probably put him to work on the ranch so you won't have to leave."

She laughed softly. "Yes, I can see Dad doing that very thing. I don't have to tell you that Dad is very family oriented. Even this trip he's sending me on is primarily a family issue. But I'm a long way from getting married or even engaged. I don't even have a steady boyfriend. I kicked my latest one to the curb a couple of months ago."

"Why? He started to bore you?"

She turned a wide-eyed look on him. "Exactly! Wouldn't you be bored with a girl who was constantly checking her appearance in the mirror? Well, turn it around. Nick was stuck on himself."

Kipp couldn't help but grin. "I take it you didn't like his preening."

She sniffed with disdain. "I wanted to date a man, not a peacock."

Chuckling, Kipp stroked a thumb and forefinger over his chin. Since he'd avoided shaving in the past four days, the stubble was as rough as a wire brush. But then, he wasn't trying to impress Beatrice. Besides, it would take more than a smooth face to make an impact on her.

"Next time I go on a date, I'll try to remember not to glance at myself in the mirror."

She laughed, and then, with her gaze still glued to his profile, she asked, "Can I ask why you aren't married? You're thirty-six, aren't you?"

He tried not to stiffen at the personal question. After all, it was only normal that she would be wondering why he didn't have a wife or family.

He countered with a question of his own. "You think a man should be married by the time he's thirty-six?"

He could tell from the look on her face that she was far from being embarrassed for prying into his personal life. In fact, she appeared more concerned for him than anything. The idea made him want to groan out loud.

Shrugging, she said, "Not all men. Some just aren't suited for marriage at any age. But you seem like a guy who'd enjoy having a wife and kids around. Or am I wrong about that?"

He tried to keep the bitterness he was feeling off his face, but it was hard to do when his thoughts were consumed with his parents' broken marriage and the farce of his father's second marriage. Why should Kipp set himself up for that sort of pain? There wasn't a woman on the face of the earth who would be worth the agony.

"I used to think about marriage," he admitted. "When I was much younger. But time passed and I never met the right woman. After a while I just put the whole notion aside."

"Hmm. So now after all this time you're thinking you won't ever meet the right woman. That's sad."

No, it was smart. At least he wouldn't have a wife

cheating behind his back or plotting his demise, he thought cynically.

"Look, Bea, my life is full just as it is. I stay busy and productive. Do I look sad to you?"

Even though he didn't glance in her direction, he could feel her blue eyes making a slow survey of his face. The feeling left him wanting to cough and squirm, to tell her to stop it and leave him alone. But he did none of those things because he wanted her to believe he was cool and calm and, above all, happy.

To his relief, she smiled at him. "Ask me that question again when we reach your place. I'll be able to answer you better then."

By the time they reached the Rising Starr, he wouldn't give a damn whether she thought he was happy or emotionally deranged. He'd be relieved that she was out of his hair and he could go back to simply being a man with a mission.

Chapter Three

By the time they reached Nephi, Utah, and stopped at a fast-food restaurant for coffee and restroom visits, the sky was completely covered with gray clouds, while cold wind was whipping across the parking lot.

Before they climbed out of the truck, Beatrice pulled on a white sock cap and wrapped a fuzzy black muffler around her neck, then slipped into a black-and-white-plaid coat.

"Thirty-four degrees," Beatrice exclaimed as she glanced at the thermometer on the dashboard screen. "I thought it was supposed to be in the forties today!"

He said, "I thought the same thing. Let's just hope nothing starts falling out of those clouds. At this temperature, it's bound to be snow or sleet."

As soon as they left the warm confines of the truck, the wind blasted Beatrice in the face. Hugging her arms around her, she took off in a run toward the shelter of the building. Kipp followed, but kept his stride down to a walk.

"Come on, slowpoke! It's freezing out here!" she shouted over her shoulder.

When he finally joined her under the wide canvas

awning that shielded the double doors, her teeth were chattering.

"Are you really that cold?" he asked.

She shot him a droll look. "If I don't get inside where it's warm, I'm going to chip a tooth! Aren't you freezing?"

He wrapped an arm across the back of her waist and pulled open the door of the restaurant with his free hand. "You're forgetting that I work out in this kind of weather," he said. "I'm fine. But let's get inside. Hadley wouldn't like it if I caused him a huge dental bill."

As the two of them stepped inside, Beatrice welcomed the warmth of the busy room, but the relief from the cold wind was only an afterthought. For the first time Kipp was touching her! And the close contact was warming her far more than the heat blowing from the vents in the ceiling.

"I see the restroom signs over in the far corner," he said. "Maybe we should visit those before we order?"

"Good idea."

As they made their way across the room, Beatrice was delighted that Kipp kept his arm against her back. But she had to wonder if he was merely being a gentleman and ushering her through the crowd. Or did he actually want to be close to her?

What does it matter, Beatrice? After tomorrow you'll never see him. Not unless he comes to Stone Creek to visit his sister. And that will probably be a rare occasion.

She was trying to ignore the taunting voice in her head when Kipp said, "I'll wait for you over there by the window."

He gestured toward a plate-glass window that overlooked a parking area at the side of the building.

Nodding in agreement, she said, "I won't be long."

Normally, when Beatrice visited the restroom, she took time to check her makeup and reapply a layer of lipstick. But this morning, with Kipp waiting, she didn't want him thinking she was going to take time to primp with each pit stop they made. Especially after that crack she'd made about Nick being a peacock.

Instead, she barely glanced at her image in the mirror as she washed her hands and then hurried out to join him.

"That was quick," he said.

She flashed him an impish smile. "We have a long drive ahead of us and I don't want to prolong your agony."

A faint smile quirked his lips. "According to you, I'm either sad or in agony. I must look like a ball of misery."

His teasing remark caused her spirits to soar, and without thinking, she reached for his hand and tugged him in the direction of the order counter. "Come on. Let's go get our coffee. I want a tall one!"

As they walked, he shot her a wry glance. "Let me guess. With sugar and whipped cream and all that kind of stuff."

She laughed. "No way! When I drink coffee I want it plain—just good ole coffee."

He shook his head. "I wouldn't let that information out, Bea. You're not in step with your generation."

She squeezed his hand. "I'll let you in on a little secret. I don't follow the crowd. I do my own thing whether it's the in-thing or not."

He paused to look at her. "You must have plenty of courage—to be your own person."

Laughing again, she said, "I'm not courageous. Just

ask Bonnie. She'll tell you that the real issue is that I'm as stubborn as a mule."

"I'll try to remember that," he said. Then, with another faint smile, he led her up to the counter where an attendant was waiting to take their order.

Ten minutes later, as Beatrice cautiously sipped her steaming coffee, Kipp steered the truck with one hand and reached for the foam cup sitting in the holder built into the console between their seats.

Frowning, Beatrice said, "I understand you're in a hurry to get down the road, but we should've stayed a few more minutes at the restaurant so you could enjoy drinking your coffee instead of downing it while you drive."

Tilting the cup to his lips, he took a long drink before he glanced at her. "Even without making any stops, the trip to Coeur d'Alene takes thirteen hours or more. That means it will most likely be getting late when we do get there. Probably too late for you to make your meeting."

Shaking her head, she said, "I honestly never expected to be able to have the meeting with Scarlett this evening. Not after making a nine-hundred-mile trip. So, you shouldn't be worried about the time. We already planned to stay the night in Coeur d'Alene anyway."

"True. But we don't know what kind of obstacles we might run into on down the road. It pays not to dawdle."

Lowering her cup, she used both hands to steady it on her lap before she glanced at him. "Is that your motto—be careful and don't dawdle? You must be a cautious man."

"It pays to be cautious, too," he said. Then, laughing, he glanced at her. "I know. I get it. You're thinking what a stuffed shirt I am. But I'm not. At least, most of the time I'm not."

Chuckling with him, she said, "Frankly, I was thinking this guy should be working for a company who needs a man to tell them everything that could possibly go wrong so they can have safety measures in place to handle any type of accident or mistake."

He laughed again and the sound was like molasses pouring over a hot biscuit. It was melting every cell in her body.

"You mean like a troubleshooter?" he asked.

"Well, trouble does seem to stay on your mind." She shifted in the seat so she could look at him directly. "Seriously, though, in the interests of being safe, don't push yourself too hard. Dad didn't ask you to make this trip with me just to be my chauffeur. I can drive, too. So, whenever you get tired, just let me know."

He arched a dark brow at her, and as her gaze scanned his rugged face, she was amazed at how totally unpretentious he seemed to be. He didn't appear to have a clue of just how appealing he might be to a woman. A fact that made him even more endearing to her.

"Are you a good driver?" he asked.

She leveled a smug smile at him. "I've never had a wreck. Or a driving ticket. Quint says that's because I'm lucky. I tell him no—it's because I'm a good driver."

"Okay, when I get tired, I'll put your boast to a test."

"When will that be?" she asked curiously. "Whenever we reach Salt Lake City?"

"No. Whenever we stop for lunch," he answered.

She glanced at the digital clock on the dashboard. It was still two and a half hours away from noon. "When will that be?"

He glanced at her and smiled. "Whenever we get hungry. How's that?"

"You're not a troubleshooter," she teased. "You're a troublemaker."

His features tightened as his gaze returned to the stretch of highway in front of them. "I hope to be one— someday."

Beatrice couldn't imagine what he meant by that remark. From what she'd seen of Kipp Starr, he was far from the troublemaking sort. But the hard set to his features made it obvious his thoughts were on something unpleasant. A woman, perhaps? One who'd broken his heart? As much as she'd like to know, she wasn't about to ask. Their trip had only begun and she didn't relish the thought of him being angry and sullen for the remainder of their time together.

By the time they'd crossed the border into Idaho, Kipp's stomach had begun to gnaw with hunger, and when the small town of Malad City appeared on the horizon, he suggested to Beatrice that they stop for lunch.

"If you'd rather wait, we could keep going until we hit Pocatello," he told her. "We'd have plenty of restaurants to choose from there."

She shook her head. "I don't need anything special to eat. If you're hungry, let's stop here."

"Are you hungry?" he asked.

They'd been traveling for hours with only that one coffee break. Since then, she'd not asked to stop for any reason. Nor had she complained that she was tired or needed to stretch her legs. So far, Beatrice had been the exact opposite of what he'd been expecting, which made him feel a bit guilty. He'd had her pegged as spoiled and perhaps a bit demanding. He couldn't have been more wrong.

"Starved," she answered. "This morning, I had one piece of toast with blackberry jam for breakfast. I'm feeling very empty."

"Why didn't you say something earlier?" he asked. "We could've stopped in Salt Lake City."

He slowed the truck as they entered the outer limits of the small mountain town. "Because I don't like whiners. And I don't want to be one myself. I knew you'd be stopping soon enough. It hasn't hurt me to wait."

"I'm sorry, Bea." His expression rueful, he glanced at her. "I guess you can tell I'm accustomed to only taking care of my own needs. If I forget to ask you about making stops, then remind me. For Pete's sake, I won't think you're a whiner."

The soft smile on her face made something flutter in his chest and he purposely darted his gaze back on the vehicle traveling in front of them.

"All right," she said in a teasing voice. "The next time I get hungry, I'll yell 'Stop.'"

On Main Street Beatrice spotted a family-type restaurant with a board-front siding and a sign with a picture of a steer hanging over the door. "Oh, there's a place that looks like it was made just for us, Kipp. What do you think?"

A place made just for *us*. Kipp understood she'd not deliberately linked them together in a personal way. The *us* part had only been a figure of speech. And yet the sound of it got to him. Many long years had passed since Kipp had actually dreamed about being in a relationship and having a woman with him through the ups and downs of life. He'd envisioned his future with a wife and children. But those dreams had died with his father.

"Looks fine to me. I'll find a place to park."

Several doors down, he spied a parallel parking slot and quickly maneuvered the truck into the empty space. Next to him, Beatrice was already preparing herself to leave the warm truck by wrapping a muffler around her neck and pulling the sock cap over the top of her hair.

"I don't know if you've noticed, but the farther north we've traveled, the more the temperature has dropped," Kipp remarked as he reached for his coat on the floor behind the driver's seat.

"Yes. I've been watching the thermometer. It doesn't bode well. Especially with the sky growing darker," she replied.

He shrugged into the wool-lined ranch coat, then cut the motor on the truck. "I've noticed the clouds, too. After we get our meal ordered I'll check the weather app on my phone. I have a feeling the radar north of here is going to look ugly."

Her brows formed a questioning arch. "Do you think we should grab a packaged sandwich from a convenience store and keep going?"

If Kipp had been traveling alone and only had himself to consider, he'd keep going as far and as fast as was safely possible. But he had to consider Beatrice, and even though she wasn't complaining, he could see she needed a rest.

"No. We've been traveling over five hours with only one short stop. We could both use a break."

He picked up the coat lying in her lap and held it up so she could slip her arms into the sleeves. As he pulled the heavy garment onto her shoulders, her long hair brushed against his hand, and for one split second he considered snaring a strand of it, just to feel its silky texture between his fingers. But he didn't. She might not appreciate him taking liberties, and besides, touching her hair would only make him want to touch more.

She finished buttoning the garment and slipping on a pair of gloves before she looked over at him. "Dad said the weather forecast for the next three days was cold temperatures, but nothing that would impact the roads. He wouldn't have allowed me to start out on this trip if he'd believed otherwise."

A tiny crease marred the middle of her forehead and Kipp could see the idea of getting stranded in a winter storm was at the back of her mind.

He tried to sound encouraging, but in truth, he was beginning to feel a bit uneasy about the darkening skies. "It won't do any good to fret over the weather. Anyway, it would take a bad blizzard to shut down the highways."

She flashed him a cheery smile. "You're right. The only thing I'm going to worry myself with at the moment is what to choose from the menu."

He helped her out of the truck, and as soon as they started down the sidewalk in the direction of the restaurant, she reached for his hand as though it was the natural thing to do. Kipp could hardly pull away without making himself look like a jerk. Besides, if he really wanted to be honest with himself, he couldn't deny that having Beatrice's little hand curved around his filled him with sweet pleasure.

"At least the wind isn't so strong here as it was in Nephi," she said, as she glanced curiously around at their surroundings. "But it does feel colder."

"At least your teeth aren't chattering," he teased.

"No. But I'm sure my nose looks like Rudolph's."

She slanted him an impish smile. "Have you been here before?"

"I have. But it was several years ago. If you drive straight west of here for about forty miles, you'd be at the Rising Starr Ranch," he told her. "From here, a narrow highway goes in that direction for maybe half the distance before it turns into a graveled road. It's rough riding. But the other route takes you on a huge circle up to the interstate, then back down to get to Burley."

Her eyes widened with interest. "Oh. Does that area look anything like this? With desert-type mountains?"

"Some of it has mountains of this type. But we also have stretches of land with thick forests and fertile valleys."

"Sounds beautiful," she said. "I'm looking forward to seeing it."

He hoped whenever they finally reached the Rising Starr, she wouldn't expect him to show her around the ranch. He didn't know how much, if anything, she knew about the circumstances surrounding the ownership of the property. Clementine or Quint might have told her, though he didn't consider it likely. But one way or the other, it would be awkward if some of the hands, or even Andrea herself, brought up the fact that Kipp was merely a working cowboy now.

And what would that matter, Kipp? Beatrice would only be hearing the truth. You can't hide the fact that your father died a suspicious death and Andrea inherited everything right out from under your nose.

By the time they reached the door of the restaurant, Kipp had managed to shove away his dark thoughts and remind himself that this trip with Beatrice was only a tiny space of time out of his life. Tomorrow evening it would probably be over, and none of what she said or did or thought would make any difference in the grand scheme of things.

Inside the restaurant, they passed through a short foyer and into a large dining area filled with small square tables and matching wood chairs. On the right side of the room, a long, polished bar was lined with tall swiveling stools with padded red seats. Presently, most of the seating at the bar was taken, while many of the tables were occupied with midday diners.

"Mmm. Smells delicious," Beatrice said with an appreciative sniff. "Just like back home at the Wagon Spoke."

"If it tastes as good as it smells, then we're in luck," Kipp told her.

As they scanned the room for an available table, a young server wearing blue jeans and a green sweater with a Christmas scene on the front paused to glance at them.

"Go ahead and seat yourselves," she told them. "We're kind of busy right now, but there's an empty table over in the front corner. Have a seat and I'll be right with you."

"Thanks," Kipp told her. Then, cupping a hand beneath Beatrice's elbow, he guided her through the maze of diners until they reached the empty table.

"This is great," Beatrice said, as he helped her into one of the chairs. "We can see the sidewalk and street and even the mountains in the distance. And Christmas music is playing in the background. I love it."

Kipp sank into the seat across from her and promptly proceeded to remove his coat and hat. As he placed the things in the empty chair next to him, he said, "It feels good to be out of the truck. I needed to stretch."

She plucked the knit cap from her head and smoothed a hand over her hair. "I'm really beginning to feel very guilty about dragging you on this mission of mine."

Her comment caused him to look at her with surprise. "Guilty? Why? You didn't drag me. I agreed to this."

Her expression rueful, she unwrapped the muffler from her neck, then slipped out of her coat. "I know. But if you'd taken a flight back as you'd first planned, the trip would've been quick and easy for you."

"Not necessarily. Someone would've had to pick me up at the airport in Twin Falls and drive me back to the ranch. So there would've still been highway traveling involved."

"There's not an airport closer than Twin Falls?" she asked.

"There's a small airport at Burley, but it doesn't accommodate the bigger airlines. It's a town of about this size."

"I see." With a wan smile, she reached across the table and placed her hand over his. "Well, in spite of feeling guilty, I'm glad you're with me. The drive would be long and lonely without you."

Long and lonely. For years now, Kipp had told himself he was content to live a single life. And most of the time he didn't dwell on going home to an empty house after working a tiring day in the saddle. He didn't let himself think too much about his cold, empty bed. But being with Beatrice was making him think about all those things and more.

Raking a hand through the side of his hair, he forced his gaze to meet her blue one. "I'm not very good company for you, Bea. I'm not much of a talker and my work buddies tell me I'm grumpy. Too bad your dad couldn't have found someone else to make this journey with you."

She frowned and Kipp didn't miss how her hand tightened around his.

"Dad wasn't concerned about me being entertained— just safe."

How was he supposed to respond to that without sounding stupid? To his relief, the arrival of the waitress with glasses of ice water and menus interrupted the loaded moment. As she placed the items on the table, Beatrice pulled her hand away and Kipp released a long breath he hadn't realized he was holding.

"How's the day going for you two?" she asked. "Hard to stay warm in this horrible weather, huh?"

A tag with the name Josephine was pinned to the left side of her colorful sweater, while her brown hair was secured back from her face with a headband fashioned with reindeer antlers. Apparently, the young woman was still celebrating Christmas, Kipp thought.

"We're trying," Beatrice told her. "Are you expecting the weather here to get worse?"

The waitress nodded ruefully. "Our local forecast is for snow later tonight. I hear it's already falling north of Idaho Falls. Are you two traveling in that direction?"

"We are," Beatrice answered.

"Let's hope it won't last long. Anyway, the snowplows should keep the major highways cleared." She gestured toward the water glasses. "Can I get you two something else to drink? Tea? Soda? Coffee?"

They both ordered coffee, and after Josephine had left to fetch the drinks, Kipp said, "I thought we'd agreed not to worry about the weather. For now, at least."

Nodding, Beatrice picked up the laminated menu.

"Sorry. The waitress brought up the subject. You know how it is. In a small town, the weather is always a topic of discussion. But I'll talk about something else. Would you like to hear about me and Bonnie going on vacation in Hawaii?"

He picked up the menu and began to scan the lunch selections. "Sure. Tell me about it."

"I wish I could. But I was only kidding. We've never gone to Hawaii."

He lowered the menu and made a tsking noise with his tongue. "A nice girl like you shouldn't be telling fibs."

She chuckled. "Okay. I'm guilty of being naughty. But truthfully now, Bonnie and I have dreamed about going to the islands. Unfortunately, Bonnie is always too busy running Dad's office to get very far away from the ranch. And besides, the both of us are trying to save our money."

He glanced across the table at her. "Saving for your old age?" he asked wryly.

She let out a short laugh. "Dad says it's never too early to start saving for retirement. But what am I going to retire from? The boutique?"

He shrugged. "Maybe one day you'll have one of those high-paying designer jobs for a famous clothing company and you'll make so much money that you won't have to worry about saving. Whenever the urge hits, you'll be able to fly out to Hawaii and lounge around on the beach with a coconut drink in your hand."

To his surprise, her nose wrinkled with disapproval. "As good as that sounds, it's not really me, Kipp. I mean, yes, Hawaii would surely be fun. Especially if Bonnie could go with me. But me with a high-paying job in a big office somewhere—no. If I ever get into designing seriously, I want to work on my own. Small scale with only a seamstress and assistant to help me."

She sounded sincere, and Kipp could believe that, presently, Beatrice believed she wanted the simple life. Living on the ranch and working in the boutique. But sooner or later her wants and wishes would change, Kipp thought. One of these days she would meet a young man and fall head over heels in love with him. Then the course of her life would expand to include more than work. She'd marry the man of her dreams and give him children. They'd make a home together. A home full of love and laughter.

The last thought left a strange bitterness in Kipp's mouth and he quickly reached for his water glass to wash the taste away. He didn't want to think about Beatrice in the arms of any man. No more than he wanted to think about driving into a blinding blizzard. But both notions were stuck in his mind, making him wonder what the night ahead was going to bring to him and to her.

Chapter Four

"This should help warm you two," the waitress said a few minutes later as she served the coffee. "Have you decided what you want to eat? The lunch special is spaghetti and meatballs, but I wouldn't recommend it. The cook got distracted and overcooked the pasta. If you ask me, it's kinda mushy."

While Josephine pulled out a pencil and order pad, Beatrice placed the menu on the corner of the table.

"I see all kinds of good things on the menu, but I think I'll just have a cheeseburger and fries."

"Same for me. With plenty of mustard on the burger," Kipp told her.

"Can't go wrong there," the waitress said with a wink that was mostly directed at Kipp.

After she jotted down the orders, then hurried off in the direction of the kitchen, Beatrice picked up her coffee and took a long, grateful sip.

"Mmm. Thank goodness this is strong and hot. I need something to revive me." She glanced across the table to see he was making a slow study of her face.

"We still have over nine hours to go before we reach Coeur d'Alene. Think you can make it?"

"Honestly, at this very moment, I don't have the energy to travel one more hour, much less nine. But don't worry. After I eat, I'll be good to go," she told him.

He shook his head. "If you become too exhausted, we'll stop. From what you've told me, Hadley has been searching for information about his father for a year or two now. I'm sure one more day isn't going to upset him."

"No. Dad doesn't expect me to speed through this trip," she replied. "But I wouldn't want to be the cause of you getting home late."

A faint grimace touched his face. "I'm not expected back at the ranch for three more days, so don't concern yourself with my schedule."

But she would concern herself, Beatrice thought. Because from the very beginning, she'd instinctively felt that he wasn't making this trip because he wanted to. He was only doing it out of obligation to her parents. The idea stung far more than it should have. Which was silly on her part. It shouldn't matter whether he wanted her company.

Trying to shake away the thought, she glanced across the spacious room filled with diners. Some of them were obviously couples and she wondered how it would feel if she and Kipp were together and he was looking at her with love in his eyes.

The fantasy traipsing through her mind was suddenly interrupted as two men at the bar erupted in laughter. Apparently one of them had said something funny, as the waitress warming their coffee was laughing with them.

Biting back a sigh, she turned her gaze on Kipp,

who seemed to be more interested in his coffee than anything else.

"Is the Rising Starr as busy as Stone Creek?" she asked. "Seems like my brothers and the ranch hands are never caught up with the work that's needed to be done. Especially during the winter season when the livestock need extra hay and feed."

He let out a long breath, but Beatrice decided the sigh hadn't originated from fatigue. It was more like a sound of regret.

"The Rising Starr isn't nearly as big an operation as Stone Creek, but it's busy. Along with me, there are two other ranch hands and the foreman. There's always work of some kind to be done by all four of us," he said.

Beatrice decided the more she was in this man's company, the more she wanted to know about him. If she asked him a hundred questions and he answered all of them, she had a feeling her curiosity still wouldn't be satisfied. The feeling was something new to Beatrice. Normally, when she went on a date with a man, she didn't really expect, or even want, to hear his life story. As long as the guy was attentive, polite and not boring, she was content to keep their conversation light and in the present. But with Kipp that wasn't enough. She wanted to know what was going on inside him. She longed to know what he was thinking and feeling.

"Did you always want to be a rancher? To work as a cowboy?"

He shrugged. "It's what I grew up doing. From the time Clem and I were able to ride a horse well, which was around five years old, we started helping our dad with the cattle and sheep. That kind of life was all we knew. The TV was rarely turned on in our house and we didn't have computers or video games. It wasn't until we started school that we learned only a portion of the other kids did the things that we did at home."

Smiling with fond remembrance, she nodded. "I understand. It was sort of that way with Bonnie and me. We were always horse crazy and we rode constantly. That was all we wanted to do until we entered high school and other interests caught our attention. We were in the school choir and I was on the debate team. And, of course, both of us took agriculture and showed steers and lambs at the livestock shows."

His lips twisted to a crooked line. "Sounds like you twins had plenty of interests. But you left out boys."

She chuckled. "To be honest, boys were my very first interest. I had a boyfriend in kindergarten, and believe it or not, he still lives in Beaver and we've remained good friends."

His brown eyes narrowed to a squint. "Just not your boyfriend?"

"No," she said with a little laugh. "He's married now. Happily, I might add."

"Ah, the one who got away." He picked up his coffee cup. "Well, as for me being a rancher, no other job would suit me. All I've ever wanted was to be outdoors caring for animals—to see the livestock and land thrive."

A knowing smile curved her lips. "To feel the wind and the sun on your face and a horse between your legs," she said. "Yes. I understand. Outside of Flint, my brothers are the same way. They wouldn't be happy doing any other job. But there's no need for me to be telling you this. You got to know all my brothers while you were at Stone Creek. You saw for yourself that they're cowboys through and through. Even Flint does

his fair share of ranching whenever his schedule with
the sheriff's department allows."

"Yeah, your brothers are all fine men. And dedicated
to helping your father keep the ranch profitable," he
replied, then cast a curious glance in her direction.
"What made Flint want to get into law enforcement?"

Shaking her head, she said, "Flint has always marched
to the beat of a different drummer."

He leveled a pointed look at her. "Sort of like you."

She wasn't sure if it was the warm light in his eyes or
the faint dimple carved into his left cheek, but something
about him was giving her the impression he was flirting
with her.

"You think I'm different?" she asked.

The coy look on his face caused her heart to chug
faster and faster, and she wasn't exactly sure why. Plenty
of guys had flirted openly with her and most of those
times she was merely amused by their behavior. But
Kipp was different. He was a man. Not a boy, but a full-
grown, experienced man.

*He's much older than you. I imagine he's left plenty
of women crying into their pillows.*

Bonnie's warning drifted through her mind and
suddenly she understood what her sister had meant. And
yet, even knowing he was dangerous to her emotions,
she couldn't resist him. Even with his long stretches of
moody silence.

He said, "I think I'd be safe in saying you're not
typical."

As soon as he spoke the words, his gaze turned to
the plate-glass window to their left and Beatrice used
the moment to study his profile. Without his hat, a dark
wave of hair was dipping over his right eyebrow, and

she thought how the rakish curl paired perfectly with the black stubble of whiskers on his face. Just looking at him was enough to send a shiver down a woman's spine and she'd been doing it for the past five hours. If she didn't start forcing her eyes to look elsewhere, she was going to suffer some sort of meltdown.

"I hope you mean that as a compliment," she told him.

His gaze landed back on her face. "I do."

Her heart thumped a little harder. "I'm not always right," she told him. "But I'd rather be wrong than boring."

His lips took on a wry twist. "I don't think there will ever be any danger of you being boring, Bea."

Was she imagining things, or was she feeling a spark of electricity flying from him to her? And if he was sending sparks in her direction, what could it possibly mean?

She awkwardly cleared her throat, then reached for the handbag she'd placed in the empty chair next to her. "I—uh, think I'll see if my phone has enough signal to send a text. I'm sure Dad would like to hear how we're faring."

"He'll be relieved to know we haven't tried to claw each other's eyes out," he said.

"Not yet," she joked, then glanced across the table to see he was watching her type out the short message. And it suddenly struck her that he didn't have a father to call or text. Nor did he appear to communicate with his mother. He did keep in touch with his sister, Clementine, but not the way Beatrice did with her siblings. It saddened her to think he didn't have family surrounding him.

"Do you think Clem is expecting to hear from you?"

she ventured to ask him. "I'm sure she'd appreciate you giving her a shout-out."

"Your parents will keep Clem updated," he said.

It wouldn't be the same, she wanted to tell him. But she kept the thought to herself. "I've not had much chance to get to know Clem. She's been sheepherding on the ranch for several months now, but the only times I've been around her were when she attended Grace and Mack's belated wedding party and then when we all gathered for Christmas. I could be wrong about this, but I get the feeling that you and your sister are very different."

His eyes narrowed. "What do you mean by *different*?"

She shrugged, while wondering why she'd spoken her thoughts out loud. Now wasn't the time to engage him in a serious conversation, she scolded herself. If she had any sense at all, she wouldn't be associating the word *serious* with Kipp in any form or fashion.

"Oh, just that you see things differently. From some of the things I've heard her say, I get the feeling that she wishes you'd move away from the Rising Starr and hang your hat at Stone Creek."

His jaw tightened. "Clem's priorities have changed over the years. Especially now that Quint is in her life. The Rising Starr isn't a driving force in her life any-more."

"And it is to you?"

"It's everything to me," he said flatly.

The cool tone of his voice struck her hard and she could only wonder why her question would have flipped such a switch in him. The way Quint had explained the situation to their parents, after Clementine and Kipp's father had died, the ownership of the Rising Starr had gone to their stepmother. Which, in Beatrice's mind, wasn't all that unusual. A wife usually did inherit her deceased husband's assets. But she could see from Kipp's chilly attitude on the subject that he wasn't happy with the legal outcome.

"Sorry it took so long to get your orders," Josephine said as she suddenly appeared with a tray laden with their meals. "I don't know what's going on today, but for some reason we're extra busy."

"No problem," Kipp told her.

Beatrice slanted the waitress a reassuring smile. "We've been traveling and needed the rest anyway."

"I appreciate you being so understanding. Some customers get irate if they're forced to wait very long on their orders. Just like us waitresses can do anything about a slow cook." The young woman placed the plates of burgers and fries in front of them, then pulled a bottle of ketchup from a pocket on her apron. After she'd added the condiment to the tabletop, she refilled their coffee cups. "Is there anything else I can get for you?"

"I'm good," Kipp told her.

Beatrice said, "This is great."

"Then I'll check back with you later."

With a sympathetic expression, Beatrice watched the waitress hurry away to deal with more waiting customers. "Poor thing. She's so cute. I wonder if she has a husband and children."

She turned her attention back to Kipp and saw his lips were stretched to a grim line.

"Even though she's wearing a pair of silly reindeer antlers, she looks a lot smarter than that," he said.

Dismayed by his remark, she stared at him. He held the notion that a woman was dumb for wanting a family. She didn't want to believe he was that cynical. She couldn't believe it. Back at Stone Creek, she'd seen the gentle way he'd dealt with her nieces and nephews.

"For your information, I love her antlers. Christmas is a wonderful holiday. We Hollisters like to stretch the celebrating as long as we can. Mom doesn't take down the tree in the house until the end of the first week of January and even at that I nearly cry to see it go," she said staunchly. "And as for your crack about how someone smart wouldn't have a husband and children— well, you have your opinion and I have mine!"

He'd made her angry. That much was obvious, Kipp thought, as he watched her shake black pepper vigorously over the mound of French fries on her plate.

Hell, he didn't know why he'd made that sarcastic remark. He didn't have anything against marriage or kids—as long as he wasn't involved with either. But for the past couple of hours, he'd been thinking things about Beatrice that he shouldn't be thinking. He'd been touched by soft feelings that could only lead a man toward trouble. And the more he'd tried to ignore these unwanted thoughts and feelings, the more frustrated he'd become.

When Beatrice had voiced her curiosity over the waitress being married, something in Kipp had snapped like a dry twig. Now she was thinking he was a first-class jerk, and that wasn't the way he wanted her to view him.

He swallowed a bite of his burger before he looked across the table at her. "I'm sorry, Beatrice," he said ruefully. "I don't know why I said any of that. I didn't mean it."

Her gaze met his and the unrelenting look he saw in her blue eyes was like a sucker punch to his gut.

"You meant it," she said with an indifferent shrug of one shoulder. "But hey, there's no need for you to apologize for being honest. Or for your feelings about marriage and children. I'd already concluded that you weren't a family man. And how you think and live is your prerogative. I just didn't like the sarcastic way you expressed it."

He picked up the ketchup bottle and squirted the red sauce over his fries. Damn it, she was too young and too much of a starry-eyed romantic to see that having a family wasn't always a rosy, happily-ever-after situation. "So now you're going to be angry with me for the remainder of the trip."

"No. I'm not angry."

He frowned. "Then you're going to hold on to your opinion that I'm a major jackass."

"No. I'm going to think you're a tried-and-true bachelor. That's all."

That's all. Sure, he thought. There was nothing else to it. Like she said, he didn't need to apologize for the choices he made about his own life.

He drew in a deep breath and let it out. "I'm glad you understand."

The wan smile that curved her lips was nothing like her usual expression of warmth, but Kipp supposed her reaction was better than a sneer.

"I understand completely, Kipp."

Deciding he'd be better off dropping the whole subject, Kipp focused on his meal and Beatrice did the same. It wasn't until Josephine returned to ask if they'd like dessert that the silence that had settled over the table was broken.

"No, thanks," Beatrice told her. "I couldn't eat another bite. Be sure and tell the cook it was delicious."

"No dessert for me, either," Kipp informed the waitress. "But I would like a coffee to go."

"Sure thing. I'll be right back with it and the check," she said.

As she walked away, Beatrice collected a leather wallet from her purse. As she pulled a credit card from a protective sleeve and laid it on the tabletop, Kipp shook his head.

"I'll pay for this."

She looked at him. "No. Like I told you when we stopped for coffee, Dad gave me this card to use specifically for travel expenses," she explained. "This trip isn't your responsibility."

"I'd be eating whether I was traveling with you or alone," he said firmly. "Put the card away. You can pay for the next meal."

She studied him for a few seconds before she picked up the card and returned it to her wallet. "Okay," she murmured. "Thank you for the meal."

"My pleasure."

Without looking his way, she took a sip of water, and as Kipp's gaze slipped over her closed features, he realized he already missed the Beatrice who'd been flashing him warm smiles and gazing at him with twinkling eyes.

But it was better this way for the both of them, he thought. She'd gotten a dose of the real Kipp Starr and she wanted no part of him.

Plucking up the handbag, she suddenly rose from

the chair. "Excuse me, Kipp. I need to visit the ladies' room before we get back on the road."

"Surely." He politely stood until she walked away from the table, but even after she disappeared into the annex leading to the restroom, he was seeing the blank expression on her face and hating himself for putting it there.

The two of them had traveled through the city of Pocatello and were leaving the northern outskirts of Idaho Falls when huge snowflakes began to splatter the windshield. Normally, Beatrice loved seeing the sky turn white with the falling ice, but considering the circumstances, now wasn't a good time to be wishing for a winter wonderland.

Across from her in the driver's seat, Kipp eased off the accelerator and switched on the wiper blades. "Looks like we've hit the edge of the winter storm."

Pulling her gaze away from the snow that was rapidly covering the landscape, Beatrice glanced over at him. Since they'd left the restaurant, their conversation had been limited and mundane. Which was for the best, she told herself. She'd been stupid to talk to him about personal things. The man was a loner and he wanted to remain a loner. She had to respect his choice.

"Did I hear you use the word *storm*? Couldn't this just be a short snow shower we're passing through?"

Without looking in her direction, he said, "While you were in the ladies' room back at the restaurant, I opened the weather app on my phone. It showed a blast of bitter temps, along with snow and wind heading straight at us. And it's predicted to stay in the area for the next few days."

Her mouth fell open as the air whooshed from her lungs. "I've been trying to get my phone to load the weather report, but I can't get a cell signal. Why haven't you mentioned this before now? Surely it crossed your mind that I'd want to know!"

He darted a glance at her. "I didn't see any point in worrying you. Especially when there's not anything we can do to stop the snow."

He was right, of course. There wasn't one thing they could do to delay the storm's arrival. Still, she didn't appreciate him keeping her in the dark.

"Thanks for sparing me," she said dryly. "I guess when we ran into blizzard conditions, I would've figured it out on my own."

He frowned. "Look, Beatrice, even if we cut over and took the western route to Coeur d'Alene, we'd still run into bad weather. The radar shows it's spreading over the state and into Montana."

Groaning, she said, "Oh, great. So much for Dad's faith in the weather forecasters."

"The way I see it, we have two choices," he said flatly. "Keep going. Or turn around and go back to the first town behind us and wait out the storm. Is that what you want?"

Scowling now, she said, "I can't believe you're even suggesting such a thing. No! I do not want to turn around. I'm not a cowering little girl who's afraid of a storm! Why should I be? Not when I have a strong man like you to take care of me."

Sarcasm was threaded through her last words and she hated herself for acting so childishly. And why was she? She shouldn't care one way or the other about Kipp's outlook on marriage and children. It shouldn't bother her if he thought she was a naive romantic.

After a moment, he said, "It's obvious that you're still angry with me."

From the corner of her eye, she could see him wearily pinching the bridge of his nose. The sight made her feel even more ashamed of herself. "I was never angry with you, Kipp," she said softly.

His brows drew together. "You could've fooled me."

She sighed. "All right. If you must know, I was disappointed in you."

When he didn't immediately respond, she twisted around in the seat to see his jaw had dropped.

"Why?" he asked. "Because I want to remain a bachelor?"

Beatrice had never felt so big of a fool. "I'm sorry, Kipp. I shouldn't be making any kind of comments about your personal life. But I— Oh, this is hard to explain. Except that—well, now that I've gotten to know you a bit, I think it's a shame—a waste that you don't want a family. You're not the kind of man who's meant to spend his life alone. And don't ask me how I come to that conclusion—I just feel it."

He was silent for a moment and then he let out a short laugh. "You sound like Nuttah now. She gets these 'feelings' about things and people."

"Nuttah," she repeated with a faint frown. "Are you talking about Clementine's friend? The Blackfoot woman who lives here in Idaho?"

"I am. She lives at Shelley, which is a short distance south of Idaho Falls. She's my friend, too," he said, then promptly shook his head. "No. That's not right—I guess you could say she's been our second mother since we were young kids."

For the past two hours she'd been telling herself that his personal life, past or present, was none of her business. But all the self-lectures had been in vain. She was still just as curious about him, just as hungry to learn what this man was all about, as she had been from the start. If that made her a fool, then she was a big one.

"Nuttah must have lived closer to your ranch at the time you were a child."

His lips twisted. "Not closer. She lived *with* us. Dad hired her to cook and clean and do whatever else needed to be done around the house. I'll have to admit that was one of his better decisions."

"What about your mom? Did she have an outside job and didn't have time for housework?"

He reached over and punched a button on the dash to turn on the defroster to the windshield. "She didn't have an outside job until the last couple of years of their marriage. But even before she got a job in town doing office work for a car dealer, she was always disorganized and sort of helpless, if you know what I mean. She was a good mother to us. At least, she tried to be. But Dad was always in charge and things had to be done his way or there was hell to pay. Anyway, after our parents divorced and Mom moved away, he hired Nuttah to make sure everything got done that needed to be done."

So, his parents had divorced and his mother moved away when he was only a child, she thought. Did their broken marriage have a bearing on Kipp's views about having a family of his own? She had to think so. Maybe he'd decided he didn't want to give a woman a chance to steal his heart, then walk away. It was a sad notion.

But it was sadder still that she was letting the thought get to her. To allow herself to imagine that Kipp could be anything more to her than a friend and her future sister-in-law's brother would be a monumental mistake.

He was a lone cowboy. And nothing about her or this trip was going to change that fact.

Chapter Five

"Are you falling asleep over there?"

Kipp's voice interrupted Beatrice's deep thoughts and she gave herself a hard mental shake before she tried to form a reasonable answer.

"No. I was just wondering—about Nuttah," she said, which wasn't far from the truth. She had been thinking about Kipp's childhood and Nuttah had obviously been a major part of it. "I believe that you said she lives in Shelley now. How long did she stay on the Rising Starr?"

"She was there from the time I was about twelve until Dad died eight years ago. After his death, Nuttah left the ranch and so did Clementine."

A few days ago, after Clementine and Quint had become engaged, she'd overheard her brother talking to their parents about the Rising Starr and something about there being a big split in the family. Beatrice had only been passing through the room and she hadn't hung around to listen. Mainly because she'd understood the information was private and had nothing to do with her. But now she was curious as to why Kipp had stayed. Especially after his sister and Nuttah left.

Squaring around in the seat, she studied his rugged profile. "Clementine told Bonnie and me that during her downtime as a sheepherder, she lived with Nuttah," Beatrice said thoughtfully. "Now I understand why. I mean, for the most part I can appreciate why the woman is like a second mother to both of you. But what about your biological mother? I—"

She paused as it dawned on her that she was doing it all over again. Asking Kipp personal things she shouldn't be asking.

"You didn't finish your question—why?"

The heater vents were directed away from her face, but her cheeks felt like they'd been blasted by a furnace. She wasn't about to look in the mirror on the visor above her head. She knew she'd see a blush on her face.

Turning a sheepish little smile on him, she said, "Only a few minutes ago I told myself I shouldn't be talking to you about your personal life. And here I am, digging in and asking you about your family. Looks like you're going to have to put tape over my lips or plugs in your ears."

After a stretch of silence passed, she watched his lips quirk with something like a grin.

"I don't believe I'll have to resort to those drastic measures." He flexed his shoulders, then settled back against the plush leather seat before he darted a glance at her. "I imagine you were about to ask if I ever see Mom?"

Oh Lord, she must be transparent to this man, she thought. The idea that he could read her thoughts was more than disarming: Especially since the last few hours they'd been traveling, she'd been dreaming and wondering how it would feel to kiss him. Had he spotted those erotic thoughts dancing around in her head?

An awkward lump suddenly settled in her throat, forcing her to swallow before she spoke. "All right, I confess. I was about to ask you about your mother. But look, Kipp, you don't have to talk about her, or any of this. Not if you don't want to. Like I said, I shouldn't be asking."

"The more I think about it, the more I believe you ought to know," he replied. "Otherwise, you'll just keep wondering. Besides, it's not like any of this is a secret. Anyone who lived around Cassia County years back and was acquainted with Trent and Ella Starr know about their divorce. And that Trent was the reason for the split. He cheated on Mom with other women. At the time of the divorce, Clem and I had no idea about his extracurricular habits. It wasn't until afterward, and the kids at school started whispering behind our backs, that we learned the hard truth. Then later, after we'd grown into adults, we learned he'd been a habitual cheater. But that's another story."

Beatrice couldn't say she heard bitterness in his voice, but there was a resolute sound to it that made her wonder if his father's behavior had hardened his heart toward love and the family unit. Or perhaps Kipp had once loved a woman and she ended up cheating on him?

Oh Lord, she was getting too invested in this man's life. She was beginning to care about his feelings, about his future happiness. And where was that going to lead her? Two or three days from now she'd be telling him goodbye. After that, it wasn't like she'd be able to pop over and see him whenever the urge struck her. Or that she could call him up and invite him to a family gathering, or even a dinner date. The hopeless thoughts drifting through her mind should've squashed her interest in him. But even those miserable circumstances couldn't dim the pleasure of being in his presence.

Shoving at the gnawing thoughts, Beatrice murmured, "Your poor mother. She must have kept the reason for the divorce hidden in order to protect you children."

He let out a heavy breath. "Years later, she admitted she kept the fact to herself—because at that time she thought things were already hard enough without hearing our father was an adulterer. But to tell you the truth, her admission made us feel betrayed all over again. Any way you slice it, deception hurts."

"Hmm. Yes. I believe that's why Dad is going to such lengths to search for the truth about his parents," she said thoughtfully. "No one wants to live under false assumptions."

"Not unless the truth is too hard to bear."

From the corner of her eye, she saw his jaw tighten. Did he know someone who was trying to hide the truth? His mother? Himself? No. Not him, she thought. She instinctively knew he wasn't the kind of man who'd be content to live a lie.

She said, "I hope you've forgiven your mother. I'm sure she believed she was doing what was best for you and Clem."

He shrugged. "Yeah. I've forgiven her. And I do see Mom, from time to time. She lives down in Boise with her second husband. He's a nice enough guy, but to be honest, talking to her is like talking to a stranger. Which is probably mine and Clem's fault—after the divorce we chose to stay with Dad rather than go live with her. Not because we loved him more. It was just that the ranch and working with Dad were our whole life. And like I told you—we didn't know he'd been an unfaithful husband."

How much more terrible could things have gotten for Ella Starr? Beatrice wondered. Her husband cheated on her and then her children chose not to make their life with her. She must've felt deeply betrayed.

"Would it have made a difference if you had known?" she asked curiously.

He was silent for a long moment before he finally said, "No. Clem and I would've stayed on the ranch no matter what. We loved every inch of that place. It was our world and everything we cared about."

Beatrice couldn't imagine being forced to make such a difficult decision. It would be like ripping her heart right down the middle.

"Well, your mother probably understood that you wanted to remain in the home where you were comfortable and would be able to keep on doing the things you knew and loved."

He slanted her a rueful glance. "Nice thought, Bea. But I'm not so sure she saw both sides of the situation. Not all parents are like yours. Be grateful."

She gazed out the passenger window, only partially registering the wintery landscape as she imagined what it must've been like for Kipp and his sister to suddenly not have their mother. Especially at the age when they desperately needed one.

"My parents aren't perfect by any means. They've gone through rough patches with the ranch and raising eight kids. But they've always given us the love and support we've needed." She looked at him. "Has it crossed your mind that you have something in common with my father—other than being a rancher?"

"Not exactly. Hadley has been married for forty-some years, has eight children and owns and operates one of the largest ranches in Utah. I don't see any common factors," he said wryly.

"I do. Both of your mothers left their homes—their families."

He grimaced. "True. But at least I can see mine and speak with her if I choose. From what you tell me, Hadley was never given that choice. Your grandmother—or whatever you call her—is a different matter. If I were in your shoes, I'd be as anxious as hell about meeting her face-to-face. Especially since it will be the first time either of you have laid eyes on one another. She probably doesn't even know that Hadley has eight children—her grandchildren." He shook his head with dismay. "If you ask me, meeting her would be worse than driving into a blizzard."

"Oddly enough, I'm excited about the whole idea." She let out a short laugh. "Most of my family calls her the—uh, *b* word. But I try not to judge her that harshly."

He shot her a look of disbelief. "Why not? I don't blame them for labeling her as a bad woman."

"Okay, I realize it looks as though she turned her back on her sons, but we don't know what really happened with her and Lionel—that was my grandfather's name. Even Dad doesn't know. Everyone speculates that Scarlett had an affair. But we have no proof of her infidelity. If anyone is still around who knew the couple back then, none of us have met them or would even know who to ask to get an account of what they knew of the Hollister marriage.

So, it's all a guessing game. Could be that Lionel was the one with the roving eye."

He was quiet for the next couple of moments as he carefully focused on passing an 18-wheeler that had slowed to a crawl. Once he was a safe distance ahead of the semitruck, he asked, "Does Hadley not remember what happened with his parents, or was he too young at that time to understand?"

Beatrice crossed her legs in an effort to ease the stiffness creeping into her back and hips. "Dad was a very young child when his parents parted. All he remembers is yelling and noises that sounded like things being thrown around the room. And he recalls seeing his mother packing suitcases. But that's all. Lionel put the three brothers to bed one night, and when they woke up the next morning, their mother was gone. He simply told them that she had to go away. Much later, when the boys grew old enough to ask questions, Lionel refused to explain anything. All he said was that she was gone and better forgotten."

"Wow. That's tough." He rubbed a hand against the back of his neck. "Sometimes it's hell being a kid."

Yes, she imagined, as children, life had been tough going for Kipp and Clementine. And she could understand how the circumstances of his parents' broken marriage had wounded him. But wounds healed, she mentally argued. Especially if a person wanted to move on and forget the hurt.

She said, "Dad never talks much about his childhood or the lack of a mother. But I'm sure it was hell for him and his brothers. It doesn't surprise me that my uncles aren't that interested in collecting information on Scarlett or Lionel. They'd just as soon forget that part of their lives."

His dark brows lifted. "I didn't meet any brothers while I was visiting Stone Creek. Do they live near the ranch?"

"No. Once they became adults, they left Stone Creek. Neither one of them was ever interested in ranching. That's why Grandfather willed Stone Creek and all its holdings to Dad. Now Uncle Wade lives in Nevada and Uncle Barton in Montana. Both are younger than Dad. We rarely see them. Dad only hears from them on rare occasions."

"Sounds as though they acknowledge each other as brothers, but that's about it," he replied.

"Right," she agreed. "The men grew apart. Not on purpose but just out of circumstances. Which is sad. I can't imagine being that separated from my siblings."

She glanced out the windshield at the open range stretching away from both sides of the four-lane interstate. To their left, beyond the pastureland, the western horizon was made up of a ridge of jagged mountains. Presently, the peaks were shrouded with gray snow clouds, while the barren foothills were dotted with patches of evergreen forests. On the right, a large herd of black cattle were sheltering next to a grove of juniper trees. The overhanging limbs weren't enough to completely shield their hairy hides from the snow, but without a barn or deep arroyo, Beatrice figured the junipers were the best refuge the animals could find.

If the snow migrated on south to Stone Creek, her brothers and the hands would be working overtime to deal with the extra chores. It was a hard time of the year for cowhands and livestock, she couldn't help thinking.

But it was a part of ranching life. A life that Kipp obviously loved.

He'd said he wouldn't be happy doing anything else, and she could believe that. There was something innately earthy about him, she thought. A quality that spoke of wide-open skies and the rhythm of a horse as it carried him across a sage-dotted range.

Would his lovemaking be as wild and untamed as his appearance? The erotic question was slowly swirling around in her head when his voice suddenly interrupted her daydreaming and she looked over at the same time he flipped on his left blinker.

"I'm assuming your uncles don't know any more about your grandparents than Hadley does," he said as he pulled over in the passing lane to avoid an SUV that was creeping along the shoulder of the highway.

"No. But Van stumbled onto some information down in Parowan that's making the whole family second-guess our family's early history."

"Where is Parowan?" he asked, while steering the truck back into the right-hand lane. "Is that in Utah?"

"Yes. It's a little town south of Beaver and happens to be the county seat of Iron County. Lionel had always claimed he was born in Parowan. So, Van decided to drive down there and search through the Iron County records. She didn't find anything concerning Lionel Hollister or his wife, Scarlett. But before she left town, she decided to check at the library to see if there might be some archived information from that time period. She didn't find any written information, but the librarian introduced her to an elderly gentleman who'd lived his whole life in Parowan. Amazingly, he was acquainted with Lionel back before he was married and built Stone

Creek. The man told Van that Lionel showed up in town around 1959 or 1960 and was searching for land to buy. From what he says, Grandfather stuck around Parowan for a year or two, then moved on."

"But you say Van couldn't find any county records of Lionel's birth. Do you know the names of Lionel's parents—your great-grandparents?" he asked. "Maybe Van could find some sort of proof they once lived in the little town."

"Supposedly, his father's name was Peter. And his mother's name was Audrey. She died when Lionel was just a toddler."

She watched his brows draw together as though he was deeply focused on her grandparents' story. A fact that surprised her. But then, she needed to remember that his sister would be marrying into the Hollister family soon. He was probably interested to know about the roots of her future in-laws.

"Why do you say *supposedly*? You're not sure about the man's name?"

"Not exactly." She slashed her hand through the air in a dismissive gesture. "Van has been digging through every genealogy site offered on the web and she can't find a Peter Hollister. Not one that fits, anyway. Also, there's no state record in Utah listing a Lionel Hollister or a Peter. Obviously, Grandfather's story of that little town being his birthplace doesn't jibe with the old gentleman's account."

"Hmm. I hate to say it, Bea, but it sounds like your grandfather wasn't being totally honest."

"Ha! You're saying it in a nice way, Kipp. Dad says he must've outright lied about being born in Parowan.

But why? Doesn't make any sense. Unless he was a fugitive. That's what Bonnie thinks."

He chuckled. "Bonnie has more imagination than I would've guessed."

She laughed with him. "Bonnie doesn't put a limit on the possibilities. Neither do I. We're both open-minded, I guess you could say."

"Hmm. I can tell that you're believing Scarlett will be willing to explain things about her broken marriage. And that she'll give you Lionel's birth date. But I wouldn't count on it, Bea."

His negative assumption put a frown on her face. "Why not? Grandfather has been dead for several years now. What would it hurt if the woman revealed things about him?"

He shot her a suggestive grin. "Maybe she was a fugitive with your grandfather."

Chuckling, she said, "Forget that reason. The statutes of limitations would've already run out on their crimes—well, most of them, anyway. Besides, deep down I figure the only crimes those two committed were crimes of passion."

He frowned. "Those kinds of crimes don't usually make a person want to hide their identity."

"No," she said wryly, "they just make a person want to hide, period."

He arched a curious brow at her and once again she felt a measure of heat rush to her cheeks. Why had she said such a thing in the first place? It was like her brain was stuck on passion and sex and making love!

"I take it that you've committed that sort of crime?" he asked drolly.

She tried to laugh, but the awkward rush in her voice

revealed her embarrassment. "No! But I've heard my friends talk. Some of them have had—heated affairs."

"And you haven't?"

Had his voice grown softer with that last question? Or was her imagination continuing to work overtime?

"No!" she blurted emphatically, then added more gently, "I've never been that serious about any guy—yet. And why start something that you feel from the very start is only going to be temporary? Right?"

His chuckle was a bit wicked sounding. "I refuse to answer on the grounds it might incriminate me."

"Okay, you're excused from the witness stand," she said with a laugh. Yet even though she was joking along with him, she wondered if he'd ever had a serious affair. After all, if he was that averse to marriage, what else did that leave, other than meaningless one-night stands or affairs that usually burned themselves out?

After that awkward exchange, Beatrice fell silent and so did Kipp, until several miles had passed and he brought up the subject of her grandparents once again.

"I've been thinking about the reason for this trip, Bea. And I'm wondering if this woman you're planning to meet in Coeur d'Alene will be—uh—trustworthy."

She glanced at him. "In what way? Are you wondering if she might not be the real Scarlett Hollister?"

"No. I figure Van has already done her homework on the woman's identity. My question is whether you think anything she says to you will be the truth. I realize Hadley is expecting you to try to get some useful information from her, but if I were in your place, I wouldn't put a whole lot of trust in anything she said."

She leaned slightly forward and peered out the windshield. The snowfall was slowly and steadily getting heavier, while patches of ice were beginning to form on the highway. For the time being, they were able to continue traveling, albeit at a much slower pace. But at this rate, she couldn't see them making it all the way to the top of Idaho before nightfall. Still, she wasn't going to let the weather or the question of Scarlett's honesty ruin the remainder of the day.

"Listen, I'm hoping the weather is going to improve and I'm also hoping that when I do meet Scarlett, she'll be cooperative and helpful—and honest. Maybe I'm being Pollyanna, but I'd rather look on the positive side of things."

"Sorry if I sound like a downer to you, but frankly, both possibilities look bleak to me," he said in an apologetic voice. Then he glanced at her. "I don't think we're far from the next town. We'll stop and get something to drink and stretch our legs. How does that sound?"

"Perfect. I am getting a bit tired," she admitted, then chuckled. "And I thought traveling this far would be easy! What did I know!"

He shook his head. "You weren't expecting this bad weather to slow us down."

No. No more than she'd expected his presence to be affecting her so deeply. How was she going to be able to go home to Stone Creek and forget all about his rugged face and sly little grins? How could she not think of his broad shoulders and long, muscular legs? Most of all, how could she push the image of his dark brown eyes out of her mind? Eyes that were shadowed with loneliness.

Turning her gaze toward the window, she swallowed down the strange emotions balling in her throat. "I guess the rule of a road trip is to expect the unexpected."

To her surprise, he reached across the console and

folded his hand around hers. Her heart gave a hard lurch before it leaped into a rapid thump.

"Don't worry, Bea. I'm not going to let anything bad happen to you."

Was he making her promises to keep? No. He was only trying to make up for his downbeat predictions.

But no matter, she decided. Having his big strong hand wrapped warmly around hers was enough to fill her heart with sunshine.

Chapter Six

Kipp wasn't surprised to see the weather worsening with each hour that passed. Even though he or Beatrice hadn't mentioned the obvious, he could tell she was growing a bit anxious about the situation. For the past half hour she'd been sitting on the edge of her seat, watching the snow grow deeper on the highway. As for Kipp, his eyes were aching from trying to see through the blur of white flakes shrouding the vehicles traveling in front of and behind them.

Earlier this afternoon, they'd crossed into Montana and stopped in the town of Dillon to refuel the truck and take a short break. While they'd sat for a few minutes sipping cups of hot coffee, they'd discussed whether to get rooms in Dillon for the night or try to make it on to Butte, which would put them much closer to Coeur d'Alene tomorrow.

Because Kipp had been doing all the driving, Beatrice had left the final decision up to him. Now, as he blinked his eyes and flexed his weary shoulders, he wished he'd not attempted this last sixty-five miles. The asphalt was becoming snow packed and slick, which made it impossible to relax his intense focus on the road for even a few seconds.

"Where are the snowplows?" Beatrice asked as she peered out at the darkening landscape. "This is the main interstate going north and south, isn't it?"

"It's the only interstate going into northern Idaho. I-84 at the bottom of the state runs through Boise and on to Oregon. Taking it would've been a superlong way around for us," he explained.

"I'd trade more miles for better weather any day," she said. "Wouldn't you?"

"Sure," he answered. "Except in this case, going 84 wouldn't have been much better. According to the radar, the winter storm is hitting that area, too."

Groaning ruefully, she squinted at the crawling traffic in front of them. "What little I can see, there aren't any kind of road workers up ahead. If they don't have a snowplow around here, you'd think they'd at least have trucks dumping salt or gravel."

"With hundreds of miles of highway to deal with, the workers can't be everywhere at once. They're probably dealing with worse conditions elsewhere."

"Worse? What could possibly be worse? I could probably walk faster than what we're moving," she exclaimed. Then, with a shake of her head, she swiftly apologized. "Sorry, Kipp. I shouldn't be ranting and raving at you, or anyone. I should be grateful we've not come to a complete standstill."

"Exactly. It would be a very cold, miserable night if we had to spend it out here on the highway."

She groaned. "I wouldn't want to try. Although it would probably be an experience to tell all my friends."

Without taking his eyes off the road, he said, "Yeah, you could recount the time you were stuck on the side of the road in a blizzard. That is, if you didn't end up turning into a chunk of ice before morning."

She outwardly shivered. "Please. Don't scare me, Kipp. I always hated those horror movies with the abominable snowman carrying some helpless person off into the icy mountains."

He couldn't help but grin. "Is that any worse than a wild animal dragging you off in the burning-hot desert?"

She said, "I suppose that depends on whether a person would rather freeze or sweat before the end came."

He realized she was trying to joke, but he could hear a thread of tension in her voice. The sound bothered him. She was probably one of the happiest, most optimistic people he'd ever met and he wanted to see her stay that way. Not drag her down with dark warnings. But they were in a precarious position, he thought, and it wouldn't be wise for her to take it too lightly. Still, he didn't want to unduly alarm her.

"Sorry, Bea. I didn't mean to scare you. I was only joking about you turning into a chunk of ice. We wouldn't freeze. I happen to know your mother packed blankets, bottled water and packaged food, just in case of emergency. And we'd have each other's body heat to keep us warm. See, even at the worst, it wouldn't be all that bad," he said while mentally crossing his fingers.

She didn't say anything, but from the corner of his eye, he could see her brows lift. What was she thinking? That she'd rather freeze to death than snuggle up to him? He didn't think so. Several times today she'd reached for his hand and walked close to his side. She'd not acted like a woman who was averse to being close to him. But she might be a bit leery of getting *that* close.

Why start something that's only going to be temporary?

Beatrice's earlier remark about having an affair unwittingly penetrated his thoughts and he realized he wasn't all that surprised by her attitude on the subject. Sure, she'd admitted that she'd been a bit boy crazy since her kindergarten days and she'd had plenty of boyfriends over the years. Yet it was plain to Kipp that she'd seen all the young men she'd dated as friends rather than as something more. He figured most of the men she'd dated had never gotten past kissing her. And the others? Well, he didn't much want to picture her having sex with any man. But oddly enough, it was easy for him to picture himself undressing her, laying her back on a soft bed. And kissing every inch of her body before he claimed it as his own.

Damn, Kipp. Before you climbed into this truck early this morning you were a man with a fair amount of common sense. Being cooped up with Beatrice for a few hundred miles has warped your brain. Sex with this honey-blonde beauty is out of the question for you. Tonight, tomorrow, or ever!

"You did promise to take care of me on this trip. So, I trust you."

Her voice interrupted the mocking words of warning going off in his head and he took his eyes off the road just long enough to glance at her face. The impish expression had him wishing he could safely stop the truck on the side of the highway and pull her into his arms.

"You do?"

Leaning back in the seat, she lightly touched a hand to his arm. "Certainly. You like my dad too much to disappoint him, and Dad happens to be partial to me and Bonnie. We're not only his only set of twins, but we're the babies of the family. He wouldn't like it if you let me turn into a chunk of ice."

Was she deliberately flirting with him?

Even if she is flirting, Kipp, you keep your mind on your driving. And don't let yourself forget you'll soon be telling her goodbye.

Clearing his throat, he pointed to a dim cluster of lights in the distance. "You don't have to worry about freezing now, Bea. Looks like we're about to arrive in Butte."

"I'll be honest. I'm going to be relieved to get off the highway for the night," she said.

"I'll be just as honest and say I'm relieved, too."

But his relief was for an entirely different reason, he thought. Getting out of this truck would give him a chance to put some distance between him and her. Otherwise, he was going to lose his grip and forget the real reason he was on this trip.

They stopped at the first respectable-looking hotel located on a service road off the interstate. After acquiring a pair of rooms on the fourth floor, they went their separate ways to settle in and relax, with plans to meet later for dinner.

Inside the comfortable room, Beatrice tossed her coat and handbag over the back of an armchair, then switched on a pair of bedside lamps. As she sank onto the edge of the queen-size bed and pulled off her boots, her stiff, aching muscles screamed in protest. She couldn't think of a time she'd ever felt this exhausted. But the idea of meeting Kipp in an hour was enough to stop her from curling up on the bed and falling into a deep sleep.

Shoving her tumbled hair back from her face, she was

about to rise and make her way to the bathroom when she heard her cell phone ringing inside her handbag. Snatching the leather bag from the end of the bed, she managed to pull out the phone and answer her father's call before he ended the connection.

"Hi, Dad. Can you hear me okay?" she asked.

"There's a bit of static in the background," he said, "but I can hear you. Are you still traveling?"

About two hours ago, she'd found enough signal on her phone to call Stone Creek and give her parents an update. However, before the conversation had ended, the connection had dropped and she'd been unable to call back.

"No. We're in Butte, Montana. We've stopped for the night. I just got into my room."

She could hear her father let out a sigh of relief.

"Good. What about the snow? Is it letting up?"

A hysterical little laugh came close to bursting out of her, but she clamped her lips together to stifle it. Not for anything did she want her father suspecting she was having a meltdown.

After taking a deep breath and blowing it out, she said, "Unfortunately, it's getting worse. Since I talked with you earlier, we've been traveling in blizzard conditions. To be frank, Kipp and I are both surprised the highway hasn't been closed to traffic."

Hadley cursed under his breath. "You shouldn't have gone on. You should've stopped earlier."

She rolled her eyes. "Dad, it's not like there are a lot of options out here. The little towns are few and far between. Some of them don't even have a motel or hotel. We talked about staying in Dillon, but when we were there, it still wasn't that bad. By the time it got dangerous, Butte was the closest option. And anyway, we both decided we wanted to get as close as possible to Coeur d'Alene before we stopped for the night."

"Well, you're still a hell of a long distance away from there," Hadley muttered, then released a heavy sigh. "I'm sorry, Bea. It's just that I've been worried about the both of you. And I'm feeling like a damned idiot for letting you start out on this trip. I should've never trusted the weather data, but it was predicting this storm to be coming much later in the week. And with Kipp needing to get back to Idaho anyway, there wasn't much wiggling time."

"Dad, there's no need for you to apologize or feel bad about this. You can't control the weather."

"I wish I *could* control it. At least until you got safely back home," he said, then asked, "How's Kipp holding up? I imagine he's cursing the day he agreed to this trip."

The thought of how exhausted Kipp must be feeling left her sighing. "He's obviously tired. He's driven for miles and miles in near-blizzard conditions. We've had to go at a crawl and it's been almost impossible to see two or three feet beyond the hood of the truck. But he's not complaining. In fact, he's been wonderful company."

So wonderful that she wished there were some way of prolonging these days with him. But she could hardly admit that to her father. He'd not sent her to Coeur d'Alene to have a fling with a sexy cowboy. In fact, if Hadley had guessed just how attracted she was to Kipp, she very much doubted he would've asked him to go on this trek with her.

"I wouldn't expect anything else from Kipp. He's

a stand-up guy. Why do you think I asked him to join you?"

Because fate was telling you to? Because it was meant for me to be with Kipp? Even beyond this trip?

The wild questions were darting through her head, even as she tried to come up with a sensible response to give her father. "Um, probably because you like and trust him."

"Darned right about that," he said. "And as soon as I finish this talk with you, I'm going to call him and see what he thinks about this whole situation. Just from looking at the map, I believe it would be pointless to turn around and head back to Utah. You've already traveled too far for that and the storm is moving southward, so that would hardly take you out of the mess."

"Go back? No way, Dad! We'll be fine. Even if we're forced to spend another night on the road, I'm determined to see Scarlett. I can't explain it, but I have this feeling that I'm supposed to meet her face-to-face."

Hadley was silent for long seconds before he said, "Believe me, Bea, in my mind, I've gone over this thing about Scarlett a million times. And each time I'm just as uncertain as to whether I'm doing the right thing. If dealing with the woman ends up causing you distress or pain, I'll never forgive myself. I love you, honey. I don't want you to hurt. Not for any reason."

Tears unexpectedly misted her eyes. "Listen, Dad, maybe I don't act it at times, but I'm tougher than you think. Even if the woman calls me every bad name in the book, I'm not going to let it get to me. I'm just going to thank her for giving me the best father any girl could ask for."

There was another long pause and then her father

spoke in a voice gruff with emotion. "Bea, why the hell do you think I sent you to do this job?"

His question put a puzzled frown on her face. "Because I was the most ready and available one of the family," she answered.

"No. Because I know you have a bit of my—you called it toughness—I'll just call it willpower. You're like a fierce little terrier. You won't quit digging until you get what you're after."

Any other time she would've laughed at his description, but tonight something was making her feel especially sentimental. Besides, it wasn't often her father gave her this type of compliment.

"Oh, Dad, you're worrying me now."

"Why? Hearing your father call you a strong woman scares you?"

"Yes. Because tenacious or not, my meeting with Scarlett could turn out to be a failure. Then what?" She wasn't going to go so far as to tell him that Kipp was doubting the woman's truthfulness. She figured her father had already considered that possibility.

"If it comes up empty, it won't be through any fault of yours. I'll bet on that. Anyway, my only concern is the two of you getting safely to Coeur d'Alene. The rest— well, whatever happens, we'll deal with it."

"Thanks, Dad. I'll do my best."

"I've never even considered you'd do anything less," he said gently. "Now I'm going to hang up and call Kipp. You get some rest. Good night, honey."

She gave him her love, then ended the connection and thoughtfully placed the phone on the nightstand.

You won't quit digging until you get what you're after.

In his own way, her father had been saying Beatrice wasn't a quitter, and he was right. It was extremely hard for her to give up on any endeavor she started. Even when the endeavor looked hopeless. Which meant she'd better not let herself get started on Kipp. Like seriously wanting him. With all her heart and soul. If that happened, she'd never be able to give him up. She'd be stuck on the man for the rest of her life. A man who didn't want a wife or children. She'd be doomed to a one-sided love.

Giving herself a hard mental shake, she pushed herself to her feet. She didn't have time to sit around pondering such silly ideas. She wasn't going to fall in love with Kipp. She was only going to enjoy his company for the next day or two. And then she'd be giving him a cheery goodbye.

Well, maybe it wouldn't exactly be a cheery parting, she thought, as she placed a small suitcase on the bed and lifted the lid. But she'd be sure to be smiling enough to convince him she was happy to be going home to Stone Creek. And why wouldn't she be happy? Back in Beaver County, she had everything a woman could want. A comfortable home, a job she adored and a family who loved her. Yeah, everything she wanted was there, she thought. Except Kipp.

After Kipp spoke with Hadley, he'd been tempted to call Beatrice and tell her he was too tired to make it downstairs to the hotel restaurant. Which was very nearly true. He was more exhausted than he could ever remember being. But that wasn't why he wanted to miss the meal. Talking with Hadley reminded Kipp that he was expected to be a gentleman. The Hollister patriarch trusted him implicitly with his daughter's well-being. Which hardly included keeping her warm by way of his bed. And the more time he spent with Beatrice, the more he was thinking about holding her in his arms. Not just for a few seconds or for several minutes, but holding her all through the night.

Somewhere between Idaho and Montana, she'd cast some enchanting glow over him. His brain was no longer working like a thirty-six-year-old man who knew about women. It had reverted to his teenage days, when his thoughts had been controlled by raging testosterone. Somehow he had to break this spell she'd put him under—and he figured sitting across the dinner table from her wasn't going to help him break anything. Except his peace of mind, he thought ruefully.

But leaving her to eat alone wouldn't be a gentlemanly thing to do. Besides, he had to admit, foolish or not, he wanted to be with her.

He was raking a comb through his hair when a faint knock sounded on the door and then Beatrice's voice called out, "It's me, Kipp."

Tossing the comb aside, he went over and opened the door to find her standing a couple of steps back from the threshold. Her black jeans and sweater had been changed to a long red skirt and some sort of silky white top covered with a furry white jacket. The dim light in the corridor illuminated the golden waves of her hair and a portion of her face. The fatigue he saw on her lovely features made him want to gather her in his arms, to cradle her head against his chest and hear her sigh with contentment.

Oh Lord, this wasn't good, he thought. This wasn't the way to start the evening or end it.

"Ready to go?" she asked. "Or am I too early?"

"Uh—no. You're not early. I'm ready." He darted a glance over his shoulder at the wide, empty bed directly behind him. He didn't dare invite her into his room. Not with such erotic thoughts running through his head. "I'll fetch my hat."

"While you're at it, you should probably get your jacket," she suggested. "It's not exactly toasty here in the corridor. The restaurant might be chilly."

Leaving the door ajar, he stepped back into the room long enough to collect his things, then carefully shut the door behind him. Thankfully, she was too busy gazing at a tall Christmas tree erected at the opposite end of the corridor to notice he was making a point to keep her out of his room.

Turning her attention back to him, she smiled. "I'm so glad most of the businesses still have their Christmas decorations on display. No matter about the storm, this time of year is such a lovely time to travel. I'm one lucky girl."

Chuckling, he shoved his hat down on his head, then pulled on his jacket. "For being holed up in Butte in a snowstorm? If that's what you consider good luck, I'd hate to see the bad."

Laughing softly, she looped her arm through his. "Think about it, Kipp. I'm getting to see all kinds of different countryside, little communities and big towns and—"

"And everything is hidden beneath a coat of snow," he finished for her.

"The snow goes along with the Christmas cheer that's still floating in the air."

"Especially in subzero windchill," he said with sardonic humor. "The freezing temperature makes it extra festive."

Pulling a playful face at him, she urged him forward. "Bah humbug. You definitely need to eat. Hopefully, some tasty food will put a smile on your face."

There it was again, Kipp thought. That strange glow that spread through him each time she smiled at him or touched him. He didn't know why this woman was causing such a reaction in him, but he certainly knew he needed to get a handle on his feelings. If not, she was going to have him wrapped so tightly around her little finger, he'd never get loose.

He darted an inquisitive glance at her. "You think I need to smile more?"

She gave his arm another squeeze. "Only if you actually want to. Otherwise, it wouldn't mean anything. Faking being happy or pleased isn't good. Not when you're really feeling like a scrooge."

"So, you consider faking a smile to be the same as living a lie," he replied, unable to keep the mocking humor from his voice.

She let out a short laugh. "Well, I don't consider it *that* extreme. But who likes fake things? I don't."

Fake smiles. Fake laughs. Fake words and promises. He'd been on the receiving end of all those things. With his father and stepmother. With the girl he'd once thought he wanted to marry. One way or the other, all of them had been deceptive. Their deceit had cut him to the very core of his being and altered the course of his life. He'd had plenty of face-to-face dealings with fake people. But he wouldn't tell Beatrice that. He didn't want to ruin this evening for her or himself.

As they paused in front of the elevator doors, he

slanted her a pointed look. "You want the real deal, huh?"

A faint smile curved the corners of her lips. "That's right. The real deal. Or nothing at all."

When the elevator doors swished open, they stepped into a large lobby furnished with plush leather furniture accented with wood. Paintings and still photos depicting scenes of the old and present-day West covered most of the walls, while cowhide rugs were scattered across the varnished pine floor. At one end an enormous fireplace was burning what appeared to be huge logs. But on closer glance the flames were originating from carefully hidden gas burners.

As they passed near the fireplace, Kipp gestured toward the flames. "You probably don't like the fire. It's fake."

Chuckling, she said, "It doesn't compare to the real crackling logs of Dad's fires. But it still looks beautiful, and the heat feels wonderful. Sometimes, Kipp, a bit of pretense is better than nothing at all."

Yeah, he used to do a lot of pretending, as a way to hang on to his sanity. He had to keep imagining and promising himself that someday he would get the Rising Starr back into his and his sister's hands, where it rightfully belonged. But eight years had passed and the reality was that his stepmother still had her claws firmly embedded in the Starr property. Now he wanted to believe that with Quint and Flint's help, they'd find the evidence needed to prove Andrea had stolen the ranch. But that might take a miracle and Kipp wasn't sure he believed in miracles anymore.

With her arm still looped through his, they walked across the lobby and through a wide entryway to the restaurant. The room was dimly lit and furnished with countless round wooden tables and chairs, plus two rows of booths padded with dark red vinyl. On the opposite wall from the entrance, a long bar was fitted with tall stools and shelves stocked with endless bottles of spirits.

As they stood inside the door, waiting to be seated, he noticed many of the tables and booths were already occupied with evening diners. Which was surprising, considering the brutal weather hammering the city. But then, the majority of these folks might be traveling and in the same predicament as he and Beatrice—desperate to get off the road.

He was gazing toward the front of the room, where plate-glass windows revealed a view of an outside courtyard landscaped with spruce and junipers, when he felt Beatrice's hand wrap around his.

"Look, Kipp, they have a bar. I'd love to have a drink before dinner. Would you?"

She was already making his head buzz, he thought. One little drink likely wouldn't muddle his senses any more than they were already. With any luck, a shot of whiskey might clear away the stardust she'd been sprinkling in his eyes.

"Sounds good to me," he told her.

At that moment a hostess approached them, and once Kipp informed her they wanted to go to the bar before they ordered dinner, the middle-aged woman with a messy black bun and brown floral dress ushered them through the maze of tables until they reached two empty stools at the bar.

"Enjoy your drinks," she told them with an easy

smile. "I'll have a booth reserved for you whenever you're ready for dinner."

The hostess turned to leave at the same time the bartender, a big burly man with bushy white hair and an equally white handlebar mustache, moved down the counter to where they were seated.

"What can I get for you folks this evening? Wine? Brandy? It's mighty cold tonight."

"Cold or not, I want a martini on the rocks," Beatrice told him.

Kipp arched a playful brow at her. "Are you sure you're old enough to drink a martini?"

Frowning at him, she looked at the bartender. "What do you think? Is twenty-six old enough to drink a cocktail?"

Chuckling, the man inclined his head in Kipp's direction. "Does he always give you a bad time?"

Beatrice laughed. "Not really. He's my protector."

Kipp gave the bartender a wry grin. "Looks like I'm falling down on the job."

With another chuckle, the bartender said, "I don't think she's going to give you any trouble tonight."

No. Not from overindulging in cocktails. But she was giving him plenty of trouble in other ways that had nothing to do with alcohol.

"In that case, I'll take a bourbon and Coke," Kipp told him.

The man gave him a thumbs-up before turning away to mix the drinks.

Beatrice swiveled the stool so that she was facing him, then casually crossed her legs. Kipp was glad her skirt was long, because he had a feeling if he ever did catch sight of her legs, he wouldn't be able to get the image out of his mind.

"Kipp, after the day you've put in driving, you definitely need a cocktail or two," she told him. "You have to be exhausted."

"I'm okay."

She tilted her head to one side and he watched a strand of her long hair fall onto the white fur of her jacket. Even in the soft lighting over the bar, the blond wave held a healthy gloss, and not for the first time, he found himself wanting to reach out and touch it.

"Did Dad call you?" she asked.

He wiped a weary hand over his face. "Yes. We talked and I agreed that it's far too late to turn around and head back to Utah. I assured him I wouldn't take any unnecessary chances. If the highway looks too bad to go on tomorrow, we'll just have to wait it out."

Her blue eyes made a slow perusal of his face and he couldn't help but wonder what she was seeing, thinking. Moreover, what was he wanting her to see when she looked at him? A man who'd basically worked most of his life for someone else? A cowboy who'd probably never have much more than a horse and saddle and place to hang his hat?

She said, "Ever since Dad talked to me about taking this trip, I've been excited about going. Which is hardly a surprise to you, I know. I just talked about enjoying traveling at Christmastime. But I—"

He urged her to finish. "You what?"

"Well, I can't help feeling bad about you." She sighed, then shook her head. "I've not said this before, but I think Dad was asking too much of you to go on this trip with me. He put you on the spot and you felt beholden to take on the task. We both know that much is true. And that makes me feel bad for you—and for me."

Maybe at first Kipp had felt roped into this journey. He'd decided there'd been no polite way of refusing Hadley, even though he'd wanted to run like hell from the whole proposition. But those reluctant feelings had left him way back in Utah. Probably before they'd ever passed over the Beaver County line. Now it was impossible to imagine not being with Beatrice. Not making sure she was safe and warm and happy.

He absently rubbed his fingertips against the smooth counter of the bar. "Like I said before, Bea, I'm still wondering why your father asked me to make this journey with you."

She frowned at him. "I told you why. He trusts you."

Kipp shook his head. "I imagine he knows plenty of men that he trusts. He's only known me for a few short days. Frankly, it doesn't make sense."

"Naturally, he has lots of friends he'd trust with his life. But in case you didn't notice while you were on Stone Creek, Dad does things his own way. Not necessarily the way others think is best."

He had to smile at that. "Yeah. I can't see anyone telling Hadley what to do or how to do it."

The bartender arrived with their drinks, and once he'd served them and moved on down the bar, Beatrice took a tiny sip from her glass. "I can't remember a time Dad ever raised his voice to us kids," she said gently. "He didn't have to. I guess we all instinctively knew he meant what he said and we'd turn out the loser if we disobeyed him."

Maybe it was the dim lighting that was causing melancholy shadows to slip over her face, or perhaps talking about her father was making her miss her family. Whatever the reason, he didn't like seeing her expression turn somber.

Pulling his gaze away from her, he took a long swig of the bourbon and welcomed the warmth sliding down to his empty gut. "You're wrong, Bea."

She shifted slightly on the bar stool. "About what?"

Staring at the liquid swirling around in his glass, he said, "About me not wanting to be here with you. I do—want to be here."

She released a long breath, but whether it was a sound of relief or something else, he couldn't guess. "I'm glad. But I still feel like I'm twisting your arm."

He swallowed another sip of the drink, then turned a grin on her. "Bea, you're not strong enough to twist my arm."

She laughed and the sound warmed him even more than the bourbon.

"No. Probably not. But you better watch out for Bonnie," she teased. "She's twice as strong as I am."

Up until a week ago, laughter was something other people did to express their amusement and joy, not Kipp. But since he'd met Beatrice, he'd caught himself laughing on several occasions. Was she turning him into a soft sap or was he beginning to be a human again? He didn't know, but the idea that she might be changing him, even just a little, was enough to unnerve him.

"You're a funny girl, Bea."

"You think so? I don't really try to be."

"I don't know anyone else like you," he told her. "Honestly."

The smile on her face carved deep crescents in both her cheeks. "I'm glad. I wouldn't want to be like anyone else. Not even my twin."

"I don't think there's any danger of that happening," he said. "And I mean that. In a good way."

She reached over and rested her hand on his knee and he couldn't help thinking the sensation was like brushing against an electric wire fence. It wasn't causing unbearable pain, but it sure as heck made him want to jerk away from the danger.

"Thank you, Kipp. Especially for calling me funny instead of silly. Like my siblings sometimes do."

Her voice held a husky note that trickled down his spine like drops of hot water.

"You're welcome."

The two words were all he could manage to push out of his throat, and it wasn't until she finally pulled her hand back that he allowed himself to breathe.

After a moment, she asked, "Do you think it would be okay if we carried our drinks over to the window? I'd love to get a closer look at the courtyard."

"I'll ask the bartender," he told her.

When the older man answered with a thumbs-up sign, they left the bar and, with drinks in hand, walked over to the wide expanse of plate glass. Footlights lit a stone pathway that had recently been shoveled clean, while the limbs of the tall spruces and junipers were sagging from the weight of the snow. High drifts of the white stuff had accumulated on the seats of two wooden park benches, yet it was easy for Kipp to imagine how inviting the little courtyard would be come spring. Flowers would be blooming and birds would be chirping and Beatrice would most likely be champing at the bit to carry their drinks outside to sit on one of the benches.

"I might be imagining it, but the snowfall appears to

be letting up a little." She glanced hopefully up at him. "Do you think so?"

"It doesn't seem to be peppering down as thickly as it was earlier. And the wind looks like it's easing up. We'll see how the highway looks in the morning."

She thoughtfully sipped the martini. "Well, whatever happens, happens. And this will probably sound a little strange to you, Kipp, but I'm getting the odd feeling that this storm was meant to happen."

He grunted with wry amusement. "Of course this winter blast was meant to happen. Otherwise, it wouldn't have. Or are you being like Nuttah again? You're having a *feeling*?"

"I must be doing Nuttah's thing again," she admitted. Then, frowning slightly, she shook her head. "The idea that my meeting with Scarlett is meant to be detained keeps running through my mind. It's an eerie feeling, Kipp."

Frowning, he took another sip of his drink. "I thought you told me you weren't worried about meeting her."

Sighing, she said, "I'm not worried about her. I'm not even sure this intuition I have directly concerns her. I just have the feeling that something unexpected is going to happen."

Something unexpected was already happening. To him. She probably couldn't see the change, but Kipp could damned well feel it. And this was after only day one of their time together. What kind of man was he going to be when she finally headed back to Utah—without him?

The question had him gulping down the last of his drink and slipping an arm around the back of her waist.

"Come on. You need to eat," he said more gruffly

than he'd intended. "Not dwell on the storm or what might happen tomorrow."

As they walked back to the bar, she said, "You're right, Kipp. We still have tonight. And I want to enjoy this time with you."

With you.

He didn't know exactly what those two words meant to her. But one thing he knew for certain; he couldn't let them mean anything to him.

No. Kipp Starr was on a mission. And his objective didn't include falling in love with Beatrice, or any woman.

Chapter Seven

After dinner, Beatrice had ordered dessert and coffee because she'd been craving brownies with a double dollop of whipped cream. And she'd wanted to prolong their time over the dinner table. She wanted to keep listening to the sound of his low, masculine voice. She wanted to continue gazing into his dark brown eyes and imagining them looking at her with desire and passion. And now as they stepped off the elevator and walked arm in arm down the corridor to their rooms, she still wasn't ready to let him go. Physically, or otherwise.

When they finally reached the door to her room, he turned a questioning look on her. "Do you mind getting up early in the morning? If the northbound lanes of the highway are passable, I think we should get a head start."

"I don't mind at all," she told him. "What time would you like to get on the road? I need a few minutes for coffee."

While he pondered her question, Beatrice continued to hold on to his arm and drink in the pleasure of standing close to his hard, rugged body.

She wasn't sure what sort of upheaval had been taking

place inside her since she'd left Stone Creek Ranch very early this morning, but the hours she'd spent with Kipp had definitely done something to her. And whatever this euphoric feeling was that had swept over her, she didn't want to let it go. She didn't want to let *him* go.

"By seven, at the latest," he told her. "But if you don't mind getting up early, we can make time for breakfast here in the hotel restaurant before we go."

"Sounds great. I'll be ready by six." Her eyes met his and the warm glint she saw in the brown orbs caused her heart to skip a beat, then jump into the imitation of a jackhammer.

"Whenever you're ready, you can ring my phone," he said, "and I'll meet you here at your door."

As he spoke, his gaze dropped to her lips and Beatrice's breath caught in her throat. Was he thinking about kissing her? As much as she was thinking about kissing him?

"I'll do that," she murmured.

He gently cleared his throat, then drew in a deep breath. "Well, we—uh—should probably say goodnight."

Her gaze still clinging to his, she turned so that the front of her body was aligned with his. She wasn't sure if it was mere physical craving or something more, but it was pushing aside all caution. At this very moment she needed to touch him. To show him how much she wanted him. "Yes. But there's something we should do first. Don't you think?"

"Something?"

"Yes—this." Her heart pounding, she rested her palms against the middle of his chest at the same time she rose on the tips of her toes and angled her lips up to his.

She thought she heard a tiny moan in his throat, but

she couldn't be sure. Not when her heart was beating so loudly she could hear it roaring in her ears, and sparks were flying behind her closed eyes. And then as their lips made contact, the sights and sounds around her dissolved into a whirling mass of sensations.

His mouth felt so perfect against hers. Firm and sweet. Gentle, yet masterful. He tasted like coffee and the chocolate mousse he'd had for dessert. But most of all he tasted like a man. A real man who was strong enough to carry her off to his warm bed. The wicked idea added fuel to the desire coursing through her and she unwittingly deepened the search she was making of his lips.

It wasn't until she felt his hand meshing in the hair at the back of her head that she realized the kiss had gone on for far longer than she'd planned. She'd wanted to simply show him she was interested in him. Not imply she wanted them to have sex!

Summoning all the willpower she could find, she eased her mouth from his and lowered her feet back to the floor.

"I—um—just had to do that." Unable to meet his gaze, she focused her eyes on a button of his shirt. "I hope you don't mind."

The hand in her hair moved ever so slightly and she closed her eyes as a rash of goose bumps covered her skin.

"Did I act like I minded?"

The huskily spoken question had her lifting her head and her heart took another hard jolt as she gazed into the brown depths of his eyes.

"No."

His lips took on a wry slant and she stared at them,

amazed that one kiss from them had tilted her senses. Had she really kissed him like there'd be no tomorrow? Oh, what could he be thinking?

"Then you shouldn't mind this," he murmured.

She watched in fascination as his head lowered until his lips were hovering above hers and then her eyes instinctively closed as the breath rushed from her lungs.

"Kipp…"

His kiss blotted out the whisper of his name, and as his lips began a slow, heady search of her mouth, she forgot they were standing in the corridor where anyone might come along and see them. She forgot that her time with him was limited and she'd soon be telling him goodbye. All she could think was that the taste of his lips was like nothing she'd ever experienced. The feel of his arms circling lightly around her shoulders was wrapping her in warm pleasure.

When he finally lifted his head, she stared at him in dazed wonder. "Was that supposed to be a payback?" she asked.

A faint smile curved his lips as he lifted fingertips to her cheek. "No. That was a good-night."

Still rattled from what had just taken place between them, Beatrice sucked in a shaky breath and tried to compose herself. But how could she gather her senses when his hands continued to rest on her shoulders and the warmth of his body was pulling at her like a strong magnet?

"Oh. Well—good night, Kipp."

Not waiting around for a reply, she turned and dug the room key from the pocket of her jacket. Her hand was shaking as she jammed the card into the slot, but thankfully, he'd already turned and walked away without seeing her shaky confusion.

Inside the room, she hurriedly bolted the door, then blindly tossed her jacket and handbag into an armchair before walking over to the bed.

Sitting on the side of the mattress, she dropped her head in her hand and closed her eyes. She'd never done anything so impulsive in her life. But surprise over her own reckless behavior was only a part of the reason she was overcome with rattled nerves.

Oh Lord, her friends back in her hometown of Beaver would surely laugh if they could see her right now. Man-crazy Beatrice, the girl who thought she knew all about the male species, had been completely blown away by two little kisses.

Wrong, Bea. Those weren't just little kisses. Those lip-locks were whoppers. And you were like a puppet in Kipp's hands.

She had to admit the mocking voice in her head was horribly right. After the first kiss, Kipp could've taken her by the hand and led her straight off a cliff if he'd been so minded to. She thanked God he'd had enough wherewithal not to take advantage of her emotional state.

Who are you kidding? You're not thankful that Kipp walked away. You're so disappointed you want to bury your face in a pillow and cry yourself into oblivion.

She was gritting her teeth, fighting against the taunts sounding off in her head, when she heard her cell phone ring.

Relieved to have her thoughts interrupted, she went over to her purse and quickly dug out the phone. The instant she saw the caller was Bonnie, she pressed the accept button.

"Hi, sissy! I know it's getting late. Did I catch you at a bad time?" Bonnie asked.

Pushing her jacket to one side, she eased into the chair, while keeping the phone pressed to her ear. "No. You timed your call just right. I've just now gotten back to my room from dinner downstairs in the hotel restaurant."

"Oh. I'm glad to hear you're safely off the road for the night."

"We've stopped in Butte. I imagined Dad would've already told you."

"He's not had a chance to talk with me and Mom. He's been on the phone for most of the evening," she explained. "Talking to a hay dealer down in Fallon, Nevada. He's trying to make a deal for twenty tons."

"Ouch. There goes that new couch Mom has been wanting."

Bonnie chuckled. "For what we'll be spending, we could have gotten a couch, two chairs and a set of matching end tables. But Mom always agrees that the livestock comes first," she said, then asked, "Is the weather letting up any? I'll be honest, Bea. I've been worried ever since I learned you were traveling through a snowstorm. Was it really blizzard conditions?"

"I'd call it a blizzard. We could hardly see the edge of the highway. Kipp used the taillights ahead of us as a guide."

Bonnie was silent for a moment before she said, "I know you had planned to be in Coeur d'Alene tonight. This has really put a crimp in your journey, hasn't it?"

"Yes. But I guess you could say we're just rolling with the flow. There's not much else we can do."

"Is Kipp upset about the delay?"

Upset? Over dinner, he'd insisted again that he didn't

regret agreeing to the trip, and after that kiss he'd given her, she had to believe him. Or did she? Could be he'd just been playing with her. Or even worse, he was feeling sorry for her, because he could see the stars in her eyes every time she looked at him. The idea made her want to crawl under the covers and never show her face again.

"He doesn't seem to be. I think—well, he's the sort that takes things in stride."

There was another pause from Bonnie, and then she said, "There's something wrong with you, sissy. Tell me what it is."

She was glad her sister couldn't see her rolling her eyes. "Why do you always think you can read my voice?"

"Ha! I'm not reading your voice—I'm reading your mind. You were full of excitement when you left the ranch early this morning. Now you sound like you've just gone through the worst day of your life. What's happened? Did Kipp tell you that he has a steady girlfriend?"

Everything inside Beatrice revolted at the idea of Kipp being serious about any woman—except her. "No. He doesn't have a girlfriend. He—uh—holds the idea he doesn't want a wife or family."

"That hardly means he can't have a girlfriend," Bonnie pointed out.

Grimacing, Beatrice rose from the chair and walked over to the window. Pulling back the heavy drape, she stared down at a parking lot located at the back of the building. Snow was continuing to fall and stack in drifts around the vehicles parked in designated slots. As she gazed at the forlorn sight, a man, woman and child emerged from a canopied covered entrance. The child was bundled in a heavy coat and furry hood and clung to the hands of both parents.

The image struck her with a question she'd only recently begun to ask herself. Would she ever have a husband and child? Would she ever find a man she could really love? Would there ever be a man who loved her enough to want her as his wife and the mother of his children?

Shaking away the nagging questions, she said, "I realize that, Bonnie. But he—"

"He what?" Bonnie prompted.

She sighed. "Nothing. And nothing bad has happened. There's a good reason I don't sound excited. I am beyond tired. Sitting for hours and hours in a truck has left me feeling like I've rolled down a cliff!"

"I can imagine. But I expected you to be chattering ninety miles an hour about Kipp. Your silence is very telling, Bea."

Grimacing, Beatrice rubbed her fingertips across her forehead. "You always were too smart for your own good, sissy," she said, then sighed. "Okay. I'm going to admit it—I have a crush on Kipp."

Bonnie laughed. "Bea, you're getting terrible at telling jokes. We both know you've had a crush on Kipp ever since he arrived on the ranch and Quint introduced him to us."

That day would forever be branded in Beatrice's mind. Quint had been away on a sheep-buying venture, and when he'd finally returned to the ranch, the family learned he'd hauled more than a huge load of merinos from Idaho. Kipp Starr, the man who would soon be his brother-in-law, had made the trip to Stone Creek with him. And when Quint had introduced the cowboy to his parents and siblings, Beatrice had been secretly blown away. Not because he'd looked like a mustang stallion. No, the jolt she'd felt had been brought on by more than his rugged good looks. She'd felt an odd sense of connection.

Her frown deepened. "You're right. As usual. So I'll just say that my crush has grown crushier and I don't know what to do about it."

"My dear sister, there isn't such a word as *crushier*. Are you trying to tell me your feelings for Kipp have grown from a crush to serious liking?"

Serious liking. Beatrice silently repeated the words. Actually, what she felt for Kipp had moved beyond liking to intense wanting, but she wasn't ready to admit that to her sister. At least, not yet.

"It's true that the more I'm with him, the more I like him. But he's—" She paused and swallowed as unexpected emotions tightened her throat. "Well, you were right all along, sissy. It's hopeless for me to think of him as a—boyfriend. Or anything remotely close to boyfriend."

"If I recall our conversation about Kipp correctly, you said all you had in mind was enjoying the cowboy's company for a couple of days."

Oh, she was more than enjoying his company, Beatrice thought. What would Bonnie think if she told her exactly how much she'd enjoyed those two kisses? Bonnie would be shocked, no doubt. Because her twin, more than anyone, realized that in spite of Beatrice's numerous boyfriends and endless gushes over good-looking men, she was mostly all talk. In fact, Beatrice had never initiated a kiss with any of her past dates.

Her hand trembled slightly as she pushed it through

a wave of hair at her temple and tried to give Bonnie a sensible reply. "You remember correctly, dear sister. And that's all I plan to do. Enjoy this trip with Kipp and then tell him goodbye."

"You're saying I don't have to worry about this crush of yours getting any crushier than it is right now?" Bonnie teased the question.

Beatrice forced herself to chuckle. "No. No need for you to worry at all," she said, then deliberately changed the subject. "How is the weather there tonight? I guess Dad and the guys are preparing for the worst."

"Nothing here yet in the way of a storm, but it is very cold," Bonnie told her. "If you can believe it, Clem and Quint are camping out tonight over by Snow Mountain. They'll be herding the sheep closer to the ranch tomorrow."

She bit back a wistful sigh. "Clem and Quint are in love. They'll never feel the cold."

"You're probably right," Bonnie replied, then added, "Those two getting engaged made this Christmas celebration wonderful for the whole family. And Kipp seemed genuinely happy for his sister."

From what Beatrice could tell, Kipp was extremely happy for his sister's plans to marry. Which seemed such a paradox given that he didn't want a family of his own.

She said, "For the past eight years, except for the couple of winter months she always stayed with Nuttah, she's basically lived alone, with only a herd of sheep, her dogs and horses to keep her company. He's happy she's decided to return to a more normal life."

"Hmm. Maybe someday she'll tell us why she decided to leave the Rising Starr and live like a nomad after her father died," Bonnie replied. "I can understand she was probably full of grief. But you'd think she'd want to stay close to her brother. Not that it matters, but it does intrigue me."

Beatrice wished Kipp would share more about his past with her, but he usually steered their conversations away from his personal life. And at this point, she didn't feel she had the right to ply him with private questions.

"From everything Kipp has told me, he's very devoted to the Rising Starr," Beatrice told her. "He wouldn't leave it for any reason."

"I imagined that was the way he felt. And think about it, Bea—all our brothers are the same way. Can you imagine any of them leaving Stone Creek? True, Hunter and Flint have jobs outside the ranch, but they'll always call it home. I can see Kipp being the same way."

Bonnie hadn't included herself when she'd talked about her brothers and the ranch, but Beatrice already knew that her twin wouldn't leave Stone Creek. Not for the love of a man or any reason.

Walking back over to the bed, she sank wearily onto the side of the mattress. "Is this your way of reminding me not to fall for Kipp?"

"Why, no! You've already assured me that you're only out for a little fun."

Fun. So why were her insides still shaking? Why was she still seeing his face drawing down toward hers? Why were her lips continuing to burn from the kiss he'd plastered on them? Oh, this wasn't good, she thought.

"Forget I asked, Bonnie. I'm very tired. I hardly know what I'm saying."

"Poor little sissy, I need to say goodbye and let you get some rest," she said. "As of now, are you two planning to drive on to Coeur d'Alene in the morning?"

"Yes. Unless things get worse in the night."

"Okay. Call me tomorrow when you have a chance. Love you."

"Yes, I'll call. And I love you, too. Very much."

Tears suddenly sprang to her eyes and she hurriedly disconnected the call before Bonnie could add anything else. Her sister wouldn't understand her overly emotional mood. Frankly, Beatrice couldn't understand it herself. Except all the talk about Kipp never leaving the Rising Starr had been a hard jolt to her senses.

Because as much as she wanted to be in his arms, she could never see herself leaving Stone Creek and her family behind.

The next morning, Kipp had been relieved to see a weak stream of sunlight shining through the windows and the snow depth mostly unchanged from the night before. He'd thought Beatrice would be happy and smiling to see an improvement in their traveling conditions. But she'd seemed rather subdued as they'd eaten breakfast in the hotel restaurant.

Now as he steered the truck onto a northbound lane of the highway and she stared pensively out the passenger window, he had to wonder if she was upset about the kisses they'd shared. As for Kipp, the word *upset* couldn't begin to describe the way Beatrice's kisses had affected him.

He'd lain awake for half the night, wondering why she'd reached for him in the first place and wondering, too, why having her lips touching his, her fingers curling into his chest, had very nearly rocked him off his feet.

He'd kissed pretty girls before and the experiences had been pleasant enough. But even kissing Evie, the woman he'd thought he might want as his wife, hadn't affected him so deeply. So why had locking lips with Beatrice knocked him silly? Everything about her was wrong for him. Why couldn't he think about all those wrong things, instead of dwelling on the sweet softness of her lips?

"You didn't eat very much breakfast," he said, while keeping his attention firmly on the road. "Aren't you feeling well?"

"I'm fine. I just wasn't all that hungry. Not after eating such a big dinner last night."

From the corner of his eye, he could see she wasn't making any effort to look at him. Instead, she was staring out the passenger window. Her passive attitude was totally out of character and more than a little unnerving to him.

A few miles passed in silence before he decided being frank was the best way to approach her. "Are you angry with me?"

The question whipped her head around and he glanced over to see she was staring at him in disbelief.

"No! I'm not angry. Why would I be angry?"

If he had any sense, he'd drop the whole matter, Kipp thought. Sometimes it was best to leave things unsaid. But he couldn't. How she felt about him—about everything—mattered.

"Okay, you're not angry," he answered. "But you are upset with me."

"No!" she repeated emphatically. "Why would you be thinking such a thing?"

Shrugging, he absently rubbed a hand against his jaw. "You're awfully quiet. And you're having trouble looking me in the face. I guess I should've shaved for you this morning. That might've made seeing me across the breakfast table a little easier on your eyes."

To his relief, she smiled.

"Don't be silly. If you'd shown up this morning without whiskers, I would've thought I was traveling with a stranger," she said.

"I didn't realize I'd been so lazy these past few days."

"Is that what you call it? Being lazy?"

He glanced over to see the corners of her lips curved into a deeper smile. Seeing her mood lift was better than the weak ray of sunshine filtering through the windshield.

"In the cold months I don't bother with shaving much. In the summer I shave more often because wearing a beard can be warm. Besides, it's not like there's anyone around who cares whether my face is smooth."

She didn't say anything to that and he kept his eyes on the highway as he carefully chose his next words.

"I should probably apologize for kissing you like I did last night. I imagine you thought I was getting out of line. And I—well, I'm sorry."

There was a short stretch of silence and then she said, "You must have forgotten, Kipp. I'm the one who kissed you first. Not the other way around."

Forgotten? Every second their lips had touched, the brief moments she'd been in his arms, all those sensations had been burned into his brain. He'd never forget them, or her.

"I remember," he murmured.

"Then you should know you have nothing to apologize for," she told him. "I wanted to kiss you, so I did. There's no need for you to feel bad about anything. Unless—you didn't like having me kiss you. If that's the case, then I apologize for putting you through the ordeal."

"Ordeal?" Kipp was sorely tempted to pull the truck off the highway and show her exactly what he'd thought about their kisses. But this thing between them was already bad enough without adding fuel to the fire. "You know good and darned well I liked it! What are you doing? Fishing for compliments?"

From a side glance, he saw her eyes widen and her mouth fall open. "Are you living on another planet?"

"I must be," he muttered. "Why else would we be having this conversation?"

Her mouth snapped shut as she turned her head and stared straight ahead. "I don't know. Why are we?"

He tugged at the brim of his hat while trying to recall one woman who'd made him feel this frustrated or stupid. He couldn't think of one.

"You seemed out of sorts this morning. What happened with us last night was the only logical reason I could come up with to explain your mood," he said gruffly. "And I wanted to try to make you a bit cheerier. That's all."

She pinched the bridge of her nose and released a long, heavy breath. "Forgive me, Kipp. I am off-kilter this morning. It's not your fault and I appreciate you wanting me to feel better. I'll be fine. I guess I'm more anxious about meeting Scarlett than I thought I'd be."

He didn't understand why, but something in her voice caused a mix of pleasure and pain to strike the middle of his chest. "Listen, Bea, there's no reason for you to be anxious. One way or the other, you're going to come out of this meeting with Scarlett just fine."

She reached across the console for his hand, and without giving it a second thought, he curled his fingers around hers.

"Thank you, Kipp. You've made me feel better," she

said. "And in case you haven't figured it out yet, I enjoyed our kisses. Very much. But they were only kisses. Nothing for either of us to get bent out of shape over."

Only kisses. He'd be much better off if he viewed them as only kisses instead of having this half-cocked notion that kissing her had put him through some life-altering experience.

"I'm glad we have that out of the way," he told her. "We have several hours to go before we get to Coeur d'Alene and I want you to enjoy this last leg of the trip."

Her smile tepid, she eased her hand from his and rested it on her lap. "I want you to enjoy the remainder of our journey, too. Do you have any idea what time we might get to Coeur d'Alene?"

Shrugging, he wondered why he suddenly felt so deflated. Because she'd moved her hand away? Or because she'd made light of kissing him?

Damn it, Kipp, you're losing it. You need to focus on your driving. You need to get these next couple of days over with and get away from this woman before she turns you into a complete idiot.

"Normally, I'd say we could make the trip in four hours. But with snow still packing the highways, I'm not going to be able to pick up much speed. With any luck, we might get there by midafternoon," he told her.

"Midafternoon," she repeated thoughtfully. "That should give me plenty of time to plan how I'm going to introduce myself to Scarlett."

He shook his head. "Is there more than one way? If I were in your place, I'd be simple and frank. Give her your name and explain that Hadley is your father. Surely she hasn't forgotten she once had a son by that name."

She tapped a forefinger against her chin. "Maybe I

should ask her if she remembers Hadley? Her firstborn son? The one she left behind when he was only a little boy?" Grimacing, she added in a sarcastic voice, "That ought to get me off on the right foot with my paternal grandmother."

"Look, Bea, this is your family business. If you think you should handle the old woman with kid gloves, then by all means, go for it. You should conduct this meeting the way you see fit. Not the way I'd do it."

She rolled her eyes in a hopeless fashion. "That's the problem, Kipp. I can't decide on the best way to approach her. I guess playing it by ear might be the best. And hopefully when I walk up to her, the right words will come to me."

"Yeah. A feeling might come over you—like Nuttah gets."

With a good-natured groan, she said, "You're teasing me now."

He shook his head. "No. I'm being serious. Nuttah does have these— I'm not sure what to call them. Mystical intuitions, I suppose. Anyway, she's been right too many times for me to dismiss them."

She looked at him. "You mean the woman makes predictions?"

"I wouldn't exactly call them predictions," he tried to explain. "She has premonitions. Mostly about people and places. For example, when Clem first went down to Stone Creek to take the sheepherding job, she told me that my sister wouldn't be back. Which turned out to be true. Clem won't be back to Idaho. To visit, maybe. But not to live."

He could feel Beatrice staring a hole in the side of

his face and then she let out a dismissive chuckle. "She was only making an instinctive guess."

"Well, I'll be honest. When Nuttah first told me about her *feeling*, I was spooked. I was afraid something terrible was going to happen to Clem. Like a fatal car crash or something. When Quint showed up on the Rising Starr and told me he intended to marry Clem, I was relieved. I knew then what Nuttah's premonition was all about."

"I'm glad you didn't view him as a problem."

He frowned as he tried to decide if he could creep around the car traveling in front of them. The snow was too thick to see the asphalt beneath, but Beatrice's truck was equipped with heavy-duty tread on the tires, which had made their slow progression down the road a bit easier than some of the other northbound vehicles.

"Your family is great, Bea. Clem is a fortunate girl. Trust me, I won't be guilty of worrying about her now. Before I was—she was on my mind quite a bit. Not that I thought she was too helpless to take care of herself. On the contrary, she's one of the most self-reliant people I know. But she lived in such isolation. The letters she sent me twice a month were my only means of staying in touch with her."

She twisted around in the seat so that she was facing him. "Do you have close neighbors on the ranch?"

He tried his best not to stiffen. After all, her question was a reasonable one. "Close enough. I live in what used to be the foreman's quarters and the main ranch house is visible from my front yard. I'm the only ranch hand who lives on the Rising Starr. Except for Warren, the foreman. He lives with my stepmother—in the main house."

He glanced at her long enough to see a thoughtful frown draw her brows together.

"Are they married?" she asked.

"No. But they've been together for a long time."

Andrea and Warren had been together even before his father had died, Kipp could've told Beatrice. But he kept that tidbit to himself. The fact wasn't something he wanted to broadcast, even though he imagined most folks around Burley had suspected the truth. As for Kipp, the thought of the woman cheating on his father while he'd lain dying was worse than trying to swallow a handful of nails. Yet when those bitter thoughts came around, he had to stop and remind himself that Trent had done his own share of cheating. And who was Kipp to judge their behavior?

Still, the idea of him and Clementine coming from a loving and loyal family was a bitter joke. And that was the main reason Kipp never wanted a wife and children of his own. Why set himself up for that kind of pain and betrayal? Why risk hurting and disillusioning innocent kids, who couldn't understand why their parents didn't love each other anymore? No, Beatrice only saw the rosy side of love, but all Kipp could see was the ugliness of lives torn apart by lies and deceit.

And yet when he looked at her sweet face and thought of her soft, giving lips, he wished he could see life as she saw it. He wished he could believe there was more for him than being alone.

Chapter Eight

After a short stretch of silence passed, Beatrice turned a questioning look at Kipp.

"Do you get along with your stepmother and the foreman? Or is that a stupid question? After all, you're living and working there."

He stared at the slowly moving traffic ahead of them. "I guess you could say we're all civil to one another. I'm only around them when it's necessary. And they don't bother with me unless I'm needed around the ranch for some reason."

"Oh my. That's sad."

"No, Bea," he said flatly. "For me, it's survival."

Survival. What did he mean by that remark? It sounded so stark and empty. Surely his life on the Rising Starr was more than merely existing.

"What about the other two ranch hands? Do you get along with them?"

"Oh, sure. They're both good men. Ben is in his fifties. He's worked on the Rising Starr since I was a teenager. He's kind of like a second dad to me. He's married and has two grown sons. Then there's Zach. He's in his late twenties and still single. He used to ride saddle broncs on the rodeo circuit, but after he broke a few bones, he gave that up to ride broncs on the ranch."

"Are they both originally from the Burley area?"

"Ben is. Zach migrated to Burley from St. Paul, Oregon. He and Ben are both hard workers. We're lucky to have them."

We? He made it sound as though he was still part owner of the Rising Starr. Was she missing something? She wanted to ask him, but they'd already started this morning on shaky ground. Now that they were back on friendly terms, she didn't want to rock the boat. If she pressed too hard on a topic he didn't want to talk about, he might shift the conversation back to something that made her uncomfortable. And she especially didn't want him bringing up those kisses again!

She'd spent most of the night thinking about her behavior and feeling more and more like a fool. Yes, she'd wanted to kiss him. Badly. But that didn't mean she should've acted on impulse and reached for him. The more she thought about it, the more uncomfortable she felt, until this morning when he'd met her at the door to escort her down to breakfast, and she'd felt so embarrassed, she could hardly look him in the eye. A fact he'd obviously noticed.

Trying to shake away the disturbing thoughts, she said, "I know what you mean. If we didn't have the dedicated men that we have on Stone Creek, Dad and my brothers would be stressed to the limit. They couldn't do everything that needs to be done. In fact, we need more workers on the ranch."

"Quint introduced me to the two men who've come up from Arizona to work the second ranch that your father purchased recently. I could tell, just by talking with them, that they weren't greenhorns. And your brothers were singing their praises."

"Yes. Dad was given the chance to expand the ranch and he's run with it. You know, I've been wondering what Scarlett would think of Stone Creek now. It's a far different place from the one she left some fifty years ago. Back when she and Grandfather were first married, it wasn't nearly as big or profitable. Though maybe her opinion of it wouldn't change either way. From what little Dad remembers about his mother, she didn't like living in the country or being near any of the livestock. The ranch is doing well now, but it's still a ranch."

"Hmm. Makes me wonder why she married the man in the first place. It sounds as though they were totally mismatched."

She glanced thoughtfully at him. "I would love to ask Scarlett so many things about her and Grandfather. About their marriage and their lives together on Stone Creek. With Lionel refusing to talk about his ex-wife, we don't even know where she was from originally or how she met Lionel. But I probably shouldn't press my luck with her. If she'd just be willing to tell me when and where her ex-husband was born, that would be a huge accomplishment."

He didn't say anything for a long moment and Beatrice thought he was concentrating on the ridge of distant mountains and the gray clouds gathering above the peaks. But then he looked at her and she couldn't help but notice his brown eyes held a strange light as they scanned her face.

"In the beginning, I thought you were making this trip basically for your father—to make him proud of you. But I'm changing my mind about you."

Her heart beat just a tad faster as she studied the profile of his face. From the very first time she'd met Kipp, she wanted him to see her as a mature woman with serious interests. And she was hoping their time together on this trip would open his eyes to the real Beatrice.

"And what are you thinking about my motives now?" she asked curiously.

"I believe you're doing this not just for your father, but for your whole family."

His observation filled her with joy and a wide smile spread over her face. "Thank you, Kipp. It makes me happy to hear you say that—because it's true. I am doing it for the whole family. When we first found out we were related to the Arizona Hollisters, us kids weren't sure how we felt about it. Or even why it should matter to us. We didn't know them. And they had never met us. But later, as we all got to know them a bit, we started getting curious as to how and why we carry the same DNA."

"It sounds like the more Hadley and Vanessa dug for answers, the more questions arose within your own family."

"Right. And now we'd all like answers. Even our relatives in Arizona. If I can help find some of those answers—well, I'd feel as though I've accomplished something worthwhile."

"And that means a lot to you, doesn't it?"

"Naturally. Most people want to be productive—in a good way. Don't you?"

"I just think of myself as a working cowboy. Most days we get up and do the same thing over and over, though sometimes, depending on the weather, our jobs change. I make sure I get done what I need to do. If that's being productive, then I guess I am."

"Yes, you are. You're making sure the Rising Starr holds together and makes a profit."

"Yeah."

Beatrice realized the Rising Starr was a touchy subject with Kipp, but if she couldn't mention it to him now, when would be the right time? Clementine might eventually explain the situation with Kipp and the ranch, and the reason he continued to stay there, but Beatrice didn't want to hear it from his sister. She wanted to hear the explanation from Kipp himself.

"While your parents were married, did your mother like living on the ranch?" she dared to ask.

He shrugged as his attention remained firmly on the slow-moving traffic around them.

"I never heard her say much about it either way. Ella—Mom—isn't much of an outdoor person. The only animals she ever interacted with were the cats and dogs. Otherwise, she was usually indoors doing household chores, and later, like I mentioned before, she took that job for the used-car dealer. Dad didn't much like her being away from the ranch during the day. But I suppose by that time, she didn't much care what he liked."

"Hmm. Do you think she might have taken the job to spite her husband?"

The grim set to his jaw told Beatrice he'd not forgotten the discord between his parents.

"Looking back on it now, yeah, she probably was trying to spite him. But at that time, Clem and I didn't know Trent was carousing around with other women. If we had, then we might have understood what was driving a wedge between them. We thought they were just two people who couldn't get along."

"When you think about it, Kipp, you were right. They really were two people who couldn't get along. Otherwise, there would've been no cheating. Only loving."

He turned his head to look at her, and instead of barking something cynical, she was surprised when he gave her a gentle smile.

"You put that in awfully simple terms."

"Because it is simple," she told him. "If you love someone, you don't hurt them. You want to make them happy."

He turned his attention back to the highway, and a few mile markers passed before he finally made a reply. "I think my parents might have been like your grandparents, Bea. They should've never been married in the first place."

His notion was a sad one, Beatrice thought. Especially when he seemed to be avoiding making a family for himself just because his parents were mismatched. But he wouldn't appreciate hearing her thoughts on the subject. And she didn't want to make this long drive on an icy highway any worse for him than it was already.

They both remained quiet, until he said, "You haven't turned on the radio yet this morning. If you'd like to hear some music or the weather, I wouldn't mind."

Since they'd begun this journey early yesterday morning, she'd been surprised to learn he liked all kinds of music. She'd imagined he stuck to the beer-drinking/truck-driving songs, so when he'd tuned in a station playing '80s rock music, she'd laughed out loud. He'd explained how as a kid he'd grown up listening to his father play the tunes on cassette tapes. She'd enjoyed hearing the tidbit about his childhood because it had given her an insight into his relationship with Trent Starr. Yet there was so much more she wanted to know and so little time left to be with Kipp.

"Okay, I'll find some music. As for the weather, I don't see any need to bother. I've been watching the clouds to the north. They're starting to look ugly. And just when we're getting a bit of lovely sunshine." She punched a list of numbers on the navigational screen until she reached a satellite station that played standards, then turned the volume to a background level. "Do you think we're going to run into snow again?"

"I've been watching those clouds, too," he told her. "Let's keep our fingers crossed that we'll get to where we're going before we see snowfall again."

Late that morning, they crossed the Montana line and reentered Idaho. Along the way, they ran into light snowfall. The closer they got to Coeur d'Alene, the darker the skies grew and the stronger the wind whipped across the highway.

When they finally entered the city, piles of snow had been plowed to the curbs of the busy streets, while drifts left mounds here and there along the sidewalks. Christmas lights and ornaments still adorned the light poles, while decorated twinkling trees were displayed in shop windows. Plenty of people were bustling in and out of businesses and waiting at the crosswalks. Most were bundled in bright heavy clothing and furry head covers.

Because Beatrice was clearly enjoying the busy sights and sounds, Kipp tried to express a little enthusiasm, but in truth he was deflated. Had this drained feeling come over him because he'd driven for hundreds of miles on slick highways? Or was it because he and Beatrice were on the last leg of their journey and their time together would soon be ending?

He was pondering the answer to that question when she said, "I've read that Coeur d'Alene is a tourist town. Especially in the winter with ski slopes located not far away. I suppose some of these people we're seeing on the streets are here for holiday ski trips."

"Probably so. The only time I was in this town it was during the summer. It was busy then, but nothing like this," he said, as he carefully braked to a stop behind a delivery truck. "How far does your map say we're from Scarlett's apartment?"

She carefully studied the screen of her smartphone, then glanced at the navigation system on the dashboard. "Looks like it's six blocks from this next intersection. When you reach the stoplight, you need to make a right."

As he neared the busy intersection, he flipped on the blinker and steered the truck into the far-right lane of traffic. "Are you sure that thing is working right?" he asked. "It looks like we're going to go down a street filled with more shops."

"Could be the apartments are old and businesses have built around the complex," she reasoned. "It makes me wonder just what Scarlett can afford in the way of housing. I'm not sure how Van found the information, but she did discover that the woman is a widow for a second time. So, who's to say? Her second husband might have been well-off."

"My guess is that your grandmother isn't rich. Otherwise, she'd be living in a fancy house of her own, with a live-in assistant."

"Hmm. Sounds logical," she said, then gave him a

lopsided smile. "And none of that really matters. I'm just hoping she doesn't refuse to see me."

Several minutes ago, when they'd reached the outskirts of town, Kipp had stopped at a coffee shop to give her a chance to collect herself before she faced her grandmother. During their brief time there, she'd disappeared into the restroom for a few moments, then returned with a fresh application of rose-colored lipstick and her hair brushed smoothly down her back. She looked lovely and respectable, and he couldn't imagine any woman not being proud to acknowledge her as her granddaughter.

"After all we've been through to get here? That would be criminal," he said. "Besides, she's going to take one look at you and her heart is going to melt."

Her eyes narrowed skeptically at him. "Kipp, all this driving has made you punch-drunk. Grandfather didn't think the woman had a heart. Or at least, that's what he always implied," she said, then pointed to an approaching side street. "Get ready to turn here and then head straight for three more blocks."

Spotting the anxious crease between her brows, he tried to joke and lighten the moment. "Is that you or the computer talking?"

"Those instructions are from both of us," she said glibly.

He made the turn, then glanced at her. "It might not be obvious to you, but if a town has more than three stoplights in it, I get shook up."

She chuckled, even though her attention was glued to the navigation map on the dashboard. "Sure, Kipp. You think I'm going to believe that? You've just driven across two and a half states without making a bobble and most of that was on snow!"

"Gosh, I didn't know I was so good. I should be wearing a cape."

She shot him a droll look before she chuckled again. "Thanks, Kipp, for trying to ease my nerves."

He flashed her a smile. "Am I making any headway at it?"

"A little." She suddenly pointed to a brick building on the left side of the street. "There it is, Kipp. The Neighbors' Place."

He turned into a wide driveway that led into a large parking lot that bordered three sides of a two-story redbrick complex. Several cars were scattered around the parking area, most of which were located near a glass double-door entrance. Snow had been carefully cleaned away from the sidewalk and the concrete floor beneath a covered portico.

Kipp parked near an enormous spruce flocked with newly fallen snow. After cutting the motor, he reached around the seat to fetch their coats from the back floorboard, then helped her into the plaid woolen garment.

While he dealt with his own coat, she pulled on her sock cap and adjusted the strap of her purse over her shoulder. Once she was finished, she looked over and gave him a wobbly smile.

"Well, we're finally here. But I'm not exactly sure I'm ready for this," she said. "I hope you're planning on going in with me."

"Sure. I'm going in," he told her. "I imagine there will be some sort of lobby. I'll wait for you there."

Her mouth formed an O. "The lobby! No, Kipp! I

want you *with* me when I see Scarlett! Please say you'll come."

She didn't sound as if she was on the verge of panicking, but he could plainly see she was getting anxious. The idea that she believed she needed him during this impactful moment in her life surprised Kipp. He wasn't family. He wasn't even her boyfriend, and yet she was treating him as though he were important to her. The idea caused his chest to swell.

"Are you sure about this, Bea?" he asked. "You might feel more comfortable facing her without me tagging along."

She reached for his hand and squeezed it tightly. "I'm very sure about this, Kipp. You don't have to talk to the woman unless you want to. Just as long as you're with me—for support."

He couldn't refuse. Not when her misty blue eyes were pleading with him. "All right. I'll stay with you."

A breath rushed out of her and then she leaned across the console and planted a soft kiss on his cheek. "Thank you, Kipp."

He awkwardly cleared his throat. "We—uh—better go on in. The truck is already getting cold."

He hurriedly departed the truck, then helped her down from the cab. Freezing wind and bits of snow slapped them in the face.

"Better hang on to me," he told her. "The ground is slippery."

She wrapped both hands around his arm and clung tightly. "Don't worry. I'm not going to let go of you."

Any other time that kind of statement from a woman would have left Kipp a bit uneasy. But this was different, he inwardly reasoned. This was Beatrice and she wasn't just any woman. He didn't know when he'd arrived at that conclusion, but at some point during the last two days his feelings about her had changed into something more.

Inside the building they walked down a short foyer that opened into a large lobby furnished with several comfortable couches and stuffed armchairs. On the back wall, two side-by-side picture windows looked out over a snow-covered yard shaded with pines and one bare-limbed hardwood. Colorful birds fed at a feeder, while snowfall blew at a slanted angle thanks to the brisk wind.

Several elderly men and women were seated near the windows. Beatrice noticed some were in deep conversation, while others were gazing at the wintery scene outside the building. On the far right-hand side of the room, a middle-aged woman with dark hair and red-framed eyeglasses was working at a desk behind a sliding plate-glass partition.

Beatrice gestured toward the reception area. "Hopefully that lady will be able to direct us to Scarlett's apartment."

As soon as Beatrice informed the woman that they were there to see Scarlett, her brows formed skeptical arches above the tops of her glasses.

"Are you acquainted with Ms. Wilson?"

"Not exactly," Beatrice told her. "I'm her paternal granddaughter. And this is my fiancé, Kipp Starr." She felt Kipp startle a little beside her at the lie, but he didn't call her out on it. She felt bad about springing this on him out of nowhere, but she really didn't want to face Scarlett without him, and she was getting the sense that only family would be allowed through.

"Do you have an ID or something to prove you're a relative?" she asked Beatrice.

Feeling both helpless and frustrated, Beatrice hurriedly dug out her driver's license and placed it on the counter for the woman to see.

"My name is Hollister," Beatrice explained before the woman could ply her with questions. "Scarlett was originally married to my grandfather Hollister before she married Mr. Wilson."

The woman, sporting a name tag that read Administrator: Tanya Farnum, hesitated, then said, "I wouldn't know about any of this. We've never been told that she had other family."

Bending his head down to the level of the office worker, Kipp said, "Ms. Farnum, I'm sure you're only following protocol, but we've traveled all the way from southern Utah to see Ms. Wilson. I can promise you that we're not here to upset the woman or cause any kind of trouble."

Tanya cautiously eyed Kipp for a long moment before she released a sigh of resignation. "Well, her children have signed a consent form for their mother to have visitors. I suppose it will be okay. But please, whatever you do, try not to get her too excited. We—uh—well, some of our patients can become stressed—if you understand my meaning."

"Patients? This establishment isn't a nursing home, is it?" Beatrice asked.

"No. It's not a nursing home. Most of our residents are mobile and only require a little assistance. Ms. Wilson is certainly able to walk, but she—well, she needs help in other ways. Just a moment and I'll show you to her rooms."

While Tanya let herself out of the office area, Beatrice

glanced uncertainly at Kipp. "For a minute I thought she was going to turn us away," she said in a hushed voice.

He said, "I wasn't going to let that happen without putting up a fuss."

"Did you catch that part about Scarlett's children?" Beatrice asked. "That means I have aunts and uncles I've never seen or heard of."

"It means more than that, Bea. It means your father has half siblings. I wonder if that possibility ever crossed his mind."

"I've not heard him mention it before. But I imagine he's thought there was a good chance his mother had other children once she left the ranch. It's—"

The remainder of her sentence drifted away as the administrator rounded a corner and walked up to them.

"If you'll follow me to the elevator, Ms. Wilson's apartments are located on the second floor. That's to avoid her slipping out the front entrance. We have guards to prevent such things from happening, but you never know. Some of the residents get to thinking they want to go outside—for different reasons, you understand."

Beatrice exchanged glances with Kipp and she could see a doubtful look in his brown eyes. But at the same time, he clasped a tight hold on her hand and the warmth and strength it conveyed to her was enough to give her the extra courage she needed.

At the elevator, the three of them stepped inside, and as the door closed, Ms. Farnum said, "I imagine you two ran into some terrible weather on your way up here. Did you see much snow?"

"In Montana we experienced blizzard conditions,"

Kipp told her. "It wasn't pretty. Coeur d'Alene is actually in much better shape than the bottom part of the state."

"Oh. That's good news. With the holidays going on, we're expecting more visitors. And we've planned a New Year's Eve party for the residents and their families. Will you two be sticking around long enough to attend?"

Beatrice once again glanced at Kipp. He looked uncomfortable, but that was understandable. She wasn't exactly feeling at ease herself. And no doubt he was still wondering why she'd introduced him as her fiancé.

"Thank you for asking, but no. We—uh—have to be home by New Year's," Beatrice told her.

"Too bad. Maybe you can make it back up for Valentine's Day. We always have a nice party for the residents then. The ones who don't have living spouses usually have someone in the building they're sweet on, so it gives them a chance to do a little extra romancing." Her pointed smile encompassed Beatrice and Kipp. "But I'm sure you two will have something special going on for that day."

Kipp winked at Beatrice. "I'm already planning it."

Beatrice wanted to smile, but she couldn't. By the time Valentine's Day rolled around, there would be several hundred miles separating her and Kipp.

"How nice. You need to hang on to him," Tanya said to her.

Feeling like a fraud, Beatrice was wondering how to respond to the woman when she suddenly stopped at a door with the number twenty-six posted next to the frame. How ironic, Beatrice thought, that her age was the same as Scarlett's apartment number.

"Here we are." The administrator punched the door-bell. "I'll let her know she has visitors."

Apparently Scarlett was mobile enough to answer the

door, Beatrice thought. Which had to be an encouraging sign. Still, she had an uneasy feeling that all wasn't well with her estranged grandmother.

As they stood waiting for the door to open, Kipp slipped an arm around the back of her waist and gave her an encouraging wink. She gave him a grateful smile, while trying to imagine herself in this stressful situation alone or with anyone else but him. She couldn't. It was as though he was meant to be at her side during this very important moment in her life. But would he be at her side later? After this trip was over and she was back at Stone Creek?

No. She couldn't let herself dwell on those questions now. She was here to gather information about Lionel Hollister. Not moon over a cowboy who was dead set on remaining a bachelor.

Chapter Nine

The rattling of the door broke into Beatrice's swirling thoughts and she watched in anticipation as it swung back to reveal a somewhat tall woman with a slender build. The rosy artificial color on her cheeks made a clownish contrast to her pale wrinkled face. Faded blue eyes peered at them from beneath sagging lids, while her iron gray hair waved to one side of her head. Earrings fashioned in the shape of red Christmas balls swung from her ears.

"Scarlett, you have visitors," Tanya announced. "Do you feel like talking?"

"I always like to talk." She motioned for the three of them to enter. "Come in, young folks. I have a new couch. You'll like how it sits."

As they all stepped inside what appeared to be a spacious living area, Tanya questioned the older woman.

"Do you recognize this young lady?"

Scarlett squinted a long look at Beatrice before she finally said, "She looks like Lori Jane."

Beatrice looked curiously at Tanya.

"Lori is one of her granddaughters," she said, then

added in a voice too low for Scarlett to hear, "She has four of them, and she gets them mixed up at times."

"No. This isn't Lori. She'll tell you who she is," Tanya said to Scarlett, then turned to Beatrice. "You two stay as long as Scarlett would like. If you need me, I'll be down in my office."

She watched the woman walk out the door and carefully shut it behind her. Once she was out of sight and Scarlett had moved farther into the room, Kipp murmured close to Beatrice's ear.

"This is going to be interesting."

"I'm afraid it's going to be hopeless," she replied in a hushed voice. "But we're here and I have to try."

"Come sit down," Scarlett said to them. "It's cold as hell in here, but I can't get anything done about it. The maintenance man says the heat works fine. Bah! I shiver all day long!"

Beatrice and Kipp took seats close together on a dark red couch with several throw pillows scattered across the cushions. Only a couple of minutes ago, Scarlett had told them her couch was new, but Beatrice couldn't help but notice a few worn spots. Had Kipp also noticed the discrepancy? But to be fair, the couch could simply be new to Scarlett.

Directly across from them, Scarlett sank into a wooden rocker cushioned with thick pads upholstered in bright yellow calico. As soon as the very slender woman was settled in the seat, a gray tabby cat with a blue collar appeared from a nearby doorway and jumped into her lap.

Snuggling the animal closer to her, Scarlett stroked a bony hand over the cat's back. "Oliver, are you cold, boy?"

Beatrice felt Kipp's hand tighten around hers and she

glanced over to see a rueful expression on his face. No doubt he'd already reached the conclusion that Scarlett Hollister Wilson was not fully comprehending the situation.

Drawing in a bracing breath, Beatrice decided to ease into a conversation. "Have you lived here long, Ms. Wilson?"

The wrinkles on Scarlett's face deepened as she frowned with bewilderment. "A year ago, I believe," she said, then quickly shook her head. "No. I guess it was last week. I got here just in time for Christmas. We had a big party for Christmas. Did you two have a big Christmas party?"

Kipp squeezed her hand again and Beatrice suddenly realized that having his warm touch encouraging and supporting her was something she would always need. Even though it was something she'd probably never receive again once the two of them said goodbye.

"It was a very nice one," she answered Scarlett. "My family was celebrating all together on Stone Creek Ranch. That's where I live in Utah," Beatrice told her.

The mention of the ranch didn't bring about any change in Scarlett's expression, but Beatrice was determined to keep trying. Hopefully, there'd be something to spark the woman's memory.

"My name is Beatrice Hollister. Does the name ring a bell with you?"

Scarlett lifted a hand from the cat's back to make a dismissive swat through the air. "I knew some Hollisters once. They had a shoe store over in Post Falls. Too expensive for my taste. I think his name was Peter. No. That's not right. It was something strange like Perth." She leaned forward in the rocker and peered curiously at Beatrice. "You sure do look like Lori Jane. Do you know her?"

Out of nowhere, a lump of emotion lodged in Beatrice's throat, and she was forced to swallow before she could speak. "No. I'm afraid I've never met her."

Scarlett appeared disappointed by Beatrice's admission and then her eyes narrowed skeptically. "I think I know who you are now."

Surprised by the old woman's sudden change in demeanor, Beatrice glanced hopefully at Kipp, then back to Scarlett.

"You do? Who am I?"

"Why, you're that girl who comes to take me to the beauty parlor to get my hair cut. Do I have an appointment today? I sure do need a haircut. It gets on my nerves when it hangs in my eyes." She patted the side of her head. "I used to have pretty auburn hair. The dark kind that looked like a black cherry. If I don't say so myself, I was a real looker back when I was your age. Those years don't last, young lady. So you enjoy 'em while you have 'em."

Yes, Beatrice could easily imagine Scarlett as a young woman in her twenties. She would've been tall and regal with smooth, porcelain skin and dark, rich hair. Her blue eyes would've been bright back then. Perhaps even the color of hers and Bonnie's. She would've been striking. She couldn't imagine Lionel marrying a plain woman.

"Have you always lived in Idaho, Ms. Wilson?" Kipp asked.

She gently scratched Oliver between the ears. "No. I think I lived somewhere else a long time ago. I had to move to Idaho for my health."

"Oh. You had health problems?"

She snorted. "They were all in my head. That's what the doctor said. Just a head thing. But Curly made me well." Her features softened as she looked at them and smiled. "I loved Curly."

"Who was he?" Beatrice asked.

"Why, Curly was my husband. He was gentle and kind. He fixed my head and made me happy."

"Sounds like he was a good man," Kipp remarked.

"Good. Yes. But he's over in the cemetery now and I don't get to visit him very much. My kids won't take me. They don't want to see me cry."

"Or more like don't want to be bothered," Kipp mouthed close to Beatrice's ear.

Beatrice nodded at him in agreement, then glanced over at her grandmother. Of all the things she'd expected to feel whenever she finally met Scarlett, none of them had been sadness. And yet that was the very thing striking her now. Overwhelming sadness at the knowledge that she'd never been given the chance to know this woman in her prime. All those years Beatrice and Bonnie had been growing up, their grandmother had been living another life. She might not have ever known she'd had grandchildren from her first marriage. And why? Had she hated Stone Creek and Lionel that much? Or had she remained hidden all these years out of fear?

"Maybe your children will take you to the cemetery when the weather gets warmer," Beatrice suggested, then drew in a deep breath and asked, "Do you remember anyone by the name of Hadley?"

"I know Harry. He lives downstairs. He likes to come up and see me and Oliver."

Beatrice tried not to feel defeated. But it was hard not to think of her father and how disappointed he was going to be when she informed him Scarlett was suffering from some type of dementia.

She threw out the name of Hadley's younger brothers. "What about Wade? Or Barton?"

As she pondered Beatrice's question, her eyes squinted and her lips puckered together. "No Wade. But a woman I once knew had a small boy she called Bartie. He had a cute little split between his front teeth. I used to think that when he grew up the girls would fawn over him."

Beatrice tightened her fingers around Kipp's as she looked at him and whispered, "She's talking about my uncle. Dad calls him Bartie and he does have a split between his teeth."

"That means—this woman truly is your grandmother. Not that there was any doubt—but there's no question now!"

Tangled emotions struck Beatrice as she glanced over to see Scarlett staring off in space. Was she seeing her little boys and the ranch she'd once called home?

"Wonder what ever happened to that woman and little Bartie," Scarlett muttered more to herself than to them. "I wish I could see him. Seems like little Bartie had some brothers, but I can't remember. None of them might be living, anyhow."

The woman looked at them and shook her head with regret, and for a short moment, Beatrice felt as if she was seeing a tiny slice of the real Scarlett.

"These days I can't remember like I used to," she said ruefully. "The doctor says I'm going to get better. She says the more I try to think, the more it will help me."

Before Beatrice could consider what she was about to do, she left the couch and went over to Scarlett. Then, bending down, she wrapped her arms around the woman's shoulders and hugged her tightly.

"You will get better, Scarlett," Beatrice told her. "Don't give up."

To her amazement, she felt her grandmother's hand gently pat the back of her shoulder. The unexpected gesture of affection brought a mist of tears to Beatrice's eyes. Which hardly made any sense. Scarlett didn't recognize Beatrice or understand why she'd traveled hundreds of miles to see her. But all the same, it felt like a grandmother's loving touch.

Blinking at the telltale moisture, Beatrice straightened to her full height and glanced helplessly over at Kipp. Their eyes connected and he immediately rose from the couch and walked over to join her.

Scarlett continued to stare at the two of them and Beatrice watched as a foggy look of confusion swept over the old woman's face.

"You're a cowboy," she said to Kipp. "I used to know lots of cowboys. They were like you, good-lookin'. One especially."

Beatrice arched questioning brows at Kipp. Was he wondering, like her, whether Scarlett was recalling Lionel in his young years? Or some other significant cowboy in her life?

"What was his name?" Kipp gently asked the woman. "Do you remember?"

Scarlett closed her eyes while a faint smile touched her lips. "Damned charmer, that's what he was," she said, then opened her eyes and looked straight at Beatrice. "What did you say your name was?"

Kipp's arm gently slipped around the back of Beatrice's waist and she realized he understood how her grandmother's confusion was tearing at her. In fact, it would've probably been easier if she'd met a Scarlett without dementia, who'd screamed at her to get out and never come back.

"I'm Beatrice Hollister. I came from Utah to see you."

Nodding with approval, she said, "That's right. You're here to take me to the beauty parlor. Good. It's about damned time I got a haircut." She pointed over her shoulder to an open doorway of what appeared to be a bedroom. "Would you get my coat from the closet, dearie? I think it might be cold outside."

Beatrice shot a look of dismay over to Kipp before she carefully tried to craft an excuse to explain to Scarlett that she wouldn't be leaving the apartment.

"It's very cold," Beatrice told her. "Too cold for you to be going outside. I'm afraid you're going to have to wait until the weather gets better to make a trip to the beauty salon. But when we go downstairs, I'll be sure to stop and tell Ms. Farnum to make you an appointment."

To Beatrice's relief, she didn't argue. Instead, she tilted her head to one side and smiled. "Thank you, sweetie. You sure are a pretty little thing. You look just like Lori Jane."

Another layer of moisture filled Beatrice's eyes while she reached down and patted Scarlett's forearm. "We have to go now, Ms. Wilson. Take care and goodbye."

Kipp's hand splayed against the small of her back and Beatrice was ever so grateful for his strong presence. He was a reminder of the good things in her life. The things that made up her hopes and dreams.

Scarlett looked down at the cat curled on her lap. "You can tell Oliver goodbye, too. He likes to be petted."

Beatrice didn't hesitate to gently stroke the tabby's head and neck. "Do you like animals?" she asked.

"Oh, I love 'em. Always have. Oliver needs a buddy."

"Would you like to have another cat to go with him?" Beatrice asked.

"Sure would. But the folks who run this flophouse won't let me have two cats."

"Maybe they'll change the rules," Kipp suggested. "When they do, we'll bring you another cat. How does that sound?"

Scarlett gave him a grateful smile. "Bless you, young man. That would make me and Oliver very happy."

After another round of goodbyes, Beatrice and Kipp let themselves out of the apartment. As soon as the door closed behind them, she leaned heavily against his shoulder.

"Forgive me, Kipp. If you don't mind, I need a moment before we walk to the elevator," she said weakly. "My legs are so shaky I'm afraid they're not going to hold my weight."

"Bea! Let me help you!" He slipped his arm around her back and lifted most of her weight off her feet. "There's a bench in the corridor not far from here. I'll carry you."

"No! I—can walk—just hold on to me."

The bench was located inside a shallow alcove, about twenty feet on down the corridor, near the elevator doors. A wall table with a small Christmas tree stood at one end of the wooden bench, while a group of red and pink poinsettias sat at the opposite end.

When Kipp lowered her to the bench, she let out a sigh of relief. "I've never been so glad to sit in all my life," she told him.

He eased down at her side and reached for her hand. "I'm sorry you had to go through that, Bea. And I'm especially sorry you had to go through it alone."

She frowned at him. "I wasn't alone. You were with me."

"I wasn't any help."

At this moment, Beatrice didn't care what he thought. She leaned over and kissed his cheek. "Just knowing you were there in the room with me was all the help I needed. I just—"

He touched the spot she'd kissed. "You just what?"

She groaned with anguish. "I don't know anything, Kipp. I've never felt so confused and torn in my life."

"Well, it couldn't be easy discovering your grandmother is suffering from some type of dementia."

"No," she said grimly. "I wonder why Tanya didn't explain that to us before we went in to see her."

"She probably doesn't have the authority to give out medical information about the residents."

"Authority! She's supposed to be the administrator of this place!" Beatrice exclaimed sharply. Then, sighing, she shook her head. "I know—I'm losing it and I'm wrong! My sister is a doctor. She's explained how she can't go around talking about a patient's health. I imagine it's the same way with Tanya. And she did sort of warn us that things weren't exactly right with Scarlett."

"Yes, she was giving us a few warning signals," he agreed. "But even if she had told us the woman had dementia, we would've wanted to see for ourselves."

"Yes. You're right." Beatrice closed her eyes and let out another long sigh. "I think—what's bothering me the most isn't the fact that Scarlett's mind is deteriorating. I mean, yes, that part is terrible and I desperately wish she was healthy. But all the while I was trying to communicate with her, I kept thinking of all the things I had missed because she'd not been in my life. Of all the things she'd missed because, for some reason we might never know, she made the decision not to keep in touch."

"I'll tell you one thing, Bea—I don't know much about your family history. And I sure can't say I know about your grandfather Lionel. He must have been a great man in many ways. He built Stone Creek into what it is today and raised three sons. That wouldn't have been an easy feat. But when Scarlett mentioned Bartie and how she wished she could see him—that was gut twisting. And a little telling. Don't you think?"

Beatrice sniffed. "Yes, I thought it was very revealing. She didn't sound like a mother who'd deliberately deserted her sons." She turned a bewildered look on him. "But perhaps that could have been guilt talking. Maybe her subconscious was trying to surface and she was wishing she'd stayed in touch with her sons."

He squeezed her hand. "Bea, we're not psychiatrists. And I doubt even a doctor that specializes in the human brain could tell us exactly what Scarlett was trying to convey. You need to find something that will give you tangible truth about your grandparents' marriage and divorce. If you could find the truth, then you might also find the information about the when and where of his birth."

She nodded. "Right. It would be a big help if I could talk with her children from her second marriage. She might have told them things about her life down in Utah. But I have the feeling that Tanya won't disclose any information about the Wilson family to me."

"We can try," Kipp told her. "Do you feel well enough to go downstairs now?"

"Sure. I feel much better."

Although she was steady on her feet, he kept his

hand on her elbow as they rode the elevator down and returned to the administrator's office.

Tanya was back at her desk, and as soon as she spotted Beatrice and Kipp standing outside the sliding glass window, she came over and opened the partition.

"Can I help you two with something else?" she asked.

"Yes. We were wondering if you could give us the name of one of Scarlett's children," Beatrice told her. "Or where we might locate one or all of them. Considering the woman's condition, it would be very helpful if we could discuss the situation with one of them."

"I'm very sorry, Ms. Hollister, but we can't give out private information regarding the families of our residents. I'm sure you can see how that might create problems."

Create problems? This woman couldn't imagine the problems Scarlett was creating for the Hollisters just by being too ill to talk lucidly.

"Yes, I understand. I just thought I'd ask. You see, I—my family—wasn't aware that Scarlett had children from her second marriage. We—uh—hadn't seen her in a very long time."

"It would've had to have been a very long time. Her oldest child is forty years old."

Beatrice darted a glance at Kipp, and even though he appeared to be staring out at the lobby, she knew he wasn't missing a single word.

"I see. Well, thank you just the same. And thank you for allowing me to visit my grandmother."

"Of course. Come back anytime. And who knows—you might just run into some of her family on another occasion. They don't come frequently. Maybe once a month."

Beatrice thanked her again, and as they walked away

from the office, Kipp suggested they walk around the lobby.

"Some of the residents might be acquainted with Scarlett's family. You'll never know unless you ask."

Beatrice glanced over to the large furnished area where several older people were sitting on the couches. The TV in the corner had been turned off and now a white-haired gentleman with heavy black glasses and a red muffler tied around his neck was playing a quiet tune on the piano. Near the end of one of the couches, two women were intently working on a huge jigsaw puzzle.

"Good idea," she said. "If we strike up a generic conversation about the weather or something first, then they might not suspect we're detectives."

He grinned at her. "Detectives? We hardly look the part."

"No. But if we start throwing out pertinent questions about Scarlett, they might start wondering."

The two of them ambled casually over to the Christmas tree and made a show of looking it over, then moved over to one of the picture windows.

Beatrice was remarking about the birds and the snow when a pair of men who looked like brothers strolled up behind them. One was chewing on a toothpick, while the other appeared to be munching on a piece of gum. Except for a few silver streaks, their hair was mostly dark brown and their eyes as gray as the winter sky. She suspected the men didn't really require assisted-living care, but chose to reside here for the company of the other residents.

"You young folks been visiting one of the residents here?" the one with the toothpick asked.

"Yes," Beatrice told him. "Scarlett Wilson. Are you acquainted with her?"

"A little," the gum chewer answered, then quickly introduced himself and the man with him. "I'm Rueben Stevenson and he's Walter. We're brothers. Just call us Rube and Walt."

Beatrice and Kipp told them their names and shook hands with both men.

"Nice to meet you," Beatrice told the pair. "Are you two twins?"

Chuckling, Kipp said, "She has a reason for asking. She's a twin."

"Oh, yeah, guess you can tell we look alike. So you're a twin, too," he said to Beatrice. "That's great. Me and Walt don't run into too many twins in here. But we don't see very many young folks like you two, either."

"Yeah." Walt spoke up. "That's why we walked over and butted in. We're nosy and wondered why you were here."

"Well, we're a little nosy ourselves," Kipp told the men. "We're wondering if Scarlett's relatives come around very often. Do you know any of them?"

Rube shook his head. "We've asked her about her children. But I guess you could tell you can't put any stock in what she says. Poor woman. She's been sick for as long as we've been here, and that's been a couple of years."

Walt said, "There's one man, looks to be in his fifties or somewhere abouts, who shows up here from time to time. He brings Scarlett down here in the lobby on occasions, and sometimes he takes her out for a few hours, then brings her back. Don't know who he is. He dresses like a businessman. You know, suit, tie, neat haircut. He doesn't associate with any of the other residents."

"Neither does the red-haired woman who comes to visit Scarlett. She's not around as often as the man. You might say she'd be in her late forties. Sort of on the haughty-acting side, if you ask me. I asked Walt if she thinks this place is so beneath her, then why don't she move the woman to some highfalutin home."

Walt frowned at his twin. "You're talking too much, T. These people are probably related to Scarlett. You're going to offend them."

"He's not going to offend us," Beatrice assured him, then added, "I'm Scarlett's granddaughter from her first marriage. She didn't— Well, let's just say my last name has slipped her memory. And we were hoping she could tell us a bit of family history. But that's clearly not going to happen."

"Oh, that is too bad," Rube said. "Did you ask Tanya for names or addresses of her children? If you could talk with some of them, they might be able to give you the information you need."

"We tried," Kipp told him. "She refuses to give out family information."

"Hardly seems fair," Rube muttered. "And it's the Christmas and New Year season. You'd think she'd be a little more generous."

"Don't worry—we'll keep our ears open for you," Walt said and elbowed his brother in the rib cage. "Get one of our old cards out, T. It has our names and cell numbers on it. This nice young couple can call us from time to time."

Rube dug out his wallet, pulled a business card from a slot in the leather and handed it over to Kipp.

"We appreciate your offer to help—very much," Beatrice told the brothers. Then, changing the subject, she smiled at them. "Have you two been together most of your lives?"

"Always," Walt said. "Except for when we were in the military back in the late sixties. Otherwise, we've always lived in houses next to each other and run a car repair business together. That lasted for more than fifty years."

"Both of our wives died and our children live out of state," Rube explained. "When we decided to retire, we sold our houses and moved in here together. Makes it easy. No lawn mowing. No fixing the roof or cleaning gutters."

"My twin and I are always together, too," Beatrice told the men. "But she didn't get to come on this trip with me."

"Are you folks from around here?" Walt asked.

At this moment, Beatrice felt as though she lived a million miles away from Coeur d'Alene. During the past two days, her emotions had been on a roller coaster and she wondered if she'd ever get back to Beaver County and the young woman who'd eagerly greeted her customers at Canyon Corral and shared a bedroom with her twin.

"I'm from Utah," she told the man, then instinctively placed a hand on Kipp's forearm. "And my fiancé is from right here in Idaho—the southern part."

Rube grinned meaningfully at the two of them. "Congratulations. Being engaged means you'll probably become an Idahoan, too, pretty soon."

Beatrice glanced at Kipp for his reaction to her continuation of her little fib, but his expression was as bland as if she'd been discussing the weather. No doubt he was probably laughing inside at her attempt to make them appear as a couple. And she supposed she deserved his laughter.

"I—uh, suppose I will," she told Rube, then followed that fib with an awkward little laugh.

"She might not sound enthusiastic about it right now, guys," Kipp suddenly said, "but she's going to love living in Idaho."

The twins laughed and Walt even clapped his approval. Beatrice felt humiliated, but tried to hide it behind a smile. These men believed that she and Kipp were truly in love and soon to be married. They had no idea that Kipp's remark was really a subtle jab at her.

Chapter Ten

Beatrice and Kipp visited with the twins for a few more minutes before he finally suggested they needed to get back on the road. After exchanging goodbyes with the talkative men, they left the apartment complex.

Outside, the sun was rapidly going down and streetlights were beginning to flicker on. Light snow fell on the two of them as they walked to the waiting truck.

"It's nearly dark," Beatrice said with amazement. "I had no idea we'd been in the Neighbors' Place so long. To tell you the truth, Kipp, I'm still in a daze."

She looked pale and totally drained, Kipp thought. With his arm snug around her waist, she was leaning heavily against his side and he realized the reality of facing Scarlett Hollister Wilson had taken a powerful toll on her. A part of him resented Hadley for laying such a task on his daughter. The man should've made the trip himself. He was the one who should have seen Scarlett's blank look and listened to her confused ramblings. On the other hand, this was something Beatrice wanted to do for her father, and Kipp figured if she had the choice, she'd do it all over again.

"You look totally beat. You need rest, Bea."

"I do feel drained," she admitted. "But don't worry. I'll be fine once I relax and have something to eat."

He helped her into the truck, then took his own seat behind the steering wheel. As they buckled their seat belts, Kipp said, "I don't know what you're thinking about traveling, but it's rather late in the day to be starting the long drive to the Rising Starr. Especially on highways with patches of snow. Eight or nine more hours of driving would do us both in."

"I agree. Getting a fresh start in the morning makes more sense," she told him. "Only when the weather forced us to stay in Butte last night, I had to cancel the hotel reservations I'd already made here in Coeur d'Alene. Do you think we can find rooms?"

"We won't know until we try," he answered.

With that decision made, Kipp drove back to the main highway to hunt for suitable lodging. After they'd passed several hotels and motels with no-vacancy signs posted in bright neon, he pulled into a grocery store parking lot and stopped the truck.

"I think we'd make more progress if we pull out our phones and see if we can locate something on the web. With it being the Christmas holiday season, plus fresh snow on the slopes, the town must be bursting with tourists and travelers," he said.

Beatrice reached for her phone. "When we talked about how busy the town was earlier today, I didn't stop to think about finding vacant hotel rooms. I was too busy concentrating on meeting Scarlett. We might have to drive to another nearby town, do you think?"

"I wouldn't want to do that unless it's absolutely necessary. To get to the Rising Starr from here, we have to travel south. For a long distance in that direction, there are only a few little tiny towns and they're probably an hour away. If we drove west to Post Falls, we might find rooms there, but it's out of the way. We'd be adding twenty more miles, at least."

"Then we need to find something here before it really starts getting late," she said.

He watched her swipe the phone. As a piece of her gold-blond hair slid against her pale cheek, an enormous sense of protectiveness swept over him. The feeling momentarily stunned him.

Yes, as Clementine's older brother, he'd always felt a sense of responsibility toward her. He'd always wanted to make sure she was protected and safe. But she was his sister. It was normal for a brother to feel those things for his sissy. This feeling he had for Beatrice was something quite different.

Not wanting to analyze the strange occurrence going on inside him, he pulled his phone out of his shirt pocket and focused on finding listings for hotels along I-90.

Beatrice finally located a hotel on the south edge of town with three rooms still available and Kipp quickly turned the truck around and headed toward the address she'd read to him.

"Does it have a pic of the place?" Kipp asked as he maneuvered the truck through the traffic as quickly as the stoplights would allow.

"Yes, but it's sort of foggy. I can't really tell how it looks. But I'm too tired to care if we have to fight off bugs or mice."

"Your father would be highly upset if I allowed you to sleep in such a place," Kipp told her.

"He'd never hear about it from me. And speaking

of Dad, he's texted me twice in the past hour. I'm sure he's anxious to hear about my meeting with Scarlett. I messaged him back and told him I'd call as soon as we got settled. The news about her condition is going to hurt him."

"You think so?"

"Naturally I think so!" she exclaimed, then turned an anguished look on him. "I understand what you're thinking. You're wondering why Dad would care about the woman when she deserted him. I understand. I even agree, to an extent. But I think he'll also be a bit torn that she's incapacitated. He is human, Kipp. And I keep thinking of him as a little boy, stealing his mother's picture from his father's things, just so he'd have some sort of memory of her. It's—sad."

Her voice thickened on the last word and he wished he could take her into his arms and hold her. He wanted to comfort her and remind her that in time all would be well again. But hell, who was he to comfort anybody? He'd lived with so much bitterness for so long, how could he show a woman like Beatrice the soft, gentle encouragement she needed?

Ten minutes later, standing at the check-in counter at the hotel, Kipp struggled not to curse as, for the second time, Beatrice explained to the concierge that they needed two rooms for the night.

The young man working the desk gave them a weary smile. "I fully understand. But we only have *one* room available. The other two were taken just before you arrived. This is an extremely busy time of the year and most of our guests made reservations."

"Sorry," Kipp told him. "We didn't know we were

going to need a room in Coeur d'Alene until a couple of hours ago."

Beatrice slanted Kipp a helpless look. "This is our only choice. We need to take it."

The two of them together in the same room? It wasn't an ideal situation. Not for him. Not when just looking at her made him ache to kiss her again. But it was as she'd just stated; they didn't have a choice in the matter. Not unless he wanted to drive half the night when neither one of them was up to more traveling.

"Right. We'll take the room."

After taking care of the paperwork, Kipp fetched their bags from the truck and they located their room on the third floor at the end of the corridor.

"Even though they only had one vacancy, the hotel is nice," Beatrice said as they entered the spacious room. "And it does have two queen beds and a couch. This will be fine with me. What about you?"

While she switched on a lamp, he placed their bags on the floor near the end of the couch.

"I can sleep anywhere." *Under normal circumstances*, he could have added. But with her in the room with him? After taking a cold shower, he was probably going to stare at the ceiling and grit his teeth all night.

"Don't worry. I won't be keeping you awake with the TV. And I don't snore. At least, Bonnie says I don't."

He took off his hat and placed it on top of a chest of drawers. "I wouldn't know if I snore. I guess if I do, you can stuff something in my mouth."

She tossed her coat on the end of one of the beds. "Are you telling me that no one has been around you while you're asleep to tell you whether you snore?"

He let out a short laugh as he walked over to the

couch and sank into the end cushion. Stretching his legs out in front of him, he asked, "Is that a trick question?"

She turned away from the bed and lifted her arms before running both hands through her long hair. The movement caused her back to arch and her breasts to strain against the thin green sweater she was wearing.

"Trick? No." Frowning, she walked over to where he sat and stood staring down at him. "Surely someone has been close enough while you're sleeping to know whether you snore or not."

He had to glance away from her as he thought of the brief encounters he'd had with women over the years. When he went home with them, he'd not stuck around long enough for sleep to be involved. Nor had he invited them to curl up in his arms afterward for a night of cozy slumber when they went to his place. No, he thought, actually sleeping with someone meant commitment and togetherness. He'd never had that with any woman. Even the one he'd fancied himself marrying.

"Let's just say I've never had anyone complain."

"Oh. Well, I'm so tired I imagine once I get to sleep the fire alarm probably won't wake me." She walked over to a wall of dark brown drapes and pulled them open enough to see out. "This is a surprise. We have a lovely view of a mountain. And there are lights on it! Do you think there might be a ski lodge up there?"

Rising from the couch, he joined her at the window. "No. From what I understand, the ski slopes are a few miles from town."

"Oh. Then those lights might be coming from a swanky restaurant. You know, the kind with linen tablecloths and glass walls so you can see for miles."

"Yeah. And the food is tough and way overpriced," he said wryly.

Laughing out loud, she turned to him, and then her laughter turned into a soft smile. "Thank you, Kipp. I so needed to laugh."

"I think we both need to laugh and eat. Are you getting hungry?"

"Yes. But I really don't have the energy to leave the hotel. And I read on a sign by the check-in desk that the only food they serve here is a continental breakfast in the mornings."

"I don't have any desire to get out in the cold again, either," he said. Then, as he raked a hand through his hair, an idea struck him. "We're not thinking, Bea. I'm sure there have to be a few restaurants in town who deliver. We could have pizza or something."

"Even when the streets are snowy?" she asked.

It was Kipp's turn to laugh. "The streets in this town are most likely always snowy."

"Okay. Sounds great," she said. "I'll eat pizza or anything you can come up with."

Kipp ended up ordering two medium-sized pizzas along with two pieces of cheesecake. While they waited for the food to arrive, he walked down the corridor and collected a bucket of ice along with sodas from a vending machine.

When he returned to the room, Beatrice had removed her boots and belt and was sitting cross-legged on the couch with her cell phone to her ear.

He put the ice and the sodas in the tiny fridge located in a cabinet beneath the TV, then sat on the end of one of the beds and removed his boots. Even though he'd left his socks on, the simple act made him feel as though he was exposing himself. But he was exhausted and needed to get comfortable in the worst kind of way.

Across the room, Beatrice was speaking into the phone. "If he's over at the barn with Cord, then he might not be back in the house for a while. I'll call him later tonight...No, Bonnie. Don't do that. Kipp and I are going to be eating. I'll call once we're finished with our supper...Right, I will. Bye, sissy."

She placed the phone on a table at the end of the couch, then looked over at Kipp.

"I tried calling Dad, but Bonnie says he's gone over to the cattle barn to help my brother Cord. If you can believe it, I think some of the heifers are dropping calves now. Cord has been the foreman of Stone Creek Ranch for several years now and he's good at handling any situation, but Dad always wants to make sure the barn is warm enough, the calves are dried and all that sort of thing."

"In other words, he's just being a dad," Kipp said.

Smiling tiredly, she leaned her head back against the couch. "Exactly. Was your father that way?"

For the past two days, the two of them had sat close together in the truck. Now, whenever they were out of the vehicle, Kipp felt an odd sense of emptiness if she got more than five feet away from him. It was damned stupid of him, but he couldn't seem to shake the feeling.

With a resigned sigh, he left the bed and joined her on the couch. "Dad gave plenty of orders to everyone on the ranch. Even to Mom and to Andrea, his second wife."

A look of dismay crossed her face. "And how did the wives react to being ordered around?"

He grunted. "Just as you'd expect. Neither of them

liked it. Obviously Mom didn't. She left. And Andrea, well, she would give him the silent treatment. Until he'd buy her a new piece of jewelry or something else she'd been wanting and all would be well—for a while."

"Sounds like it was a vicious merry-go-round."

He grimaced. "While Dad was alive, there was plenty of drama going on in the house," he admitted, then purposely changed the subject. "Did you tell Bonnie about Scarlett's condition?"

Nodding glumly, she said, "Bonnie says Dad will be crushed by the news. But he's a strong man and he has Mom at his side. She softens his disappointments and he eases hers."

The few days Kipp had been on Stone Creek Ranch hadn't been long enough to learn much about Hadley and Claire's relationship, but even the short time he'd been there he'd noticed how devoted the couple were to each other. And he'd thought how lucky Clementine was to be getting such a mother- and father-in-law.

"Your parents have set a high example for you and your siblings. I imagine you want a marriage like theirs."

He'd thought his comment would put a smile on her face. Instead, she looked more downtrodden than when they'd left Scarlett's apartment.

"It takes a lot of dedication and love to have what they have. It's not something you find just anywhere."

He studied her downcast expression. "You're not expecting to find that sort of relationship for yourself?"

A resolute glint sparked her blue eyes. "I'm not expecting it to be easy to find that sort of dedication and love, but I won't give up until I find it! Before I'd settle for a lukewarm marriage, I'd live the rest of my life single."

Lukewarm? He couldn't imagine any man feeling tepid in her arms. In fact, she'd make sure her man felt plenty of heat.

"You have nothing to worry about in that regard," he said drolly.

Her brows lifted and then she glanced to the opposite end of the room. "I need to apologize to you, Kipp. For introducing you as my fiancé back at the Neighbors' Place. I— It just came out. Because I—"

As he waited for her to answer, her hands nervously rubbed against her thighs, and then as silent seconds ticked away, he decided to speak for her.

"Because it was an easy way to explain us being together."

She groaned and spread her hand in a helpless gesture. "Sort of. Which was silly of me. But I could tell by the way the building administrator first looked at us she thought we were—together. Really together. So did the twins. And I thought it would make it easier for you to accompany me to Scarlett's room, if I introduced you as family—or soon-to-be family."

"Does it bother you that those people might have thought we were lovers?"

The word jerked her gaze back to his and she stared at him in dismay. "No! It would've bothered me more to have them thinking I'm incapable of getting a man of my own—in any capacity."

He looked at her with wry amusement. "Now, that is a silly idea. But you sure don't need to give me an apology. You can call me whatever you'd like. Even a dirty word, if it makes you feel better."

She studied his face for a moment as though she needed to make sure she could believe him, and then she laughed. The soft sound lifted some of the heavy fatigue from his shoulders.

"Truly?"

He crossed a finger against his chest. "Truly."

"You're being very generous, Kipp. You're the one who should be calling me a blatant liar. I'd better not tell Bonnie about this. She'd give me a darned good scolding," she added with another little laugh.

During the long hours they'd spent in the truck, she'd talked a lot about her life back in Beaver County and her conversations had been full of Bonnie and the things they'd done together, making it obvious to Kipp that the sisters were like entwined fingers. He'd seen their closeness firsthand while he'd been visiting Stone Creek and he wondered how, or if, the two women could make separate lives for themselves. But it could be that they weren't planning on being apart, he thought.

The Hollisters' ranch was massive. Even once the twins married, there would be plenty of room for the two women to have homes close to each other and the rest of the family. Yes, he could easily see that happening. The twins would remain together and happy. Just as Rube and Walt were still together after all these years.

Together and happy. You need to remember the only way Beatrice can be happy is living close to her family. Especially her twin. You'd mostly likely pay hell, Kipp, if you ever tried to pull her away from those she loves.

His deep thoughts were suddenly interrupted with a knock on the door and he quickly rose from the couch to answer it.

"That must be our food," he said.

"Great," she replied. "I am so ready to eat."

* * *

Nearly an hour later most of the pizza was gone and Beatrice was sitting on the couch, sipping coffee she'd made in the small coffee maker supplied by the hotel. With her cell phone against her ear, she listened to her father's voice, while wondering what he would think if he knew Kipp and his daughter were sharing the same room.

Why should that matter, Bea? You and Kipp are just friends. There's nothing wrong with friends sharing a room. Besides, you're a grown woman. Your father doesn't dictate any relationship you have with a man.

The voice going off in her head very nearly drowned out what her father was saying and she had to mentally shake herself in order to focus on his voice.

"Bonnie gave me the news about Scarlett's dementia," Hadley said. "It was hardly what I was hoping to hear, but it is what it is. We can't change the facts, Bea."

"I know, Dad. But I had my hopes up that I'd be able to give you some credible information. Now I have this horrible feeling we might never get to the bottom of Grandfather's birth records."

"Is this my stubborn little Bea talking? Listen, honey, just because Scarlett is incapable of giving us information doesn't mean anything is over or hopeless. We'll figure all of this out somehow."

He sounded far more confident than Beatrice was feeling, but she did her best not to sound dejected about the situation. Especially with Kipp sitting a few inches away, hearing every word she was saying. She didn't understand exactly why, but more than anything, she wanted him to see she was a positive person.

"You're right, Dad. I'm not giving up. And maybe

Van can find the whereabouts of Scarlett's other children. After all, she did track down Grandmother."

There was a pause and then Hadley said, "You called Scarlett Grandmother. Is that how you think of her now? After you've met her?"

He sounded dismayed. As though he'd not expected Beatrice to consider Scarlett a part of the family.

Massaging her forehead with her fingertips, she glanced over at Kipp. He was bent forward with his elbows resting on his knees as he scrolled through something on his phone. The guy had no idea what the sight of the maroon-colored shirt stretched across the back of his broad shoulders was doing to her. Or how sexy he looked with a heavy hank of dark hair falling toward his eye. He'd still not shaved and her palm itched to feel the stubble against her skin.

"Bea? Are you still there?"

Hadley's slightly annoyed voice penetrated her thoughts and she fought hard to get her mind back to her father's question. "Honestly, Dad, I'm not sure what I'm thinking of Scarlett. If she'd been able to communicate lucidly and explained why her marriage to Grandfather crumbled, then I might not feel so torn—it would be easy to let go of any sense of attachment if I knew she deliberately turned her back on our family."

"Doesn't sound as though she recognized the Hollister name."

"Unfortunately, no. And she didn't seem to connect with your name or Wade's. But something sparked her mind about Barton. She called him *little Bartie* and said he had a split between his teeth." Beatrice tried to swallow away the swelling in her throat. "When she spoke of him I knew she was my grandmother—at least, biologically."

"I can understand why she was able to recall Bartie. Of the three of us, Bartie was the baby. Guess that's why he stayed in her thoughts," he said, then added, "I do have a few old pictures of us brothers when we were small. I should have sent them with you. Scarlett might have recognized her sons. But before you and Kipp left the ranch, the idea of her suffering from dementia never crossed my mind. Which was negligent on my part. She has to be in her eighties now. Even if she didn't have dementia, her memory might still have needed some prodding."

Beatrice looked over at Kipp and he glanced up and gave her an encouraging smile. She did her best to smile back at him, while thinking the last thing she wanted was for him to form the idea that she was an emotionally weak person.

"I won't lie, Dad. It was really hard seeing her—listening to her ramblings. She said she recalled a woman with a little boy by the name of Bartie and how much she wished she could see them again—as if the woman wasn't her, but someone else. And then she said she figured they both might be dead. It was sad. Really sad."

Hadley was silent for long moments, and in the background Beatrice could hear her mother and Vanessa talking together, along with the crackle of the fire in the fireplace. Apparently her brother Jack and sister-in-law Vanessa were there for a visit. And she didn't have to ask to know that Bonnie was close by, making sure everyone had after-dinner coffee and dessert. Which was always a ritual at the Hollister house.

Kipp had none of those things going on at the Rising Starr, she thought sadly. His family and the ranch had been splintered into pieces and control of the ranch taken from him. She was beginning to understand so much more about him now and why he was shying away from becoming a husband or father.

Hadley said, "I'm sorry I put you through this, Bea. I shouldn't have sent you to face a woman we know nothing about."

Her father's delayed response caused her to straighten her backbone and scoot to the edge of her seat. "Don't say that, Dad. Besides, you're the one who's gone without a mother for more than fifty years of your life. If Scarlett did that to you deliberately, then I can't really think of her as my grandmother."

He let out a heavy breath. "We'll probably never know what was deliberate with Dad or Scarlett. And it's a little late to be trying to find answers now. We sure as hell can't change the past."

"No. But you must wonder why they parted and why she never returned. We all wonder. And if you'd heard Scarlett—the sound of her voice—well, I'm just not sure that she wanted to leave her sons. Kipp heard it, and he thinks as I do. And now—well, I'm beginning to feel skeptical about Grandfather and the way he described his ex-wife. Do you think there might be a chance he didn't tell us the true story about his divorce?"

"Are you asking if Dad might have lied about Scarlett? Hell, Bea, why? What sort of reason would've made him hide the truth from us for all those years? Just to make himself look like the good guy? The martyr who raised his boys alone?"

Beatrice honestly didn't know if her grandfather had

been one to slant the truth. The Lionel Hollister she remembered was a staunch, righteous man who expected his children and grandchild to be equally upright. To imagine him lying about his private life seemed absurd and yet Beatrice couldn't help feeling that something was off with the story of her grandparents.

"You'd know the answer to that better than me," Beatrice said. "But Scarlett is unable to tell us anything. And like you just said, the past can't be changed. But I'm thinking that if we could figure out what happened with your parents, then we'd discover his birth records."

"You could be onto something. But in this case, *if* is a huge word," he said, then roughly cleared his throat. "So, now that we got that out of the way, tell me how things are going with you two. Are you settled for the night? Is Kipp holding up?"

She looked over at Kipp and the little flip she felt in her stomach had nothing to do with eating too much pizza.

"We're both tired," she answered. "But we're in a nice hotel—we'll get plenty of rest before we start off in the morning."

"And the weather?" he asked.

"So far there's only light snow falling here in town. But the weather forecast is predicting more to move in. We're hoping we'll make it all the way to the Rising Starr before any major weather hits."

"I'm hoping so, too, Bea. I'll be glad when you get back home. So will your mother," he said with a gruff little laugh. "You being gone has reminded us how much we love you."

She chuckled softly. "I love you two just as much. And there's no need for you to worry. I'll be home soon enough," she told him. Then, after a promise to call again tomorrow, she hung up the phone and placed it on the coffee table in front of her.

"I'm glad that's over with," she said to herself as much as she was speaking to Kipp. "Thank goodness Dad didn't make the call FaceTime!"

"How did he take the news about Scarlett?"

"All in stride. That's the way Dad takes most everything. Unless he really gets angry. Then everyone hears him." Sighing heavily, she rubbed her fingers over her closed eyes. "So much has happened today. I don't know how I'm going to stop my mind from whirling."

"Since we arrived in Coeur d'Alene, you've had a lot to take in," he said gently.

Dropping her hands, she looked over to see concern in his brown eyes, and the idea that he truly had taken her feelings into consideration made her very nearly burst into tears.

The tightness in her throat lent a huskiness to her voice. "You know, Kipp, I've always prided myself in being a strong woman. Not that I've had to face many tough issues in my life. I'm only twenty-six. But I went through a few trials during my college years and I never let them get me down. My motto has always been *chin up and soldier forward*. But this thing with Scarlett—or Grandmother—dear Lord, I'm so mixed up I don't know what to call the woman anymore. And now learning anything about Grandfather all seems so hopeless."

To her surprise, he moved close enough to wrap one arm across her back, and the inviting touch caused her head to instinctively fall against his shoulder. With her cheek pressed against his warm flesh, her nostrils pulled in the delicious scent of man, while her hand rested against the gentle rise and fall of his chest.

"Bea, you can't allow this one meeting with the woman to make or break you. I imagine this is just the beginning—a mini breakthrough on the road to the truth about your family. Later you're going to look back on this time in Coeur d'Alene and be glad it happened."

His words brought her head up and she found herself gazing directly into his face. Her heart thumped hard and her mouth suddenly turned as dry as desert sand.

"I'm glad right now, Kipp," she murmured softly. "Because I'm with you. Because we're here together. Alone."

His nostrils flared as he drew in a deep breath, and then his eyelids drooped until she could see only a tiny portion of the dark brown orbs.

"Your mind is spinning. Way too fast," he said.

"You're wrong. When I look at you, Kipp, it all slows down to focus on one thing."

"I have the feeling I shouldn't ask you what that one thing is."

His voice was thick and she could feel his hand move ever so slowly against her back. Beneath her sweater, goose bumps erupted on her arms.

"No," she whispered. "You shouldn't bother asking, because it's much better for me to show you."

"Bea—"

She didn't give him the opportunity to say more. The need in her was too great to let him interrupt this precious moment.

Chapter Eleven

Leaning into him, she spoke against his lips. "Say my name again, Kipp. I love hearing you say it. I love feeling it on your lips."

Groaning, he slid both arms around her and tugged her upper body tightly against his chest. "Bea. Bea. This is—not good!"

Even as he said the words, his mouth was crushing down on hers, consuming it with a hunger that stole her breath.

She wound her arms around his neck and parted her lips. After that everything became a delicious blur, until his mouth lifted a fraction above hers and his warm breath fanned her cheeks. "You don't know what you're doing," he whispered.

Her smile was dreamy. "I'm not exactly experienced at this. I'm counting on you to show me what I'm doing wrong."

"What's wrong is you trying to seduce me."

Her hands curved over the ridges of his shoulders and she marveled at the hard strength beneath her fingers. "Am I succeeding?"

He muttered a curse word under his breath. "What do you think?"

"That you—this—feels wonderful," she murmured.

"Right now it does. Later you'll think different."

"Later? Like fifty years from now? You can ask me how it feels then," she said huskily. Then, with a hand at the back of his neck, she pulled his head back down to hers.

If he was reluctant to kiss her again, it didn't show in the searing search he was performing on her lips. And after a few seconds she forgot all about his warning of later regret. Her mind was on the here and now and the incredible sensations flowing through her body.

Kissing Kipp, having her arms wrapped tightly around him, was a whole new experience for her and she realized this wasn't just a light embrace with a casual date. It was an all-out meeting of a man and a woman. And the heat it was creating was already close to melting her body and her senses.

Groaning, he lifted his mouth from hers and sucked in a harsh breath. "Bea. You need to let me go."

She watched his lips form the words and heard them with her ears, but her brain had no intentions of following his suggestion.

"Why? Is there someplace else you'd rather be?"

The whispered question caused him to let out another helpless groan. "No. Damn it. I don't want to be anywhere except here—with you."

She breathed his name, and then, with a resigned grunt, his mouth returned to hers.

This time when they kissed there was no holding back for either of them. This time she could taste hunger and need and even loneliness in the plundering search of his lips. And each of those cravings urged her to deepen the contact between them.

Only seconds passed before his hands began to roam across her back, over her shoulders, then down to the mounds of her breasts. And when his hands cupped their weight in his palms, she moaned with pleasure and opened her mouth to invite his tongue inside.

While it probed the edges of her teeth and the ribbed roof of her mouth, she instinctively strained to press herself closer to him. As a result, the upper halves of their bodies began to list to one side. When they finally toppled onto the cushions, he quickly lifted her legs onto the couch, then stretched out next to her. Once they were lying flat along the couch, his arms tightened around her and he slung a leg over her thighs as though to make sure she couldn't move away from him.

The sensation of lying prone against the length of his hard body shot her with so many sensations she lost all ability to think. Her brain was on fire and so was the rest of her. Desire burned from the top of her head to the bottom of her feet. The heat was so all-consuming she thought she would melt right there in his arms. But even if she turned into a helpless puddle, she wouldn't care. These moments of having him make love to her were worth every second.

Eventually his hands found their way beneath the hem of her sweater, and the contact of his rough palms gliding over her stomach and up her rib cage pulled a needy groan from her throat.

The sound caused him to lift his head and he looked at her with a mix of anguish and passion. "This is wrong, Bea. We're headed for trouble. Real trouble."

Closing her eyes, she cupped her palm against his

cheek. The days-old beard felt soft and rough at the same time and she rubbed her hand back and forth, loving the friction beneath her skin.

"How can it be trouble, Kipp? I've wanted to do this from the minute I first laid eyes on you. So there. Now you know I'm a brazen hussy."

His lips twisted to a wry slant. "Brazen, huh. I wasn't aware those thoughts were up there in your pretty head. Why didn't you let me in on your secret?"

In spite of being crushed in his arms with her face only an inch away from his, she felt a blush sting her cheeks. "I didn't want to hear you laugh at me."

She'd thought her admission would pull a chuckle from him, but instead, his expression grew stone sober. "Oh, Bea, I don't know what to say. Except that I—" He pressed his cheek to hers as his hands splayed against her back and held her tightly to his chest. "Want you, too. More than I ever thought I could want anybody."

She pulled her head back as a sob of joy rushed out of her, and then he was kissing her with desperate abandon and Beatrice reacted with equal recklessness.

The dance between their lips went on and on until he finally lifted his mouth away from hers and buried his face in the curve of her neck. She ran her fingers through his hair, then slid her hands down his back. When her fingers bumped into his belt, she reached around to the front of his waist and began to fumble with the buckle.

The signal that she wanted the two of them to be connected completely must have shocked his senses. All of a sudden he straightened away from her and bolted to his feet.

"I—uh— We can't do this, Bea! Not now!"

He turned and walked to the other side of the room.

Beatrice was so stunned by his rejection, all she could do was stare after him.

But after a moment, the shock wore off and her body was flooded with frustrated heat.

"Not now? Then when? I'll be going back to Utah soon. There won't be any more nights like tonight!" she exclaimed.

He looked over his shoulder and glared at her. "Exactly my point. This will get us nowhere."

The flat desolation in his voice chilled her and she shivered as she rose and walked over to where he stood. "Nowhere?" she repeated in a soft, incredulous voice. "Is that how you think of me? Of making love to me?"

He turned his face toward the window. "Forgive me if I'm not saying this as a gentleman would," he said dully. "I'm not exactly experienced with this kind of situation."

She gasped as she was struck with the urge to grab his shoulders and shake him. But she wasn't capable of moving a mountain, not physically and/or emotionally.

"You think this is my regular behavior with a man?" She tossed the question at him.

Grimacing, he said, "I see you as a woman too young to know what she wants or what is good for her."

To tell him to go to hell was on the tip of her tongue, but she bit back the words. She didn't want to hurt Kipp. All she wanted was to love him. But his wants obviously didn't match hers.

"Thanks," she said hollowly. "I appreciate your honesty, Kipp."

Swamped with helplessness, she turned and walked over to the bed she intended to use for the night. As she sat down on the end of the mattress and reached to remove her earrings, she told herself she couldn't think of this day as one of disappointments. True, she'd discovered her estranged grandmother had lost her mental faculties and she'd learned that Kipp had no intentions of having sex with her. But she wasn't going to let either fact break her spirit. She had to believe tomorrow would be better.

Reaching for the suitcase on the floor near her feet, she tucked the earrings safely away in a small compartment, then dug through her clothing until she found her robe and pajamas.

"Do you plan on leaving early in the morning?" she asked as she placed the stack of nightclothes near her side. "I need to set the alarm on my phone."

Still standing near the window, he said in a clipped tone, "By seven, if possible."

Her throat was aching, but she did her best to speak around the lump of emotion. "Don't worry. You won't have to wait on me. I'll be ready."

Earlier in the evening, the quietness of the room had been a relief to Beatrice's ears. After listening to the truck humming for hours on end and the drone of the radio playing in the background, she'd welcomed no sound. Now the silence seemed eerie.

Rising from the bed, she gathered up the nightclothes and a few toiletries. "Do you need the bathroom? I'm going to take a shower so I won't have to do it in the morning."

"Go ahead. I don't need it."

His remark caused her to pause. What did he need or want? she wondered. Just to get back the ownership of the Rising Starr? That didn't sound like much of a life, she thought sadly. But apparently it was enough for him.

Blocking out the dismal thoughts, she started toward

the bathroom, but only managed to make it halfway across the room before he intercepted her.

She looked up at his dark, brooding face and felt her stomach clench with longing. Had she lost all her senses? This man had just rejected her, and yet here she was, wanting to throw herself into his arms.

"You changed your mind about needing the bathroom?" she asked.

A muscle ticked in his cheek. "No. I—wanted to— say something—else."

She frowned. "Don't you think you said enough? We're heading nowhere, remember?"

"Bea, that isn't—"

"Don't bother, Kipp. I get it." She didn't want to be curt with him, but it was impossible to hide the hurt he'd caused her. "You don't have to give me detailed explanations. A man and a woman either click together or they don't. You obviously didn't feel the click that I did. That's all there is to it."

"Damn it, Bea, I felt the click! I felt it way too much!" He savagely raked a hand through his hair, then lifted his gaze toward the ceiling. "Don't you understand that I'm trying to think of you? I don't want you hurt. And that's what would happen if you got mixed up with me."

She began to shiver all over again and she clutched the nightclothes tightly to her chest as though the bundle of fabric could possibly warm her. "Really? And how do you know I'd get hurt? Have you ever thought getting mixed up with you might make me happy?"

"Happy?" He repeated the word as though he'd never heard it before. "You're not seeing things clearly, Bea! Haven't you stopped to think we live hundreds of miles apart? And what about the gap in our ages? When you look at me, don't you see the ten long years between us?"

"In case you've forgotten, there are highways and skyways between Beaver and Burley," she said. "And when I look at you I don't see years. All I see is a man who's become very special to me."

If possible, his expression turned even more anguished.

"Then you're making a mistake, Bea. I'm nothing but a ranch hand. I'd never be able to give you the things your father gives you."

"I'm glad to hear it. Because *things* aren't what I want from you."

His eyes roamed her face. "It's easy for you to say that now—tonight. But later—well, sex wouldn't be enough."

Was he saying sex was all he'd have to offer her? If so, he was right. It wouldn't be enough for her. She wanted love and passion. She expected devotion and a lifelong commitment from her mate. Anything less wasn't acceptable. But she couldn't believe he had so little to offer.

"Aren't you selling yourself short, Kipp? Don't you believe you have more to offer a woman than just a roll in the hay?"

"You're not just any woman, Bea. You deserve the best. And more than anything, I don't want you to be angry with me. Not tonight or anytime."

He reached out and gently cupped his hand alongside her face. The tender contact caused her eyes to mist over and her chest to ache.

"I'm not angry with you. And the way I see it, you are the best—for me."

His head shook slightly back and forth, and then, with a heavy groan, he rubbed his cheek against hers.

For long moments he stood with the side of his face resting next to hers before he finally said, "It's getting late, Bea. Go take your shower. We need to get an early start in the morning."

He straightened away from her and Beatrice watched him walk over to where he'd left his boots. After he'd tugged them on, then shoved his hat on his head, she had to ask, "Are you going out?"

"I need a little air. I'll be back in a bit," he told her.

After grabbing his jacket, he went out the door, and for a long moment, Beatrice remained standing in the same spot. Her lips were still burning from his kisses, while the imprints of his hands had left a trail of heat all over her upper body.

She'd never had an embrace with a man shake her so deeply. She'd never wanted anything as much as she'd wanted Kipp.

I imagine he's left plenty of women crying into their pillows.

Bonnie's warning about Kipp suddenly drifted through Beatrice's thoughts and she now realized what her sister had been trying to tell her. Kipp was dangerous in more ways than one. Falling in love with him would expose the deepest part of her heart. Was she ready to open herself up to that sort of risk? Especially when he refused to give her all of himself?

If she had any sense, she'd keep a safe distance between them. Emotionally and physically. But how could she manage to do such a thing when her body was still aching for him to make love to her?

More than an hour had passed before Kipp finally forced himself to return to their room. Except for one small lamp burning near the head of his bed, the room was dark. Beatrice had gone to bed. With her back to him, it was impossible to tell whether she was asleep, and frankly, it didn't matter. He had no intentions of striking up another conversation with her tonight. And he sure as hell couldn't make the mistake of kissing her again. Yet the need to hold her in his arms and taste her sweet lips still continued to gnaw at him.

Hanging his coat and hat on the back of a chair, he sank onto the edge of the bed and tugged off his boots. Once they were sitting side by side at the foot of the bed, he slipped out of his shirt, then glanced over at Beatrice. The idea of getting undressed with her lying so close left him uneasy. Which was damned ridiculous, he thought. It wasn't like she was going to sleepwalk and climb into bed with him. And he sure wasn't going to slip beneath the covers on her bed. No, he'd already given her all the reasons why they couldn't be together. He couldn't be changing his mind now or ever.

He was gazing at her long hair spilled upon the pillow and the curved shape of her body beneath the blankets when she suddenly stirred and turned to face him.

Even in the semi-dark room, he could see her eyes were open and staring at him.

"Did you get the air you needed?" she asked.

The husky sound of her voice slipped over him like fingers against his skin. "I walked outside for a few minutes. It's still snowing. The rest of the time I was down in the lobby. I called Ben to see how things were at the ranch. I told him if everything went well, we'd be there tomorrow evening."

She levered herself up on one elbow. "Did he say the weather was bad there?"

"No. They've had a bit of snow, but nothing that should keep you from driving on to Utah."

The mere thought of their time together ending was making him feel all twisted up inside. Like he was coming down with some sort of sickness he'd never had before.

"My parents will be relieved."

"I'm sure."

She suddenly tossed back the covers and climbed out of the bed. Kipp couldn't help but see she was wearing flannel pajamas with red and white stripes. In keeping with the Christmas holiday, he supposed. The utilitarian garments should have been a turnoff, but her sexy little curves made them look like sensual lingerie.

"I hope you don't mind, but I need to turn up the thermostat," she said. "It's cold in here."

Cold? How could she be chilled, when he was about to combust into flames?

"I don't mind."

She went over by the window, where the control for the heating and cooling system was located. As he watched her punch buttons to adjust the temperature, a reckless sort of resignation came over him. To hell with the right or wrong of it—he needed to be close to her tonight.

Pushing himself to his feet, he walked up behind her and wrapped his hands over her shoulders. The contact had her twisting around and she looked up at him with wide, questioning eyes.

"Is something wrong?"

Any other time her question would have been laughable. What wasn't wrong? She wanted to make love and he was losing his grip. In more ways than one.

"No. I just think—let's go lie down together," he said softly. "Just to sleep and keep each other warm."

To his relief, she didn't push him for explanations or ask for anything more. Instead, she simply nodded. With a hand on the back of her arm, he ushered her back over to the bed. After she'd slipped between the covers, he turned off the lamp. Then—still wearing his jeans—he climbed in beside her.

When he pulled her into the curve of his body and anchored an arm around her waist, he thought he'd never felt anything so perfect. And with the scent of her hair in his nostrils and the warmth of her body chasing away the chill in his heart, he fell into a deep sleep.

The next morning Beatrice woke to find herself alone in bed and the sound of the shower running. Although it was still dark outside and she was tired enough to sleep for another hour, she climbed out of bed and went over to the closet.

Last night, while Kipp had been out of the room, she'd hung up the clothes she planned to wear today. Now she placed the wide-legged jeans and cropped purple sweater on the end of the bed and hurriedly changed into them.

She was sitting on the side of the bed, pulling on her boots, when he emerged from the bathroom fully clothed in jeans and a heavy green plaid woolen shirt. His wet hair was brushed straight back from his forehead and his face clean-shaven. He looked very different from the Kipp she'd gotten to know these past few days. But then, sleeping in his arms throughout the night might have her seeing him in a different way no matter how he actually looked, she thought. Either way, he was achingly handsome and the sight of him was enough to send her heart into a happy flutter.

"I'm almost ready," she told him. "Just give me a few minutes to do something with my face and hair."

"No problem—take your time. I need to go down and check out the truck anyway."

He walked over to the chair and reached for the oiled canvas ranch coat he'd left lying in the seat. As he pulled on the garment, Beatrice rose from the bed and went over to where he stood.

"Do you think we'll be able to make it to the Rising Starr by this evening?" she asked.

"I hope to heck we can. Driving on snow-covered highways is beginning to get old."

She nodded glumly, while thinking their trip together would soon be ending and she'd be back in Beaver County. Then what? How was she going to jump back into the normal swing of her life? After being so close to Kipp these past few days, she was fairly certain she was going to feel empty and aimless. And she wasn't looking forward to going through the painful withdrawals of losing his company.

"Well, I appreciate all that you've done for me on this trip, Kipp." Her voice sounded unusually husky and she attempted to clear her throat before she went on. "And I want to thank you for last night."

His eyes narrowed slightly as he looked at her. "Last night? What are you thanking me for? Stopping you from having sex with me?"

"No!" She gasped the one word as embarrassed heat flooded her cheeks. "I didn't want to stop! You did!"

His sigh was heavy. "One of us had to use some common sense."

Common sense. That was something she'd worked hard to project to her family and to him, but apparently Kipp wasn't seeing her effort. A layer of moisture sprang to her eyes and she quickly turned her back so he couldn't see how much he was affecting her.

"You know, Kipp, it never seems to matter that I've earned a college degree, held down a job and helped around the ranch. My siblings have always looked at me as the silly, immature one of us. And my parents—well, they love me dearly. I've never doubted that. But they see me as the baby who needs to be watched over and protected. That's why I was so thrilled when Dad gave me this task of meeting with Scarlett. I felt like he was finally seeing me as dependable and responsible. And last night—for a few minutes I thought you were seeing me as someone you could trust to know her own mind."

His hands came down on her shoulders and she closed her eyes as the pleasure of his touch poured through her. Surely he'd not forgotten the hot kisses they'd exchanged, the sighs and touches that had passed between them. If she lived to be a hundred, those moments of their shared passion would still be burned in her brain.

"Bea, honey, I don't think you're immature. And I do trust you. I just think where I'm concerned you're misguided."

She wanted to argue the point. But the gray morning light was already filtering around the drapes of the window and she knew this wasn't the time to show and tell him how much he'd come to mean to her. And even if it were a good time to express her feelings, he probably wouldn't want to hear about them. She was certain he was going to be damned relieved to get this day over with and see the last of her when she drove away from the Rising Starr tomorrow morning.

Turning back to him, she tried her best to give him a smile. "Thanks anyway," she said solemnly, "for sleeping next to me through the night. I—uh, needed to be close to you."

His brown eyes softened and then his hands meshed in her hair as he lowered his head and placed a kiss on her forehead. "Oh, Bea, don't you know by now that I needed to be close to you, too?"

Her eyes met his and she felt a hard jolt in the middle of her chest. "Really?"

"Yes. Really," he said gruffly. Then, before more could be said on the subject, he stepped away from her and reached for his hat. "Better get your things packed. I'll be back in a few minutes."

Under normal conditions, the trip down to Burley from Coeur d'Alene could be made in nine hours. But on several occasions throughout the day, they drove into snow showers and encountered more slick highways that forced them to take it slow.

By the time they reached Burley it was growing dusky dark, giving Beatrice only a dim glimpse of the little town near Kipp's home. Once they passed through the small cluster of businesses, and back in the open country-side, he slowed the truck and turned onto a narrow dirt road.

"This takes us straight to Rising Starr. It's twelve miles and a little rough," he warned.

She laughed softly. "Kipp, have you forgotten we drive more than twenty miles on dirt road to get to Stone Creek? In fact, I do it five days a week going back and forth to work at the boutique. And then we usually drive out on Sundays to go to church. That's why none of us own cars. In a few months' time they'd be rattling like tin cans."

"Yeah. I guess I wasn't thinking," he said.

"You've been driving all day with very few stops," she reasoned. "You're tired."

"At least we're not being snowed on," he replied. "And from what I can see, there's not much snow on the ground through this area."

Peering out the passenger window, she strained to see past the shadowy clusters of sage and evergreen trees. "I wish it weren't dark. I was really looking forward to seeing your ranch."

She supposed she'd be able to see this part of the property when she drove back out in the morning as she headed home to Utah, but it wouldn't be the same then. Kipp wouldn't be with her.

A stretch of silence passed, and then he said in a flat voice, "You shouldn't call it *my* ranch, Bea. It's not mine. It belongs to my stepmother, Andrea."

"Yes, I understand that. But your father and you and Clem all made it what it is today. Even if your name isn't on the deed, you should still call it your ranch. That's my opinion."

He grimaced. "Calling the ranch mine is hardly the same as actually owning the place."

She said, "Bonnie informed me that Flint is looking into the legalities of your father's will. Of course, Flint is a deputy sheriff, not a detective, but he knows how to collect evidence and information. You can't know what he'll find."

He negotiated the truck around a stretch of washed-out ground before he glanced over at her. "I didn't realize you knew so much about the situation with the Rising Starr."

"I didn't. But from the pieces you've told me and the bits of information I've gotten from my family, it's obvious that you blame Andrea for your father's death and you think she somehow finagled a new will. Am I right about that much?"

"Yeah. The will was a shocker, Bea. Even the savings Dad had acquired and all the stocks and bonds. Everything went to her."

She heard him draw in a deep breath and blow it out. The weary sound had Beatrice trying to imagine how she and her siblings would feel if her father ever did such a thing to his children. It was unthinkable. One of the reasons he drove himself to make Stone Creek better was so it would be something worthwhile to pass to his offspring.

Frowning thoughtfully, she glanced over at him. "Do you really think the woman harmed your father?"

After a moment of silence passed, he shrugged and said, "That's a question I've asked myself over and over for the past eight years. Each time I'm ready to swear she's a murderer, a slither of doubt creeps in and I wonder if I'm all wrong. I ask myself if circumstances make her look guilty, or my bitterness over losing Dad makes me look at her as a suspect."

Beatrice had never heard the exact details surrounding Trent Starr's death. She only knew that Clementine and Kipp both viewed it as very suspicious.

"Hmm. You have doubts and questions about your father that you need answered. And the Hollisters have a mystery about our family. Scarlett's dementia was certainly a setback for us. But I still have hope that someday we'll fill in the missing pieces of our family tree. Just like I believe you'll eventually learn the truth about your father's death."

"And get my ranch back?"

He practically sneered the question, but Beatrice didn't let his sarcasm stop her from answering exactly how she felt about the matter.

"Maybe. Maybe not. But your happiness—your future—shouldn't hinge on getting the Rising Starr back in your name. The way I see it, you're still on the ranch. You should consider that a blessing."

His grunt was mocking. "Do you remember me telling you that at one time in my younger years, I considered marriage?"

How could she forget? She was still trying to picture Kipp loving a woman enough to want to marry her. "Yes, I remember. But you didn't really explain why you changed your mind."

His lips spread to a thin, straight line. "Too much happened in my life, I guess. Mainly the girl I thought would make me a great wife turned out to be more interested in bettering her financial security."

Questions regarding the woman in his past rushed at Beatrice. She must have been beautiful and charming. Why else would he have been so blinded to her faults?

"Are you saying she was more interested in money than you?"

"Exactly. Money—security—however you want to label her wants, she had plenty of them."

Frowning, she asked, "You didn't know this about her? Before you became engaged, I mean."

Faint surprise was on his face as he glanced at her. "You thought I was engaged?"

She shrugged. "You said you were planning on marrying the woman."

He shook his head. "I was considering buying Evie a ring when Dad first became ill. But after his doctors couldn't pinpoint what was wrong with him, everything seemed uncertain. I felt like I needed to concentrate on him and keeping the ranch going before I jumped into marriage."

"Had you already asked her to marry you?"

"No, it was just sort of a mutual assumption between us. So it wasn't like I postponed our wedding or anything like that. We continued to date and I believed she was sincere about wanting to be with me. I thought she'd take to ranching life. She seemed to care about Dad and Clem. But I misjudged her badly. Once Dad died and the ranch fell out of my hands, she made it clear that getting hooked up with a simple ranch hand wasn't the future she had planned for herself. She couldn't tell me goodbye fast enough."

Beatrice could see how that broken relationship would've humiliated his masculine ego. On the other hand, he should know by now that all women weren't cut from the same mold.

"If you ask me, you made a lucky escape. No man should be measured by his material assets. Money and the things it can buy are fleeting. What's in here is all that matters."

She reached over and tapped a finger against his chest and he responded with a shake of his head.

"That's easy for you to say, Bea. Your family has always had plenty."

"Not always," she countered. "We've gone through some lean years with droughts and the bottom falling out of cattle prices. But if a person works hard enough, profits can be recouped. And it's never hurt me or Bonnie to cut down on our spending."

"You mean like only getting one new dress a week instead of four or five?"

She pulled a face at him. "If I thought you really meant that, I'd kick your shins with my cowboy boots."

A wry smile crossed his face. "I was exaggerating. But—"

"But what?" She urged him to finish.

"I'm not saying you've always had things easy. I just don't think you understand what living here on the Rising Starr—the way I live—would require of you."

Why was he telling her this? To warn her not to expect his home to be big or fancy? Or was he subtly trying to tell her she was wasting her effort if she was thinking about tying herself to him for any length of time?

She let out an exaggerated sigh, then did her best to joke. "So, along with being silly, I'm also lacking fortitude. What does a woman have to do to impress you? Keep her distance?"

He chuckled under his breath. "You know, Bea, I'm getting the feeling that I'm going to miss you once you go back home."

Something in the middle of her chest squeezed into a painful knot. At this moment she wasn't going to think about going home to Utah. She still had tonight with Kipp. And who knew—maybe he'd wake up in the morning with a change of attitude and ask her to stay for another day or two. Miracles did happen.

She looked over at him and smiled. "I hope so. Because I'm going to miss you."

Chapter Twelve

After another eight miles, they passed a cluster of lights about a quarter mile off to the right of the frozen dirt road.

"Does someone live over there?" she asked.

"Andrea and Warren. That's the main house—it used to be my and Clementine's home."

His voice was flat and emotionless, and Beatrice figured he'd purposely made it that way for her sake. Perhaps it was male ego that made him want to hide his feelings from her, or it could be he simply didn't want her to think he had a vulnerable side to him. Either way, she figured he had to feel a little sick each time he looked at the main ranch house.

"Is it on a hill? The lights look like they're higher than us."

"Yes. It's on a little foothill. In the daylight you'll be able to see a ridge of mountains running behind the house and down to the western boundary of the ranch."

She said thoughtfully, "While we were still at Stone Creek, I overheard you telling Dad that you don't run sheep on the Rising Starr anymore. Why is that? They weren't making a profit?"

"Dad and Clementine were the sheepherders. Once

they were gone, I was the only one around who knew much about caring for them. Warren urged Andrea to sell the flock and they've never been replaced."

She glanced at his somber profile and it dawned on her that once they'd driven onto the Rising Starr his demeanor had changed. Because the place held bitter memories? she wondered. Or could he be thinking he'd reached the end of his part of the trip and this would be their last night together? No, she decided. He had far more important things on his mind than telling her goodbye.

"Hmm. Would you like to have sheep on the ranch again? I know how much Clementine and Quint love being around the animals."

He shrugged. "I would. But I'm not in a position to express my views on the matter. Not that I want to. I'm just biding my time here anyway."

Even though he wasn't looking in her direction, she scowled at him. "You're flat-out lying to me now, Kipp. Or maybe you're lying to yourself. You're here on this ranch because you love it. Because the welfare of this land and the livestock mean everything to you. No. You're not just biding your time—waiting for something to happen or fall your way. You're here because you want to be."

Groaning, he said in a sardonic voice, "A man travels fifteen hundred miles or more with a woman and she ends up thinking she knows everything going on in his head. Spending hours in a truck cab doesn't necessarily make you a psychologist or an expert on me."

She shot him a challenging look. "Okay. Convince me I'm wrong."

His expression turned sheepish. "I can't, damn it. Because you're right."

She was wondering how to respond to his admission when another, smaller cluster of yard lights appeared on the left-hand side of the road. Once they reached the illuminated area, he slowed the truck.

"This is where we're going," he told her.

As he pulled onto a graveled drive, Beatrice peered through the windshield at the modest L-shaped house. The house was illuminated by a yard light, and she could see the structure was built with a native rock foundation and cedarwood siding. A pair of huge spruce trees towered over the west end of the house, while some sort of hardwood tree stood in the front yard. The long bare branches made fingerlike shadows against the tin roof. A walkway made of flat stepping stones led up to a wide porch with large cedar posts supporting the roof. A light sifting of snow covered the ground and the branches of the spruces, making the whole scene appear as though it had been adorned with white lace.

"This is lovely, Kipp."

"It's home."

The narrow graveled drive circled around to the back of the house, where another yard light illuminated a small yard cordoned off by a wood rail fence. Farther behind the house stood a small barn with connecting corrals.

Before she could ask about those, he said, "I keep two of my working horses here. Ben's been taking care of them while I've been away."

"Do you have any pets? I've already learned that Clem is a dog person."

"We use dogs here on the ranch, but none of them

stay with me. I have two cats. Let's hope that Ben saw fit to clean their litter box. Otherwise, the house isn't going to smell so nice."

He parked the truck near a small gate, then helped her to the ground before gathering up their luggage.

Once they started to the house, she walked by his side until they reached a small covered porch, then stood behind him while he dealt with unlocking the door and flipping on the light.

When she stepped inside, she found herself standing in a small kitchen equipped with white appliances and a yellow chrome-and-Formica table that looked right out of a 1950s home-and-garden magazine.

"Oh, my word!" she exclaimed, as she rushed over to the table. "Mom would go crazy over this table and these chairs! She's been trying to find a red one! Where did you get this?"

He chuckled. "I wouldn't know where it came from. I remember it being here when I was still a little boy. It's kind of a permanent fixture. Along with the rest of the furniture in this house. The way the history of this ranch goes, this little house was the original ranch house. That's before Dad bought it and turned it into the Rising Starr. Before then, the place was called the XO Ranch. So, some of the furniture you'll see in the rooms came from those owners years ago."

"Age gives everything more character." She walked over to a single white porcelain sink and peered out the window. From this angle she could see a tiny portion of the barn and half of one corral. It would be a lovely view in the daylight, she thought, with the mountain range in the distance and the evergreens growing up to the timberline. "Mom says that about her face and sometimes we tease her about getting older, but honestly, she hardly has any wrinkles for her age."

"Your mother is a lovely woman. It's hard for me to imagine her raising eight of you children. And the last two of you at the same time."

"Bonnie and I are both hoping we have twins. It's possible that genetics might pass the twin thing on." She turned a smile on him. "Did I ever tell you that the Arizona Hollisters also have twins in the family? Blake, he's the oldest of the sons, has two sets of twins. The last set of boys were born about two years ago. Proof that twins have to be in the Hollister DNA."

"Must be." A sober look crossed his face as he reached down and picked up their bags. "Come on. I'll show you the rest of the house and build a fire. The thermostat is turned down, so it's cool in here."

The subject of twins must be annoying to him, she thought, as she followed him out of the kitchen. He'd changed the topic fast enough. But she could hardly blame him. During their trip, she'd spoken many times about Bonnie and how she'd always leaned on her twin for guidance and support. He was probably sick of hearing about it. Could be he was sick of hearing her chatter, period.

She followed him into the living room area furnished with a leather couch and two stuffed armchairs all done in the same butterscotch brown. A small fireplace was built into one end of the room, while opposite it was a huge picture window that looked over the front yard. As she walked over to glance at the view, she said, "Kipp, I won't mind a bit if you tell me to be quiet. I know I have a motor mouth that runs too much at times."

He gave her a faint smile. "Your motor will run down soon enough. We've had a long day."

Any other time, she would've been run down by the time they'd driven through Idaho Falls. But now that they were in Kipp's house with the night ahead of them, she felt like she'd had a heavy dose of caffeine.

What are you getting so worked up about, Bea? Kipp refused to make love to you last night. What makes you think tonight will be any different? Just because he's on his own turf, you think he's going to go all soft and loving? You're dreaming.

"Bea? Did you hear me?"

His voice penetrated the scolding voice going off in her head and she turned away from the window and walked back over to where he stood holding their bags.

Shaking her head, she said, "I'm sorry. Were you saying something?"

"Just that if you'll follow me down the hallway, I'll show you the bathroom and the bedrooms and then I'll build a fire."

"Oh, sure. Sounds good."

She followed him down a narrow hallway to where two bedrooms were next to each other with the bathroom located at the very end. When he placed her bag in one of the bedrooms and carried his to the other, she wanted to put up a protest, but they'd only been here a few minutes and she didn't want to put him off before the night even got started.

While she visited the bathroom and changed her boots for a pair of fuzzy house shoes, Kipp built a fire in the fireplace. When she entered the living room short minutes later, the flames were crackling and two cats, an orange tabby and a solid gray, were stretched out on the rock hearth. Kipp was bent at the waist as he levered the position of the logs with a long black poker.

As soon as the cats spotted her, both animals dashed behind the couch.

"I take it your cats aren't used to you having company."

He straightened to his full height and dropped the poker into an ash bucket.

"Ben and Zach are the only other humans they see," he said.

She walked over and stood next to him. Holding her hands toward the warmth of the flames, she said, "Mmm. This is nice."

"Well, it's real," he said with a wry grin. "Not fake."

"I haven't seen anything in your house that looks fake," she told him. "The floors look like real oak and the tongue-and-groove walls are genuine wood, too. Which tells me this house was probably built a very long time ago."

He turned an indulgent smile on her. "You know about architecture?"

"Not really. But Van is a longtime friend of the Arizona Hollisters, and she told me their house, which is a huge three-story structure, has tongue-and-groove walls exactly like ours on Stone Creek. And I was so intrigued I read a bit about it. Nowadays it would cost a fortune to have a carpenter do this much work."

He looked away from her, and not for the first time tonight, Beatrice felt as though something was bothering him. Exactly what, she couldn't begin to guess.

"After Dad married Andrea, he spent quite a bit of money remodeling the big house to suit her fancy. She wanted the wood floors covered with carpet and the walls in every room painted gray. If I never see another gray wall again, it would make me a happy man."

She had to chuckle. "It obviously wouldn't take much to make you happy."

"I don't know. There are lots of gray walls around in the world," he said, then asked, "Would you like coffee or something? It's been a while since we ate. I can't tell you what's in the kitchen, but there might be cookies or cupcakes that are still fresh."

"Coffee would be nice. If you'll show me where things are, I'd like to make it for you."

"All right," he said. "I'll see if this coffee you make is any better than what you made in the hotel room in Coeur d'Alene."

He started toward the kitchen and she followed, saying, "Oh, that's so unfair, Kipp. What can anyone do with a coffee pod and bottle of water? This might surprise you, but I even know how to make camp coffee."

"I don't believe it. You've made coffee over an open campfire? Who taught you, Clem?"

They entered the kitchen with the yellow table and red gingham curtains on the windows, and as she joined him at the cabinet counter, she realized she could make herself feel right at home in the cozy room.

While he gathered the coffee makings from a cabinet near the gas range, she answered his question. "No. Bonnie and I used to go on the spring roundup. And sometimes the fall one. I usually made the coffee because Bonnie is a better cook than I am. She knows how to bake biscuits and cobblers and all that kind of good stuff in a Dutch oven. See, we're real ranching girls, Kipp. Not—"

"—fake."

He spoke the word at the same time she did, making both of them laugh.

"These past few days you've learned all the wrong things about me," she told him.

"No. I think I've learned all the wrong things about myself," he said huskily, then cleared his throat. "If you can handle this, I need to go make a phone call to Ben."

"Sure. Go ahead. I need to call my family, too."

He left the kitchen, and once she had the coffee brewing, she dug her phone from the purse she'd left lying in the seat of one of the dinette chairs.

When Hadley didn't answer, she tried her mother's number. Claire picked up on the second ring and Beatrice smiled as her mother's dear voice sounded in her ear.

"Bea. I'm so glad you called. We've been wondering how far you made it down the state today."

"All the way to Kipp's house. I'm happy to say we're finally off the highway and about to have coffee."

"I'm probably happier about it than you are. I can't turn on the news without hearing about these strong winter storms crippling the Northwest."

"*Storms*, as in plural? Don't tell me another one is coming!" Beatrice exclaimed.

"Haven't you been keeping up with the weather forecast?"

"Frankly, after we reached Coeur d'Alene, I quit looking at the weather. There wasn't much I could do about it anyway. But today was fairly nice. Cloudy and windy, but not much snow. The highways did have some icy patches, but nothing impassable."

Claire let out a breath of relief. "Your father will be thrilled to hear you're safe. Now, if you can just make it the rest of the way back to Utah, we can breathe easy."

"I rang Dad's number before I rang yours. He didn't answer. What's he doing?"

"What do you think? He's over at the barn with the heifers. Cord sends him home to rest and warm up, but you know your father—he goes right back."

Yes, Beatrice could easily picture the whole scene. When the heifers started calving, it was an extremely busy time on Stone Creek. Even Flint helped out when he was off his duties as deputy sheriff.

"Are Clem and Quint still out with the sheep? Kipp will want to know."

"They were supposed to be back here at the ranch tonight, but I've not seen any sign of them yet. Jett, one of the ranch hands, is keeping an eye on them, so I'm sure they're fine," she said, then asked, "How's Kipp? Glad to be home, I'm sure."

Her mother's comment caused her heart to squeeze. "Yes. This whole trip has been trying for him—what with the weather and all."

"Well, don't think your father will forget everything Kipp has done for you. I imagine he's going to send him a check. Although we both know money can't make up for his time and trouble."

Time and trouble. Beatrice wondered if that was how Kipp really viewed these past days he'd spent with her. She hoped not. She hoped— Well, where he was concerned, she hoped for too much.

"Dad shouldn't do that, Mom. It would insult Kipp if he tried to pay him." Beatrice didn't add that it would insult her, too. She was probably being delusional, but she wanted to believe Kipp made the trip for her. To be with her and no other reason.

"Then what do you suggest Hadley give him for compensation?" Claire asked.

"Just a thank-you from one man to the other."

There was a long awkward pause before Claire replied, "Oh. Okay. I'll tell your father what you said."

"I'd be grateful." She looked over to see the glass carafe sitting on the coffee maker was full.

"Bea, is anything wrong? You sound different—like something is worrying you."

Something *was* worrying her, she thought dismally. The crush she'd first developed for Kipp had now grown to mammoth proportions and she didn't have a clue what to do about it.

Fighting back a heavy sigh, she said, "Nothing is wrong, Mom. I'm just exhausted from riding in the truck these past three days. There were miles and miles we had to travel at a crawl."

"Do you think you'll be rested enough to start home tomorrow?"

The word *no* very nearly burst past Beatrice's lips. The thought of leaving Kipp was beginning to weigh on her heart. But she could hardly confess such a thing to her mother. Claire wouldn't understand how her daughter had fallen so quickly for a man she'd only met a few days ago.

"I'll feel better in the morning," she answered.

"Well, with it being New Year's Eve tonight, it's best that you're off the highway."

Beatrice gasped. She hadn't paid attention to the date, and if Kipp had remembered the holiday, he'd kept it to himself.

"New Year's Eve! I hadn't stopped to realize it was

the last day of the year! Is the family gathering at the house tonight?"

"Yes. As far as I know, everyone will be here. Dad asked Jett and Chance to join us, and the brothers from Arizona are supposed to be coming, too. At the moment, Bonnie is helping me put together snacks and Van and Maggie are bringing food. Grace is bringing desserts and Dad sent Chance into town to the liquor store, so there's no telling what we'll have to drink."

Sounded as though her family was getting ready for their traditional get-together. The image of what would be going on in the Stone Creek ranch house was a stark contrast to Kipp's quiet home.

"Everything will be great, Mom. It always is. Be sure and tell everyone hello for me."

They talked another minute or two, and once the call ended, Beatrice found mugs in the cabinet and filled them with the hot brew. After adding creamer to his, she carried both mugs out to the living room. Kipp was sitting on the couch with his ankles crossed out in front of him and his head resting against the back of the cushion.

A phone was jammed to his ear, but as soon as he spotted Beatrice entering the room, he ended the conversation.

She handed him the steaming mug. "I didn't mean to interrupt your call."

He thanked her for the coffee, then placed the phone on an end table on his right. "No problem. Ben and I were finished talking anyway." He sipped the coffee. "According to him, another round of winter weather is on its way. Do you want me to turn on the TV so we can catch the forecast?"

"No!"

The word burst out of her, causing his brows to arch with faint surprise. "Wow! That was plain enough."

Sighing, she settled her shoulders against the back of the couch and took a careful sip from her mug. "Sorry. I guess I was close to shouting. It's just that I'm totally sick of thinking and worrying about the weather. I just talked to Mom and she informed me another storm is on its way. I wanted to remind her that someone far higher up than me controls the weather."

He reached over and covered her free hand with his. The unexpected touch surprised her. It also eased some of the anxiety she was feeling about the rapidly approaching morning. Kipp and her family were all expecting her to start the drive back to Utah. But she wasn't ready for the last leg of her journey. How could she be ready when, to her, it felt like the journey was just beginning?

"Did you speak with your father?"

"No. He was over at the cattle barn again. Mom and Bonnie are getting things ready for the New Year's Eve party they're having tonight. I can't believe I had totally forgotten about the holiday."

Even though she was focusing on the fire, she could feel his gaze studying the side of her face.

"And you're going to miss the celebration. I imagine that's bumming you out."

Under different circumstances, she would be feeling a little down about missing the family party. But these past few days had changed her. Right now, being with Kipp was all she wanted. Yet she could hardly admit to him that her feelings had reached such a point. He'd probably run to his bedroom and lock the door.

"Not really. There will be other parties."

He eyed her closely as he sipped his coffee. "What would you normally be doing on New Year's Eve?" he asked. "Painting the town with a boyfriend? Or celebrating with your family?"

"I've done both. Last year I was out with a boyfriend. Dinner and dancing and all that sort of thing. I felt awful about the night, because he spent tons of money on the date and I was secretly bored to tears."

His lips twisted. "The entertainment just wasn't good enough for you, huh? Or he wasn't good enough?"

Smirking at him, she reached over and playfully pinched his forearm. "I'm not a diva, Kipp. He was a nice guy and the entertainment was fine. I just wasn't feeling it—with him. I tried, but there just weren't any sparks."

He leveled a look of amused indulgence at her and Beatrice found her gaze slipping downward to his lips. Last night, after they'd kissed so passionately, she'd not been able to look at him without thinking about those moments and wondering if he wanted to repeat them as badly as she did.

"Is that why you haven't been engaged?" he asked. "You haven't felt sparks?"

His question surprised her. These past days they'd spent together, he'd kept their conversation mostly impersonal, except when answering her direct questions. "No. It would take more than physical attraction for me to accept a man's ring and pledge the rest of my life to him."

"Like what?"

Did he truly want to know? she wondered. Or was he merely making conversation? Either way, she knew if he mocked her answer, it would cut her deeply.

She glanced toward the fire. "First of all, I'd have to

be madly in love with him. And I'd have to know he was a good person on the inside. Honest. Compassionate. Strong. Honorable. Most of all, I'd want him to love me as much as I loved him. That's not too much to ask, is it?"

"It's too much to ask from a lot of men," he said quietly.

Including him?

Why even bother to ask yourself that question, Beatrice? He's already made it clear that he doesn't want a wife. He doesn't even want you in his bed.

Not liking where the voice in her head was taking her, she placed her cup on the coffee table, then went over to the fireplace and stretched her hands toward the warmth.

"Do you keep spirits in the house?" she asked, as she watched a flame lick around a large log.

"Only the kind with alcohol."

Glancing over her shoulder, she shot him a droll look. "Seriously, Kipp. We'll need to make a toast before the New Year arrives. I suppose we could do it with coffee or a soft drink, but it wouldn't be the same."

"There might be a beer in the fridge. Or we could drive back to Burley and get a bottle of wine or champagne," he suggested.

Aghast that he would even suggest such a thing, she turned and stared at him. "Are you kidding? Climb back into that truck tonight? No way! I'd toast the New Year with water before I'd do that. But—" She paused as another thought struck her. "I'm sorry, Kipp. I wasn't thinking. Now that you're home, you might have something else you want to do—someone you want to see tonight. If so, don't worry about me. I'll be fine here by myself."

His eyes narrowed with disbelief as he left the couch and came to stand at her side. "Do you honestly think I'd leave you here alone tonight?"

She shrugged as her heart took off in a rapid thud. "If you'd rather be somewhere else, that's exactly what I'd want you to do. Come on, Kipp. Be honest. I've been a thorn in your side from the moment we left Stone Creek. I know it will be a relief to you when the thorn is pulled out and the pain is gone."

"Hmm. You view yourself as a pain?"

"To you? Yes. Especially after—" Her throat closed around the words and her eyes grew watery as she continued to stare into the hot flames. She swallowed hard, then drew in a ragged breath. "Last night."

He didn't reply and she glanced up to see he was frowning at her.

"I tried to explain why I put an end to things," he said. "If I had let things continue as they were, we would've wound up in bed together."

"We wound up in bed together anyway," she pointed out.

Raking a hand through his hair, he looked away from her. "Yes. And all we did was sleep. We're both better off for using some common sense."

"Are we?" she asked softly. "I don't feel so wonderful about it. And I don't believe common sense was the reason you ended what was happening between us. I think it was fear."

Incredulous, he stared at her. "Fear? You think I was afraid to have sex with you?"

She very nearly winced at the word *sex*, but somehow she kept a stoic expression on her face.

"Yes, I do think so! You were afraid you might like

it. Afraid that you'd want to repeat it. And afraid that once I was gone, you'd be wishing I was still here."

His dark eyes reflected his skepticism. "You don't know what you're talking about!"

"Go ahead. If it makes you feel better, keep thinking of me as the silly twin with no common sense," she said flatly. "Keep telling yourself that you're happy hiding away your feelings. Running from the joy that I—or some other woman—might give you."

She didn't wait around to hear his response. She walked over to the coffee table with the intentions of picking up her mug and carrying it to the kitchen when his hand came down on her shoulder and spun her around to face him.

His lips tight with frustration, he muttered, "Who do you think you are? You don't know what I'm feeling! But since you think you do, maybe it's time I show you how wrong you are!"

Wrong? About what? The questions hardly had time to flash through her brain before he tugged her into his arms. She landed with a thud against his chest and was trying to suck in a breath when his lips came down on hers.

Her first instinct was to shove him away and tell him she didn't want his mockery or his kisses. But that thought flew out the window as the pleasure of his lips had her groaning and wrapping her arms around his neck.

Being close to him and having his hard lips plundering hers was filling her with undeniable pleasure, and all she could think to do was hold on to him and never let go.

When he eventually lifted his head, he murmured against her cheek. "I hadn't planned on ever kissing you again. Or holding your body next to mine. But this is all I can think about, Bea. It's all I've wanted ever since we first kissed. Since even before we kissed."

The raw, vulnerable note in his voice told her that this time there wasn't going to be any stepping back or stopping, and the realization caused hot desire to rush to every cell in her body.

"Every thought I have is full of you, Kipp. You and this and the way it feels when we're together."

"Yes. Together."

He whispered the words before he brought his lips back to hers and she tightened her arms around him and opened her mouth to receive the probe of his tongue.

The flames from the fire couldn't begin to compete with the flames that were racing through her body, and she groaned with relief when he finally bent down and lifted her into his arms.

She pressed her face to the side of his neck and held tight to his shoulders as he carried her down the short hallway to one of the bedrooms. When he set her down beside the bed, she glanced around at the shadowy space and realized it was the room where he usually slept. Cowboy boots were lined against one wall, while higher on the wall above them, an assortment of hats dangled from hooks. The reality that she was in his private domain somehow made the moment even more special.

Holding her loosely in the circle of his arms, he said, "It's cool in here away from the fire. Are you too chilly?"

She slipped her arms around his waist and snugged her body close to his. "No. It feels wonderful. *You* feel wonderful."

He rubbed his cheek against hers. "Bea. My sweet Bea. You never complain. Not about the little things."

Her hands gripped the sides of his waist. "But I'd complain very loudly if you didn't make love to me. Now. Tonight."

His hands moved down her back, then slipped beneath the hem of her sweater. As his fingers walked their way up to her shoulder blades, he brought his lips close to hers. "You won't have to complain tonight. But tomorrow might be a different matter."

She laid a forefinger up to his lips. "We're not going to talk about tomorrow. We're going to concentrate on now."

"Mmm. This is the last night of the year," he said. "We should spend it like this—together."

"You're so very right."

As soon as the last whispered word passed her lips, he captured them beneath his, and for long, long moments he kissed her with fiery hunger while his hands continued on a heated foray of her body.

When the need for air finally forced them to end the kiss, Kipp didn't waste any time pulling her sweater over her head and tossing it aside.

Turning back to her, he slid his palms over the tops of her shoulders, then down her bare arms, before he reached to her back to unclasp the lacy bra covering her breasts. When the undergarment fell away, his fingers went straight to her pink nipples, causing them to turn into hard buds.

"I was beginning to wonder if you had any skin beneath all the heavy winter clothing you've been wearing."

A soft laugh rushed out of her. "You'll find I have more, the lower you go."

"Ah, so I'm finally going to get a look at your legs."

"They're bowed," she teased.

His hands cupped each breast. "I'm sure they're beautifully bowed. I can rightly say this top part of you is perfect."

Bending slightly, he nestled his face between the soft, plump orbs and kissed the satiny skin there. The tender caress of his lips caused her head to loll backward as she gave way to the pleasures rippling through her.

By the time his mouth wrapped around one nipple and his tongue laved the hardened flesh, she was beginning to ache to have her body connected to his.

Mindlessly, she unsnapped his shirt and pushed the garment apart. Beneath the heavy fabric, his flesh was bare and scorching hot. She pushed her fingers up his washboard abs, then on to the muscles padding his chest. He felt hard and strong and oh, so male, and she couldn't wait to feel his naked body driving into hers.

"Kipp. I want you," she whispered against his shoulder. "So much. So much."

He stepped back and reached for the waistband of her jeans. "I want you just as much, Bea. Let me show you."

After opening the fly on her jeans, he laid her back on the bed and reached for the hems. Once he slipped the denim garment down her legs, he tossed it behind him, then went to work removing his own clothing.

While she waited for him to finish undressing, she pulled back the covers on the bed and slipped between the sheets. The bedclothes smelled like him, and as she drew in the male scent, it wrapped around her senses like warm velvet.

When he joined her beneath the covers, he was still wearing a pair of dark-colored boxer shorts, but the thin fabric did little to hide his erection. And she was shocked at how much she wanted to wrap her hand around that intimate part of him, to touch what would eventually be inside her.

But she didn't want to rush him or appear brazen, so she waited for him to reach for her. Once she was ensconced in the tight circle of his arms and his bare limbs were tangled with hers, she realized there wasn't any part of him that she didn't want to explore. Or any spot on her that she didn't want him to kiss and caress.

"This is your bed. Your room," she whispered against his cheek.

"How did you guess? You didn't exactly inspect the bedrooms when I pointed them out to you."

With an arm around his neck, she drew herself close enough that her breasts were nestled flat against his chest.

"Because it feels like home."

With one hand thrust into her hair, he tilted her head back far enough to gaze into her eyes. The lights and shadows she saw flickering there were contradicting, and she knew that somewhere deep in his heart, he was fighting a battle, struggling to resist needing her for anything more than sex.

"It shouldn't feel like home. This house doesn't even belong to me. Not legally."

"I don't belong to you legally, either. But I feel real to you, don't I?"

With a helpless groan, he wrapped a hand around her chin and lowered his mouth to hers. "Yeah. Too real."

After that, she gave herself up to his kiss, and as his hands and mouth searched out places she'd never had touched before, she closed her mind off to everything but him and the night ahead.

Chapter Thirteen

Minutes passed as desire pushed them to a heated frenzy, and when she felt his hand slip between her thighs, she knew she couldn't allow him to prolong the agony.

"Kipp—I—can't keep going. I need you—inside me. Don't make me wait," she whispered hoarsely.

Quickly, he tugged off her bikini-cut panties and returned his hand to the soft folds of her womanhood. She was already moist and aching, and when he slipped his finger into the throbbing flesh, she cried out with helpless pleasure.

"I don't want you to wait, beautiful Bea," he whispered against her lips. "Let yourself go."

Just as she was trying to utter his name, he slipped a second finger into her and gently stroked the heated flesh. The erotic contact was more than she could bear, and all of a sudden her body was no longer hers. It belonged to him and he was sending little pieces of her flying off in all directions.

"Kipp! Oh! Hold me!"

With his face buried in her hair, he spoke next to her ear. "I have you, darlin'. Right here in my arms."

Undulating waves of pleasure gripped her body until finally her senses slowly drifted back together and she managed to open her eyes and see Kipp's handsome face hovering above hers.

Lifting fingers to his cheek, she said, "I didn't know I could do that."

His lips twisted to a wry slant. "I didn't know I could do it, either."

"Don't fib to me. Not like this."

"Who's fibbing?" he asked. "Taking a woman to bed isn't something I do on a regular basis."

"Go look at yourself in the mirror, Kipp. You can have any woman you want."

His grunt was full of amused disbelief and then his expression sobered as he traced a fingertip over the curves of her lips. "You're the only woman I want, Bea. That makes it different."

Her heart brimming with emotions, she slipped her arms around his back and held him tightly. "You're the only man I want," she murmured. "And that makes it all better."

"Better. Hmm. Show me how much better."

His lips came down on hers, and like the sudden burst of a flame, the desire between them was hot and instant. She couldn't touch him enough, kiss him enough, to satisfy the need burning deep inside her.

When she began to push his boxers down around his hips, he pulled back and swung his legs over the side of the bed.

"What's wrong?" she asked, hating the cold emptiness of the space beside her.

"I need to find a condom and I'm not sure I have any."

Groaning with disbelief, she stared at the middle of his back. "I hope you do find one."

Twisting around, he looked at her with dismay. "Why?"

"Because I don't need to take pills or be fitted with a device to keep me from getting pregnant when there's no chance of that happening."

His brows shot up. "Are you telling me you're a virgin?"

There was such a look of surprise on his face that she very nearly laughed. "No. I'm admitting I don't have much of a sex life. I learned a long time ago that meaningless sex isn't for me."

She could see his thoughts were swirling and then he leaned closer and gently stroked a hand through the hair at her temple. "Are you sure this—you and me—is right for you? This might not be what you really want or need."

She couldn't tell him that her heart was guiding her body and it was already full of feelings for him that were soft and tender. No. He wasn't ready to hear that much from her.

"You're what I need and want, Kipp."

She pulled his head down and let her lips convey how much she wanted him. After a moment, the kiss must have convinced him, because he eased away from her and climbed off the bed.

"I'd better look for those condoms."

Down the hall, in the bathroom, Kipp breathed a sigh of relief when he found the box of protection stashed away in a cabinet drawer. A few months ago, he'd purchased them on a whim when he'd dated a woman who'd come to Burley on a temporary job. As things turned out, they hadn't had much chemistry and the condoms had been a waste. Now he was more than glad he'd bought them.

Back in the bedroom, with the condom covering his shaft, he slipped under the covers and reached for her. She went willingly into his arms and he marveled at the softness of her body yielding to his and the womanly scent emanating from her hair and skin and filling his head.

"I found the protection," he told her. "No more interruptions. No more talk."

"Aww, and here I was thinking about reciting a speech I gave in high school speech class."

Chuckling under his breath, he clamped a hand on the back of her thigh and pulled her leg over his. "No speeches, sweet Bea. Just pleasure."

Her reply was to wrap her mouth over his lips and press the front of her body next to him. Kipp's senses were overwhelmed with the feel of her breasts flattened against his chest, the satin smooth texture of her skin gliding against his.

He couldn't remember ever wanting a woman the way he wanted Beatrice. She was consuming him, pushing every thought from his mind except loving her, holding her in his arms and never letting go.

When the lack of oxygen forced their lips apart, he didn't waste the chance to plant a trail of kisses down her throat and on to one breast. Touching his tongue to her skin was like licking sweet cream from a spoon and he couldn't taste enough to satisfy his hunger.

Soon, though, her fingers speared into his hair and lifted his head, while her hips arched into his erection.

"Don't keep me waiting, Kipp. You're torturing me."

The guttural sound of her voice was like an accelerant sloshing on a fire that was already blazing inside him. With a needy groan, he closed his hands around the sides of her waist and pulled her downward until her hips were perfectly aligned with his.

"All I want is to give to you," he said. "And keep giving to you. That's all I want."

His hand touched her inner thigh and she opened her legs, while at the same time she wrapped her arms loosely around his waist.

Positioning himself over her, he supported his weight with a hand on either side of her head, then slowly and surely lowered his hips and entered her sweet, warm body.

The sensation of being totally connected to her was so stunning that sparks lit the backs of his eyes. For a moment he struggled to breathe. *This is too incredible to be real.* The thought was dashing through his brain at the same time he felt her hands slide down his back and onto his buttocks.

"Am I dreaming?"

His awestruck question caused her hands to tug his hips toward hers and pull him deeper into the hot folds of her womanhood.

"This is real, Kipp. So, so real."

He blinked and her face became clear and vivid. And as his gaze took in her flushed cheeks and swollen lips, the tangled hair around her head, he thought he'd never seen so much beauty in his life. He also thought how undeserving he was to have her in his bed, his arms.

His throat was so thick with emotion he had to swallow before he could whisper, "Yes, my darling Bea. Real and true."

Slowly, his body aching with need, he began to move deep within her, and as she met his thrusts, he lost all thought of everything except her and the desire to give to her, until he had nothing else to give.

Time ceased for Kipp as the give-and-take of their bodies went on and on, and all the while he could only think he couldn't let the incredible pleasure end. He had to keep it going until her warmth filled every cold, empty spot inside him. Until her kisses and caresses made him forget the lonely nights and years he'd spent since he'd lost his family and his home.

Yet even though his mind wanted to remain in the wild throes of their lovemaking, his body was protesting, arguing that it needed relief before it splintered into helpless pieces.

The end came when he heard her cries of pleasure reach a peak and felt her hips drive upward into his. After that, he felt himself spinning violently off to a place he didn't recognize. An inky black sky was filled with thousands of stars glistening and twinkling like Christmas lights shining on golden tinsel. It was blindingly beautiful and the air was like soft velvet swooshing around and over him. If he was flying, he didn't want to land, he thought. He wanted to keep floating and sailing as long as he had her safely wrapped in his arms.

Even when his senses fell back to earth and he managed to open his eyes, he still struggled to orient himself, and it took him a minute to realize his cheek was resting between her breasts and his lower body was still connected to hers. Except for the shallow rise and fall of her chest, she wasn't moving or speaking.

Knowing his weight was surely crushing her, Kipp

rolled to one side. After tucking her into the curve of his body, he pulled the covers over them.

"Mmm. I don't have to move, do I?" She leaned her head over just enough to press a series of kisses over his damp biceps. "This feels too good. And you taste delicious."

A smile tilted his lips. "Then you shouldn't need to eat for the next week."

Laughing softly, she turned in his arms so that she was facing him, and Kipp took pleasure in using his fingers to comb her long golden hair away from her face and letting the strands fall upon the white pillowcase.

"Did I leave teeth marks on you?"

No, he thought. She'd left tiny little brands all over him—not on the surface, but under the skin, until there was no doubt that she owned him. At least, for tonight.

"I don't think so." Sighing, he nuzzled his nose against her forehead. "But you are probably hungry. We haven't eaten since early this afternoon."

"I've forgotten about eating. Are you hungry?"

Not for food, he thought. Just hungry for her and all the things he was getting just by having her lying next to him, touching him, loving him.

And yes, he was thinking of it as love. Even though he'd never felt it with any woman, he knew this was different and real. He'd tasted it in her kiss. Felt it in her hands as they'd roamed over his flesh. As for what he was feeling…he didn't want to ponder the emotions swirling around inside him. He didn't want to worry and wonder about tomorrow, or how crushed he'd be when she was gone.

"No. But if my inner clock is working, I figure it's nearing midnight. We ought to toast the New Year. I have some packets of hot chocolate," he suggested. "That would be better than nothing."

"Mmm. Hot chocolate would be great. I'll fix it."

He chuckled. "You mean you know how to boil water?"

She reached up and playfully pinched his cheek. "I even know how to pour it into a cup."

They climbed out of the bed, and while Kipp pulled on his jeans, Beatrice went to collect a robe from her suitcase. Once they were in the kitchen, she filled a teakettle with water and switched on the burner beneath it. Kipp dug the chocolate mix from the cabinet and placed it within her reach on the counter.

"Your kitchen is cute," she said.

As she glanced around the room, Kipp couldn't help but compare the spacious Hollister kitchen to this one. There was no long work island with a built-in chopping board or rows of carved cabinets. No stainless-steel appliances or a china hutch filled with fancy dishes. He figured she could see the obvious differences, but she was too nice to mention them.

"Cute, huh?"

"Very. It's just the right size. And the table is priceless. I wish I had a poinsettia to sit in the middle of it. A red one to go with the curtains."

He cast her a faint grin. "Still in the Christmas mood, I see."

"Why not?" she asked. "If people stayed in the giving mood all year round, just think how wonderful the world would be."

Giving. Generous. Gracious. She was all those things and more, Kipp thought as his gaze traveled over the sexy picture she made standing there with her wavy hair tousled around her face and over her shoulders and her lips still swollen from his kisses. The soft fabric of her blue robe clung to her body and he could see the outlines of her nipples and the perfectly rounded shape of her breasts. Even with the cool air of the kitchen wafting across his bare torso, he was still on fire for her. He could hardly wait to get her back in bed and have her soft body writhing beneath his again, hear her needy whimpers and feel the urgency of her hands roaming over him.

Would this insatiable need he felt end by the time the sun came up? Would he be able to look at her blue eyes and plush lips and not feel as if his whole world was wrapped up in her?

Not wanting to dwell on the days ahead, he pushed the thoughts aside and opened the cabinet to collect a pair of mugs. When he placed them on the cabinet counter, she tore open the packets of cocoa mix and dumped them into the cups.

"Because it's New Year's Eve, I think I should make these drinks a little decadent, don't you?"

Kipp had never been easily amused. In fact, most of his friends believed it was impossible to make him laugh. But since he'd met Beatrice, he'd found himself chuckling at the simplest things she did or said. He didn't understand how or why, but it was like she'd opened something inside him and allowed a happy light to shine in.

Chuckling now, he asked, "How are you going to make hot chocolate decadent?"

She pulled a playful face at him. "Sugar. It makes everything extra yummy."

She reached for the canister of sugar and spooned a generous measure of granules into each cup.

He cast her an indulgent grin. "That should keep us awake."

She slanted him a provocative look. "You weren't planning on sleeping, were you?"

He chuckled again. "You know, I'm not exactly a young guy."

"You could've fooled me."

Moving closer to her, he slid a hand beneath her hair and traced his fingertips along the tender skin of her neck.

"I'm ten years older than you, Bea."

Her eyes were luminous as she smiled up at him. "Thank goodness."

"What does that mean?"

Sighing, she rested her cheek against the middle of his bare chest. "It means I like you just the way you are."

He slipped his arms around her and it was on the tip of his tongue to tell her they needed to forget the hot chocolate for a while. But before he could utter the words, the shrill whistle of the teakettle interrupted his plans.

"It's boiling," she announced unnecessarily.

So was he, Kipp thought, as he released her and stood to one side while she finished mixing the drinks.

"And if the clock on the stove is correct, we're just in time for a toast. Do you have any marshmallows?"

"Sorry. I rarely keep that sort of thing in the cupboards," he told her.

Picking up both mugs, she turned and handed one of them to him. "This will be yummy even without marshmallows," she assured him, then touched her cup to his. "What do you want to toast to? The New Year?

Clem and Quint's engagement? Higher cattle prices? All the nitrate the snow is putting into the ground?"

He smiled at her. "Whatever you'd like," he said. "Maybe we should just make a toast to our trip and the fact that it brought us together."

At least for a little while, he thought glumly.

"Mmm. Yes, that's the perfect toast," she told him, then clinked her cup to his. "To our trip and us."

"I'll drink to that," he murmured.

As he took a long sip of the hot, rich drink, their gazes met, and suddenly he felt as though his whole body was filled with warmth and a feeling that was all too close to love.

After a few more sips, Kipp suggested they go sit in front of the fireplace to finish their drinks. After switching off the light, they left the kitchen and walked out to the living room. An amber glow from the fire filled the dark room, while beyond the picture window, a yard lamp illuminated the view of the front yard.

Seeing it, Beatrice gasped. "Kipp! Look! It's snowing! It's already put a thick coating on the ground!"

They both walked over to the window and gazed out at the wintery scene. The snow wasn't just a few flurries. It was falling so fast and thick it had turned the air into a wall of white.

"If that were rain instead of snow, we'd be having a gully washer."

Her lips parted in wonder as she watched the white flakes forming drifts against the porch posts. "What does it mean, Kipp?"

Snaking one hand around her waist, he turned her away from the window. "That it's time for us to go back to bed. By morning we'll know exactly what it means."

Five minutes later, with their cups emptied and the snow still falling heavily over the little ranch house, Kipp had Beatrice's warm body lying snug in his arms.

"Happy New Year, Bea," he murmured against her temple.

With her arm slung around his rib cage, her hand made lazy circles upon his back. "Mmm. So far, it's the happiest one I've ever had, Kipp."

"Me, too," he admitted. Then, finding her mouth in the darkness, he let her kiss carry him away to a place where there were no tomorrows to worry about, only the here and now.

The next morning, as dawn was just breaking, Kipp stirred and realized with somewhat of a start that the warmth in his arms wasn't coming from a furnace, but Beatrice's soft little body.

Oh hell, this was not good, he thought, as he gazed down at the crown of golden hair resting on his shoulder. This wasn't the way he normally dealt with a woman he'd had sexual encounters with in the past. No. Those occasions had been brief and there'd been no afterglow involved. And he certainly hadn't woken to a warm body lying next to his. Not even with Evie. So how and why had he let this thing with Beatrice get so out of hand?

His anxious thoughts must have telepathed themselves to her, because she suddenly stirred and opened her eyes. When they focused on his face, she smiled as though everything in the world was right. The precious greeting made something in the middle of his chest hurt.

"Good morning," she said huskily.

He touched his fingertips to her face and felt her goodness and sweetness pouring through him. "Good morning," he greeted her. "Did I wake you?"

"No. Is it still snowing?" she asked.

He glanced toward the window to where the curtains were partially opened to a view at the back of the house. "Yes. Heavily, it looks like."

"Oh my. Will I be able to drive out to the highway this morning?"

So she didn't have her heart set on staying, he concluded. That was good. He'd been half-afraid she was going to make an awkward scene about how she wanted to stay with him longer. Or at least, stay until it was time for her to return to work at the boutique. But apparently she was already thinking ahead to driving home to Utah. The fact should have made him want to leap out of bed and dance a jig of relief. Instead, he felt dead and empty. Oh God, what kind of fool was he turning into?

"I don't know," he said dully. "Let me look."

Easing from beneath the arm she'd draped across his chest, he threw back the bedcovers and pulled on his jeans.

At the window, he stared in stunned fascination at the high drifts of snow piled against the horse barn and weighing down the limbs of a nearby spruce. Snow in the winter months was a normal occurrence for this area. But the amount that had fallen during the night was totally out of the ordinary. It was like fate had stepped in to keep Beatrice here on the Rising Starr. What did it mean? Damn it, what *could* it mean? He couldn't let himself think of her in future terms. Not the two of them together!

"You're not going anywhere, Bea. Not for a while. I

don't think I've ever seen this much snow on the ranch before. Not even as a kid."

She hurriedly climbed out of bed and slipped on her robe as she walked over to join him.

"Oh my! This will be a New Year's Day you won't soon forget!"

It would be one he'd *never* forget, Kipp thought. Not because of record-breaking snowfall. But because she'd walked into his life and changed him into a man he didn't recognize.

Turning, she slipped her arms around his waist, and Kipp couldn't resist lowering his head and placing a soft kiss on her lips. "I—uh—have to get to work." He spoke against her cheek. "I told Ben I'd be in the ranch yard by six."

She didn't question him or argue how the snow was too deep or the wind too freezing for him to work. She knew a rancher's work couldn't stop for any reason.

"I understand, Kipp. The livestock need you now more than ever. Don't worry about leaving me here alone. I know how to entertain myself."

For a split second, Kipp thought about saying to hell with it all and taking her back to bed. But he had responsibilities on the ranch and he wasn't about to give Andrea or Warren an excuse to fire him. Not that either of them had ever threatened to send him packing. But Kipp didn't trust his stepmother. With her, it was best to be ready to expect the unexpected.

He eased out of the circle of her arms. "I'll just grab a cup of coffee and be off."

"No breakfast? I can fix something quickly. Toast, at least?"

"No. A cup of coffee will be plenty."

Nodding, she said, "I'll go make the coffee while you get dressed."

He patted her cheek. "Thanks, Bea."

Fifteen minutes later, Beatrice watched Kipp wade his way to a white work truck with a hay winch on the back. As he backed out of the driveway and headed the four-wheel-drive vehicle in the opposite direction of the big ranch house, she thought how much she'd been praying for some miracle to keep her here on the Rising Starr with Kipp. And the miracle had happened in the form of two feet of snow.

Think about it, Beatrice! What good is this snow miracle? Another day or two isn't going to change Kipp's mind about having a serious relationship with you. Just because he had hot sex with you for most of the night hardly means he's fallen in love with you. Get over it!

Determined not to let the mocking voice going off in her head dampen her spirits, she went to the kitchen and cleaned the cups she and Kipp had used last night and this morning, then moved on to Kipp's bedroom, where she picked up their clothes from the floor and made up the bed. Once she'd finished tidying the room, she hurriedly dressed in dark brown corduroy jeans and a thick mustard-colored sweater with a high turtleneck.

If only she'd known she was going to be staying a few more days than originally planned, she would've packed more clothes. Especially heavy winter clothing. But she couldn't have foreseen that she'd be traveling through a blizzard, then snowbound on a secluded ranch. Still, she had enough for now, and if she was stranded for very long, she could always wash a few things.

Stranded. Somehow she didn't think of herself as being stuck or trapped in Idaho. No, she was simply spending more time with Kipp and she couldn't help but think the snow was a late Christmas miracle, a gift she would never forget.

Once Beatrice was dressed, she made herself a piece of toast, and while she finished off the last of the coffee, she called her mother.

Claire answered on the second ring. "Hi, honey! Are you already on the road this morning?"

She very nearly laughed. "Mom, you can't imagine what's happened. I'm still here at Kipp's place and we're under a mountain of snow. Probably more than two feet and it's still snowing. I thought I'd better let you and Dad know that I won't be starting home today. I'm not sure when the roads might be clear enough for me to travel."

"Oh my, this trip has certainly turned into an experience for you," Claire replied.

In more ways than her mother could ever guess, Beatrice thought.

"Yes, but being here on Kipp's ranch is wonderful. From what I can see beyond the window, it's beautiful, with jagged mountains and lots of spruce trees. In a few minutes I'm going to go outside and explore—if I can wade through the drifts."

A smile sounded in Claire's voice. "You sound excited and—happy. Are you enjoying your time with Kipp?"

Her throat was suddenly thick with emotion and Beatrice realized there was no point in trying to hide her feelings from her mother. And why should she? Kipp had become the most important thing in her life, and she wasn't used to hiding the things that mattered to her from her family.

"Oh, Mom, he's been— I can't explain how these past days have been. I—think I'm falling in love with him."

There was a long stretch of silence before her mother finally replied, "I've never heard you talk like this."

She let out a breathless laugh. "That's because I've never felt like this, Mom. It's—it's the most incredible thing! But then, I'm sure you've not forgotten how it was when you fell in love with Dad."

"No. And I know how it feels to still be in love with him. But, Bea, I hope you're not being too hasty about this and jumping too fast into something that is— already full of obstacles."

Beatrice frowned as she carried her coffee cup over to the sink. Beyond the kitchen window, she watched snow continue to fall. Obviously there wouldn't be any melting on the roads today. The fact made her want to dance around the kitchen.

"I suppose you're talking about the differences in our ages."

"No. I hardly consider that a concern. I'm talking about the many miles between you. Your home and job are here in Utah. His are there in Idaho."

Beatrice had no intentions of bringing up the subject of relocating, even though the idea had already gone through her mind many times. Especially now that she and Kipp had made love.

"Oh, Mom, you're getting way ahead of things. Kipp is— Well, we've not reached that point yet. We're just getting to really know each other. But I'm hopeful about— us—and everything."

There was a slight pause, and then Claire said, "Okay, sweetie. If you're happy, then I'm happy for you."

"Thanks, Mom. I'll let you tell Dad that I'm perfectly safe, just snowbound. And, Mom—maybe you shouldn't mention anything about me and Kipp just yet. He already has enough on his mind. I don't want him worrying unnecessarily."

"I wasn't planning to tell him, Bea. But I do think you should talk to Bonnie about this."

So that she could advise her to get home as fast as she could and forget about Kipp Starr? No, this was one time Beatrice was going to follow her heart.

"I will," Beatrice assured her mother. "When the time is right."

After exchanging goodbyes, Beatrice pulled on the heaviest coat she'd brought with her, wrapped a woolen muffler around her neck and covered her head with a thick sock cap. Before she left the house, she tucked the hems of her jeans into her boots, then waded out to her truck to exchange her cowboy boots for a pair of waterproof galoshes that would protect her legs up to her knees.

In spite of a brisk wind blowing from the west and snow falling at a steady pace, the cold air wasn't unbearable to Beatrice. She supposed she was too excited and happy to be cold. Her heart was singing and she refused to let a negative thought pull her down.

Once she managed to walk to the road, she found the tracks of Kipp's truck, along with another set of tire tracks, had plowed nice little trails in the snow for her to follow. She chose to walk in the direction of the big ranch house in hopes of getting a closer look at what had been Kipp's family home before his father's death had taken it all away.

She had traveled close to a quarter of a mile when she approached an entrance that led to the house and, beyond it, a ranch yard with several barns and holding pens. Compared to the ranch yard of Stone Creek, it was small, but still a nice size.

As Kipp had described, the family ranch house rested on a foothill and looked out over a wide meadow skirted with a few evergreen trees. Presently, she didn't see any cattle or livestock of any kind on the snow-covered fields. And if the men were working around the ranch yard, she couldn't spot them from the distance of the road.

Once she reached the entryway, where an iron arch with the star brand hanging from the middle spanned over a wide cattle guard, she stopped her forward motion and stood gazing at the rambling log structure. Several spruce trees dotted the yard and towered over the north side of the house, while the south side appeared to have a long covered porch. On the far west end, smoke spiraled from a wide stone chimney.

From what Beatrice could see beneath the coating of snow, the house and the fenced yard surrounding it were beautiful. But was this property beautiful enough to kill for? she wondered. Was Kipp's stepmother really as evil as Kipp suggested? Evil enough to end her husband's life in order to inherit the Rising Starr? The notion was far more chilling than the snow peppering Beatrice's face.

If Andrea did actually harm Trent Starr, then who was to say whether she might try to permanently get rid of Kipp? Fatal accidents happened on farms and ranches every year; it would be easy for his stepmother and her foreman lover to cook up a scheme. From what Quint had said, Clementine wanted nothing to do with Andrea or trying to recover the Starr inheritance, so that left only Kipp to dig for the truth. For Andrea, taking Kipp out of the equation would be one way to make sure doubts about Trent's untimely death would never be raised. But, and this was a big but in Beatrice's mind, was the woman truly guilty of harming her late husband, or had circumstances just made her look that way?

While Beatrice thoughtfully continued to study the homeplace, Kipp's earlier remarks drifted through her mind.

...the girl I thought would make me a great wife turned out to be more interested in bettering her financial security.

He'd talked rather bitterly about losing his father, the ranch and his sweetheart all within a short span of time. And Beatrice didn't need a psychologist to explain to her that losing so much in Kipp's young life had made him shun reaching for anything meaningful. If she ever expected to gain his love, he was going to have to believe and trust that he wasn't meant to be unhappy his whole life long.

A piercing cry suddenly sounded high above her head and she glanced up to see a hawk circling the snow-covered field. The bird's chances at finding prey for lunch looked rather slim. Almost as slim as her hopes of convincing Kipp that the two of them were meant to be together.

Chapter Fourteen

It was well past dark when Kipp stepped into the house by way of the kitchen and was instantly struck with the scents of delicious cooked food. After working in the cold all day, the room felt as warm as a July afternoon and he welcomed the heat wrapping around him.

The yellow Formica table was set with plates and silverware and tall glasses filled with ice and water. Several condiments sat in the center, along with a wooden bowl filled with salad greens.

Beatrice was standing at the cookstove stirring something in a saucepan. As soon as he shut the door behind him, she looked around and gave him a wide smile.

"Welcome home."

Home. He'd never thought of this house as home, but rather a place of last resort. However, Beatrice was rapidly making it feel like home and the realization left him uneasy. The more he liked having her here, the worse it was going to be once she was gone.

"It's good to be in out of the cold," he said.

"I hope you're hungry. And I especially hope you

like meat loaf. I found lots of hamburger meat in the freezer, but nothing else. You must like it."

"I get a big order from the butcher shop at a time, and I ate all the steaks and roasts first. The hamburger meat is all I have left."

He walked over to where she stood and sniffed, then quickly realized she was the most delicious scent in the room. He had to fight the strong urge to pull her into his arms and plaster a kiss over her lips. But he was afraid if he got that close, they'd never get to the food she'd prepared.

"So you do actually know how to cook," he said as he peered over her shoulder at the simmering green beans. "I thought you might've been exaggerating a bit about knowing your way around the kitchen."

She shook a playful finger at him. "By the time you go wash up, this will be ready, and then you can decide for yourself if I was exaggerating. Oh, and take a look over there in the corner. I've made new friends."

As he started out of the room, he spotted his cats curled up on a blanket. "How did you get them in here? And that isn't their normal cat bed!"

She laughed. "I promised them if they'd keep me company I'd make them a comfy bed and give them a can of tuna. It worked."

"Cat spoiler!"

"I couldn't help myself," she said with another little laugh.

After washing and changing into a clean flannel shirt, he went back to the kitchen and found Beatrice placing the dishes of food on the table.

"Is there something I can do?" he asked.

"No. You sit and make yourself comfortable." Wearing

a pair of oven mitts, she carried the casserole dish with the meat loaf over to the table and placed it on a hot pad. "Before I sit down, is there anything else you need or want?"

"This is plenty. Let's eat." He pulled out a chair and helped her into it. "You shouldn't have gone to all this trouble, Bea. Just because you're here doesn't mean you have to earn your board and keep."

She smiled as she spread a napkin across her lap. "Don't be silly. When Dad and my brothers come in at night tired and hungry, they don't want a cold sandwich. And Mom makes sure they don't get one. I guess it's a good thing she decided she didn't want a job outside the ranch. She'd rather focus on spoiling her family."

He began to fill his plate with the meat loaf, then piled a small mountain of mashed potatoes next to it. "What about your job, Bea? I recall you telling me you had extra vacation time, but now that you're stuck here, are you going to miss work?"

She shook her head. "No. I have plenty of vacation time. If I'm still stuck after that time, my boss will understand. She's great to work for. I can't ever remember a time she was sharp and bossy with me or the other girl who works at the boutique. She's one of those people you'd just hate to disappoint. You know what I mean?"

Oh yes, disappointing Beatrice would crush him. And yet he knew that ultimately he would fail her and there wasn't anything he could do to change the fact.

"Yeah. I know."

She served herself some salad greens and then handed the bowl to him. "I took a walk this morning," she said.

His jaw dropped. "In this snow?"

"I had my tall rubber boots on and your truck tracks

cut out a nice little path down the road." She looked at him and smiled. "It was easy walking. And I went all the way to the entrance of the big house. I wanted to get a closer look."

He managed to shut his mouth, but he couldn't stop his brows from shooting up his forehead. "You went that far? Why?"

"I was curious to see what your—former home looked like. It's very beautiful. In fact, what I've seen of the ranch is just gorgeous. I'll be honest—I've always thought no place could be any prettier than Stone Creek. But when it comes to beauty, the Rising Starr is right up there with our ranch."

"Nice of you to say, Bea. But it's rather bittersweet for me to hear it." He reached for a bottle of salad dressing. "It's probably good that you've seen part of the ranch. It might help you understand why I'm still here and why I'll never leave—unless Andrea runs me off."

His comment put a faint frown on her face. "Is that something you always worry about? I don't think I could bear up under that kind of constant uncertainty."

Shaking his head, he drizzled the dressing over the bowl of salad. "After Dad's death and the will was read, I was so stunned I didn't know what to expect. Surprisingly, Andrea asked me to stay on and help work the ranch. Even though I had already made it clear that I blamed her for Dad's death."

"Oh wow! That must've been an awkward ordeal."

His mocking grunt couldn't begin to describe the horrible situation he'd endured. "It wasn't easy. I didn't trust her and she deeply resented me for accusing her of harming Dad. For weeks afterward, I expected her to change her mind and tell me to get lost. But she never did. And now after all these years have passed, I guess you could say we have a guarded truce between us."

"Hmm. And Clem? Andrea didn't ask her to stay?"

"She did. But Clem was so broken by all that had happened that she just wanted to leave and get away from the whole ugly mess."

"Yes, I can imagine." She finished filling her plate, then spoke again. "I can't help but wonder why Andrea asked you to stay. Especially knowing how you felt about her and your father's death. I'm sure you've wondered about her motive."

"Hell yes, I've wondered. The only reason I can come up with is that she knew running me off the ranch would make her look heartless and guilty to the folks around here. Or I should say, look even *more* heartless and guilty."

After that, she went quiet and turned her attention to the food on her plate. Kipp was thankful she'd dropped the unpleasant subject of his stepmother. But after a couple of minutes, he saw her looking at him in a questioning way and knew she wasn't finished.

"I can see something else is on your mind," he said. "What is it?"

"I'm not sure how you'll feel about this, but I'd really like to meet Andrea. Would you care to introduce me to her before I—go back to Utah?"

Everything about her question twisted his insides into sick knots. Especially the part about her going back to Utah. But damn it, she had to go home. He couldn't give in and ask her to stay. In no time at all she'd be miserable and regretting ever getting involved with a cowhand who had nothing to offer her.

"I can't imagine why you'd want to get near the

woman," he said flatly. "Haven't you heard anything I've said about her?"

She reached over and wrapped her hand over his forearm. The gentle touch made him want to tug her onto his lap and feast on her lips. The intensity of the passion they'd shared last night had stunned him. And all day today he could think of nothing but repeating it.

"I've heard," she said. "Remember when I told you I get these feelings and you said I was like Nuttah?"

Frowning, he nodded. "I remember. What does any of that have to do with Andrea?"

"I'd like to see what kind of vibes I get from the woman. I have the feeling there's more to this whole issue with her that you've never stopped to consider."

He rolled his eyes in disbelief. "You must think you're a cross between a PI and a criminal psychologist. Is that it?"

She pulled a face at him. "Okay, go ahead and make fun of me. Call me silly and immature if you want to. I don't care. You're not going to change my mind about this."

Kipp wasn't exactly sure why any of this mattered to her. It wasn't like the Rising Starr meant anything to her. It wasn't like *he* meant anything to her.

Like hell, Kipp. You can see she loves you. No, she hasn't said those exact words to you, but you've felt them in her touch, her kiss, heard it in her voice. That's why you're trying to run from her. From the tender feelings she's stirring up in you.

Shoving at the condemning voice in his head, he looked over at the soft, hopeful expression on her face and relented. "Okay. I'll introduce you to her."

She squeezed his arm. "Thank you, Kipp. And I promise I'll be very discreet about what I say to her."

Evie was the only woman Kipp had introduced to his stepmother and that had been long before his father had died, nearly nine years ago. Since that time, he'd not had any woman on the ranch, which made him wonder what Andrea would think about Beatrice. But he figured, in the end, what the two women thought of each other would hardly matter. They'd never meet again.

He gave her a faint grin. "I do have something else to say."

"About Andrea?"

"No. About you. This food is delicious. I thought you were supposed to be a fashion designer, not a cook."

She laughed lightly. "Thanks, Kipp. I appreciate the compliment. Bonnie tells me I need a lot more work in the cooking department. And I tell her she needs to get her fashion sense pulled together. We've always made each other try harder."

"I imagine you've been missing your twin."

"I always miss her when we're apart for any length of time. But she's glad I'm here with you. And you know what?"

All he knew was that she was surprising him at every turn and he was surprising himself at how much he liked it.

"No. What?" he asked.

"I'm glad, too."

Even though Beatrice tried to shoo Kipp out of the kitchen while she cleaned the dishes and put away the leftovers, he insisted on helping her.

Once everything was neat and clean again, they went

out to the living room and Kipp threw more logs on the low-burning coals.

While he stoked up the fire, she said, "I found the firewood in a box on the back porch. But I only used a couple of the smaller logs today, just to keep some coals going. I didn't know how hard or expensive it is for you to get firewood. So I didn't want to use the logs frivolously."

"I'm sorry. I should have explained before I left this morning that you should feel free to use all the wood you want. There's an endless supply of firewood on the mountains on the south side of the ranch. I hope you turned up the thermostat on the central heating."

"No problem. I've been toasty. Actually, I went back out this afternoon and looked over the barns behind the house. I was a bit disappointed, though, that I didn't find your horses stalled in either one of them."

He eased down next to her on the couch and she wasted no time in snuggling up to his side.

"While I was gone, Ben took my horses to one of the barns in the ranch yard so it would be easier for him to take care of them. Plus, in weather like this, we keep a heater going where the livestock are housed."

"Oh, they should be warm and comfy, then."

He reached for her hand and folded it between his two. "Did you let your family know you were snowed in?"

"Yes. I had a talk with Mom. She's going to explain to Dad what happened."

"I wonder what he thinks about you staying here with me," Kipp said.

She looked at him with surprise. "I'm sure he's relieved that I'm with you instead of stuck alone in a hotel in some strange town."

"You don't think he's worried that I—we—might get too cozy with one another?"

Beatrice couldn't help but laugh. "Kipp, I'm twenty-six years old—a grown woman. Dad took the reins off Bonnie and me a long time ago."

"Yes, but I'm sure your father wants—well, he wants you to have an ambitious, respectable man in your life."

"No, you're wrong, Kipp. Dad wants me to have a *good* man in my life."

"Look at your sister Grace. Mack is an ambitious veterinarian running his own business. Don't tell me that Hadley wants anything less for you and Bonnie."

"Dad is happy for Grace because Mack is the man she loves. That's what Dad is most concerned about. After all, if you don't have love, what good is ambition and money going to do for your life?"

His lips took on a sardonic slant. "You're living in a dream world, Bea."

She sat up, then twisted around to face him. "You're wrong, Kipp. I'm living my dream—with you."

She watched a myriad of emotions parading in his brown eyes and she knew he was fighting the undercurrent of desire that had been flowing between them ever since he'd walked through the door.

"Have you ever stopped to think you'll have to wake up in a day or two?"

Smiling, she leaned into him and wrapped her arms around his neck. "I'm not a fool, Kipp. I know what's coming. The sun will eventually melt the snow and you'll send me on my way. But that hardly means we can't enjoy the here and now. Does it?"

He groaned with misgivings as she slanted her mouth toward his and tightened her hold on his neck.

"If you're trying to seduce me—again, then you're doing a good job of it," he muttered.

Chuckling, she brushed her lips against his. "I told you I could do more than cook."

"You can do too damned much," he said with a growl.

After placing a long, hungry kiss on her lips, he rose from the couch and pulled her to her feet. As she walked alongside him to the bedroom, a foolish mist of tears covered her eyes.

Perhaps she *was* dreaming to think this connection between them could last. That this night might not be the last she'd spend in his bed. But for now, he and tonight were all she had. And she was going to cling to both with all her might.

By midmorning the next day, the snowy clouds parted and the sun came out to make a brilliant glare on the snow-covered fields and mountains. And later that afternoon, Beatrice watched with a sinking heart as rivulets of water began to run off the roof of the house while the snow on the road shrank to little more than white patches.

The inevitable had come and her temporary miracle was over. She tried not to feel sad or disillusioned. She tried to tell herself that Kipp cared enough to ask her to stay. At least for a few more days. But deep inside, she knew he wasn't ready to accept her love. Maybe he never would be ready. And that was the fear that was weighing on her the most.

Since she'd made friends with the cats, the two of them had taken to following her around the house. Beatrice enjoyed their company and they seemed to like the conversations she carried on with them. This afternoon they had joined her in the kitchen and now they were stretched lazily at her feet as she stood at the cabinet chopping vegetables for stew.

When she heard a truck stop and then footsteps crossing the back porch, she and both cats looked around as the door opened and Kipp stepped into the kitchen. With at least an hour of daylight left, she knew this time of the evening was a busy one for the ranch hands.

"You're quitting work early today?" she asked.

"Ben's handling the last of the barn chores. Get your coat and things. We're going to the big house."

She stared at him and he frowned.

"Why are you acting so surprised? I told you that I'd take you to see Andrea before you left for Utah."

Yes, he'd told her last night at dinner, but this morning when he'd left for work, he'd not mentioned anything about it. In fact, he'd been quiet and preoccupied, and she'd decided not to press him with questions about anything. "I'll be ready in two minutes," she told him.

After hurrying out of the kitchen, she gathered her coat and gloves from the bedroom, then took a moment to swipe a bit of pink lipstick onto her lips. She didn't have time to do anything about her messy bun or pale cheeks. But it didn't matter what sort of impression she left on Kipp's stepmother. Beatrice was more interested in sizing up the woman who'd caused the Starr siblings so much distress.

On the short drive to the main ranch house, Beatrice went over in her mind the things she shouldn't say to Andrea. As for the things she should say, she decided to play that part of the meeting by ear.

"Are you nervous about this?" Kipp asked as he steered the truck over the wide, bumpy cattle guard.

She looked at him, and as always when her gaze collided with his, she felt a tiny jolt. "Nervous? No. Are you?"

"No. But if anyone else had asked me to do this, I would've refused."

His remark disappointed her as much as the melting snow. "I appreciate you taking time out to do this for me, Kipp. And I'm sorry I'm causing you to do something you don't want to do."

His short laugh was full of sarcasm. "You've said that several times these past few days."

"I guess I have," she said dully. "Because there've been plenty of times you've made me feel like an albatross around your neck."

He grimaced. "Have I? I guess I just don't have a gentleman's finesse when dealing with a lady."

Suddenly she'd had enough and she burst out, "Stop it! If this is the way you're going to behave, turn this damn truck around and take me back to the house. I don't need this from you. Especially not now! What's the matter with you, anyway?"

He softly banged the heel of his hand against the steering wheel, then shook his head. "I don't know, Bea. I'm sorry. Truly. I have lots of things on my mind. That's all."

Things like her and everything that had happened between them, she supposed. Did he think any of this was easy for her? These past few days she'd been learning what it was like to lose her heart completely and irrevocably to a man. And all the while fearing he didn't want it.

With a heavy sigh, she shook her head. "I'm sorry, too. I realize I'm asking a lot from you. But I hope— one of these days you'll understand why I'm doing this."

"Yeah. One of these days," he murmured.

Near the front of the house, he drew the truck to a halt. Beatrice waited for him to help her down from the cab, and as they started toward the porch, she instinctively reached for his hand.

"Does Andrea know we're coming? Or is this going to be a surprise?"

"I talked to her earlier," he said. "She's expecting us."

As they stepped onto the wide porch, Beatrice noticed it had been swept clean of snow and a welcome mat lay at the foot of the door.

Kipp punched the doorbell and only a few seconds passed before the door swung wide and Beatrice found herself staring in fascination at Andrea Starr.

Somewhere in her fifties, she was tall and slender with brunette hair that was pulled up at the back and fastened with a clip. From the bits of remarks Kipp had made of his stepmother, Bea had imagined her with hard features. Instead, they were delicate and pretty.

She smiled at the both of them and pushed the door open wider. "Hello. Please come in."

Beatrice entered the house with Kipp following directly behind her.

"I have coffee waiting in the living room," she said as she dealt with the door. "You know the way, Kipp."

Beatrice felt his hand curve beneath her elbow and she glanced up at him as he urged her down a long entryway. His face was stoic, but she'd learned enough about him to know there was a swirl of emotions going on behind his unmoving features.

At the end of the foyer, he guided her into a spacious room filled with two couches and four armchairs all covered in copper-brown fabric. Bright serape-striped throw pillows added splashes of color, while a wide picture window exposed a view of the mountains to the north. A long coffee table made of varnished split logs sat in front of one of the couches, while a tray holding a large thermos, three cups, a small pitcher of cream and a sugar bowl sat near one end.

Earlier, as they'd traveled up the long drive, Beatrice had spotted smoke spiraling from a chimney, so she'd expected the room to have a fireplace, but it didn't. Which led her to believe there was most likely a den somewhere in another part of the house.

The three of them paused in the middle of the room, while Kipp quickly introduced the two women. "Andrea, I'd like for you to meet Beatrice Hollister," he told her. "And, Bea, this is my stepmother, Andrea Starr."

The fact that Kipp had introduced the woman as his stepmother caught Beatrice off guard. She'd expected him to simply say Andrea's name and leave off the stepmother connection. And because she was a bit rattled, it took Beatrice a moment to react to the woman's outstretched hand.

"I'm glad to meet you, Beatrice. This is so nice of you to come."

Andrea's hand was soft and smooth and perfectly manicured, with her ring finger adorned with a square emerald surrounded by diamonds. Her handshake was firm and welcoming.

"Thank you, Ms. Starr. I'm glad to meet you, too. I hope I haven't interrupted anything important."

"Not at all. When Kipp told me you two would be stopping by, I was thrilled." She gestured toward the couch by the table where the coffee was waiting. "Please, you two have a seat."

Beatrice and Kipp took a seat together on the couch, while Andrea dealt with the coffee.

"Cream and sugar?" she asked Beatrice.

"No, thank you. I drink it plain."

She handed Beatrice the cup she'd filled with coffee, then poured another cup and added cream to it before she served it to Kipp. Which told her that the woman knew her stepson far better than she'd first expected.

After Andrea poured herself a cup, she sat directly across from them in one of the big armchairs. Dressed warmly in a pair of jeans and a heavy cable-knit sweater, she wore ankle boots that were an abbreviated form of cowboy boots. She was clearly attractive and stylish and Beatrice could easily see why Trent Starr had made her his wife.

"I didn't know until today that Kipp had company," she said to Beatrice. "I think it's nice you were here for the New Year holiday. What do you think of our ranch?"

Our ranch. Not *my* ranch. Beatrice wondered if Kipp noticed Andrea's wording, but she didn't bother to glance at him. She knew without looking that he wouldn't be expressing much emotion in front of his stepmother.

Beatrice smiled at her. "I was shocked to see all the snow. But the ranch is beautiful. I imagine in spring it's even more so."

"Oh yes. The fields are full of wildflowers and most of the time you can see deer and elk feeding among the cattle." She sipped from her cup, then asked, "Are you going to be staying with Kipp for a while?"

Was her question simply a cordial one, or was she trying to pry into Kipp's personal life? "I—uh—"

"Bea has to get back to Utah. She's only waiting for the roads to clear."

Beatrice might have imagined it, but Andrea actually looked disappointed at Kipp's news.

"Oh, that's too bad. I was hoping you were planning on staying awhile. Kipp needs your company and I'd enjoy having another woman around here to talk to. What do you do, Ms. Hollister?"

"Please call me Bea," Beatrice told her.

Andrea smiled. "Okay, Bea. As long as you call me Andrea. I'd like for us to be on a first-name basis."

"I'd like that, too," Beatrice told her, then answered her earlier question. "I work in a boutique called Canyon Corral. We carry women's clothing and footwear, along with fragrances and jewelry and some household items. Everything in the store has a Western or bohemian flavor."

"Sounds like a fun place to shop. We have some nice boutiques in Burley. You should take the time to visit them before you leave."

Beatrice had been hoping that once the weather improved, Kipp would take her on a little tour of the nearby town, but she wasn't holding her breath and waiting for that to happen. The signals she'd been getting from him today were anything but inviting.

"Bea is a fashion designer." Kipp spoke up. "She's probably going to make a name for herself someday in the fashion world."

Beatrice turned a look of disbelief at him. Where had that come from? she wondered. With an awkward little laugh, she said to Andrea, "Kipp is exaggerating a little. You can tell by the way I look today that I'm hardly a fashionista. But I do have a degree in fashion design. I don't have big plans, though. I only want to create clothing, mostly ranching and Western themed, on a very small scale."

"Oh. I'm impressed. I'd love for you to design something for me. My niece is getting married this summer. A huge affair on a ranch near Reno, Nevada. I need something special to wear for the wedding."

Was this woman serious? Or was all this friendly conversation just a mind game she was playing with Kipp? Beatrice wasn't sure. One thing for certain: she was definitely having a hard time imagining Andrea as a murderess.

"If you're serious, I'd be glad to work up a sketch," Beatrice told her.

Andrea bestowed a wide smile on her. "I'm very serious. And I'd be happy to pay whatever you think the job is worth," she said, then asked, "Is this the first time you've been to Idaho?"

"Yes. I learned I had a grandmother living in Coeur d'Alene. She's the reason for my visit to your state."

Andrea glanced from Beatrice to Kipp and back again. "Oh. I thought you were only here to spend time with Kipp."

Oddly enough, the whole purpose of the trip had ended up feeling as though it was to bring her and Kipp together. And maybe in the broader scheme of things it had happened for that reason. But why would fate bring them together, only to have it all end with a painful goodbye? She didn't want to ponder the answer to that question.

"Uh—no. But Kipp has been a wonderful host."

Andrea eyed her stepson as she carefully sipped her coffee. "I'm glad to hear it. I rarely see Kipp. Warren sees him every day, of course. But Kipp is a stranger here at the house."

Beatrice hardly knew what to say to that and Kipp didn't offer any sort of remark. After an awkward stretch of silence, Andrea asked, "How is Clementine? Warren tells me you visited her over the Christmas holiday."

"Clementine is good," Kipp said in a matter-of-fact voice. "She's going to marry Bea's brother."

The look of surprise on Andrea's face couldn't have been an act, and it was clear to Beatrice that he'd not discussed anything about his sister with this woman. How sad, she thought. The Starrs had once been a family. Now they were distant.

After a moment, Andrea said, "I'm glad to hear she's happy."

Next to her, Beatrice could feel Kipp growing stiff and tense, and for his sake, she promptly changed the subject. After a few more minutes of conversation, they finished their coffee and Kipp announced they needed to leave.

As Andrea saw them to the door, she said, "I do hope you'll come back for another visit, Bea. It would be fun to take a shopping trip over to Idaho Falls. You could give me all kinds of fashion pointers."

Come back? Beatrice didn't want to leave. She was afraid that once she did drive away, Kipp would forget her and everything that had happened between them.

Clearing her throat, Beatrice said, "Yes. That would be fun."

Andrea reached for her hand, and as she shook it, Beatrice thought she saw a faint mist of tears in the woman's eyes. But surely she was mistaken. Andrea was supposed to be greedy and unfeeling. She supposedly cheated on her husband and eventually caused him to take his last breath. Why would she be sentimental over saying goodbye? It didn't jibe with the picture Kipp and Clementine had painted of the woman.

"Goodbye, Bea. Take care and thank you for coming by."

"Yes. I'm glad I did. Goodbye, Andrea."

Kipp reached for her hand, and as he led her across the porch and out to the truck, she wondered if the truth about his father's death would ever come to light. But more importantly, would Kipp ever be able to push the pain aside and accept the love she was offering him?

Chapter Fifteen

Kipp was a bit surprised when Beatrice remained quiet on their way back to his house. He'd expected her to be rattling on about Andrea and telling him the kind of vibes she'd gotten while talking with his stepmother. In any case, he was relieved that she didn't seem eager to talk about the meeting. His mind was too wrapped up in tonight and how he was going to tell Beatrice their time together was over.

When he braked the truck to a stop at the back of the house, he left the motor running. "I'm going back to the ranch yard to help the guys finish the evening chores," he told her.

Frowning slightly, she looked at him. "Are you okay?"

"I'm fine," he lied. "Why do you ask?"

Shrugging, she reached for the door handle to let herself out. "Never mind. I'll see you later."

Kipp watched her walk partway to the back porch before he turned the truck around and gunned it down the road to the ranch yard. The snow was melting fast and his dreams along with it, he thought miserably.

* * *

Since early this morning, Beatrice had known something was wrong with Kipp. It wasn't until the two of them had eaten the stew she'd made for supper and migrated to the living room in front of the fire that she finally learned exactly what was on his mind. Yet even then, her mind couldn't absorb exactly what he was telling her.

Frowning with confusion, she stared at him. "Did I hear you right? You want me to sleep in the guest bedroom tonight?"

When he didn't look at her, Beatrice wanted to reach over and yank his chin around and force his gaze to meet hers.

"You heard right."

"What's the matter? My snoring been keeping you awake?" she attempted to joke.

He didn't laugh. "You don't snore."

"Oh. Then why don't you want me to sleep with you?"

He huffed out a breath of frustration. "Because we wouldn't sleep. Not much. And you'll be leaving in the morning and—"

"I will?" she asked softly.

"The roads are fine," he said curtly. "You can drive home now."

A heavy weight struck her chest and made it difficult to breathe. "What if I don't want to go?"

Frowning at her, he said, "Damn it, Bea, don't make this harder than it already is. We both knew this—thing—this lust between us would have to end. Well, going cold turkey tonight is the simplest way to end it."

The weight in her chest turned to all-out pain. "Lust? Is that all you've felt for me?"

He left the couch and walked over to stand on the fireplace hearth. Beatrice followed him.

"Is it?" she demanded.

He shook his head. "Don't push me for answers. I don't have any to give you. I only know that your life is back in Utah. Your job is there."

"I can find a job in Burley."

He scowled. "Your family is in Utah. Your twin is in Utah. You wouldn't be happy away from them."

"I'd be happy here if you wanted me," she said simply.

He let out a loud groan. "Oh, Bea, you're being naive. I have nothing to offer you. This house, the barns, the livestock. None of it is mine. All I own is two horses and two saddles and a truck."

Her expression hopeful, she rested her palms against his chest. "I'm not being naive. I know the situation with the ranch. Do you think that matters to me? I don't care what possessions you have. Or what you don't have. You are the important thing to me."

"And how long do you think I would remain the most important? It wouldn't take long for you to realize you'd given up too much." He practically sneered the words at her, then shook his head with regret. "I'm sorry, Bea. I don't want to hurt you. I only want you to understand— why it has to be this way."

"Understand? I do, Kipp. I see it all very clearly. Especially now that I've talked with Andrea."

His eyes widened and she could see that her remark had jolted him. Good, she thought. He needed to be shaken until the scales of bitterness fell from his eyes.

"Leave her out of this. She has nothing to do with you and me."

"You're wrong, Kipp. Indirectly, she *does* have something to do with you and the way you've been living these past years since your father died. You blame her for everything. You've never stopped to consider that your father was the one who did you wrong by willing everything to Andrea."

He sucked in a sharp breath at the same time red color flooded his face. "That's a hell of a thing to say to me! I don't believe Dad had that will made. He wouldn't have done that to me and Clem! Andrea falsified it! I'll believe that until the day I die!"

"If that's so, then Flint will uncover the truth. In the meantime, you need to quit living in the past. You need to make a life of your own—you need to quit being afraid of the future. Afraid to include me in your life."

His nostrils flared with anger. "Damn right I'm afraid. Dad's life was ruined by two women. I don't want to follow in his footsteps!"

Sickened by what she was hearing, she turned away from him. "Don't worry. You won't have to."

She started out of the room and he called after her.

"Where are you going?"

"To pack. And to make sure I don't leave anything of mine behind. I wouldn't want you to be bothered with any reminders of Bea Hollister and the hell trip you took with her."

The last of her words were gruff with tears, but she managed to get them out before she hurried from the room and away from the sight of him.

Kipp slept very little that night. Without Beatrice by his side, the bed felt cold and empty, yet all the while he tossed and turned, he told himself it was something he'd get used to. He'd lived alone for all this time. He could do it again.

Long before daylight, he heard Beatrice stirring in the next room, and by the time he'd climbed out of bed and pulled on his jeans, he heard her walking out to the kitchen.

He found her there with her two bags sitting by the door. The cats were watching her every move as she pulled on her coat and wrapped a muffler around her neck.

"Isn't it kinda early to be leaving? The sun isn't yet up."

Her blue eyes were cold as she turned and looked at him. "I shouldn't have to remind you that my truck has headlights. You drove it for several hundred miles."

It wasn't like her to be sarcastic. The stone-faced woman standing before him wasn't anything like the Beatrice he'd fallen in love with. And yes, he did love her. He could admit that much to himself now. But even admitting his feelings didn't change facts. He wasn't the right man for her and she'd soon come to that realization, too.

He took a few steps toward her, then forced himself to stop. He feared if he went too close, he'd forget everything and drag her into his arms. He'd kiss her until they were back in his bed and the plan of her leaving was discarded.

"Yes," he said dully. "Your truck is well equipped. If all goes well, you should be safely back on Stone Creek by midafternoon."

"Back where I belong. Right?"

Why was pain consuming his whole body? Her leaving was for the best. She'd be happy back with her family and friends, her job and life on Stone Creek. She had so much there and would have so little here. He couldn't ask her to stay. He couldn't do that to her.

"That's the way I see it."

Her gaze momentarily clashed with his and the tears he saw forming on her lashes made him sick. He might be a bastard for hurting her now. But at least he wasn't going to make his father's mistake and try to hang on to a woman who was all wrong for him.

"That's the way you'll always see things as long as you keep wearing blinders." She opened the back door, then bent over and picked up her bags. "Goodbye, Kipp."

"Let me carry your bags out to the truck for you," he offered.

"No, thank you. I'm traveling alone now."

She slipped out the door, then shut it firmly behind her, and when he caught the sound of her truck firing and driving away, he decided it was the worst sound he'd ever heard in his life.

Two weeks later, a cold rain had been falling for most of the morning. As a result, the customer traffic in Canyon Corral had been extremely slow. Beatrice normally loved having the boutique filled with customers. She liked interacting with the women and helping them make decisions about purchases. But this morning she was grateful for the quiet time. She'd woken this morning feeling even more despondent than she had when she'd first arrived home. Maybe because after two weeks, without one word from Kipp, it had become painfully clear that whatever had been between them was now well and truly over.

Since she'd returned to Stone Creek, she'd confided to her mother and Bonnie that she'd fallen in love with Kipp, but he'd not been interested in having a woman in his life on a full-time basis. As for her father, Beatrice hadn't told him about her heartache or even hinted to him that Kipp had been anything more to her than a traveling companion. She knew that Hadley liked and respected Kipp and she'd not wanted to change her father's opinion about him.

Your life is back in Utah.

Kipp's words drifted through her mind as she strolled over to the front of the store and stared out at the wet street. This little town and her home on Stone Creek had been her life for twenty-six years. But now she felt as though a part of her was missing. It was still back in Idaho on the Rising Starr with Kipp and she wondered if the pain of that reality would ever go away.

With a heavy sigh, she went to another part of the store and began to hang newly arrived merchandise on a round rack. She'd worked her way through half of the box when the bell over the door rang.

Turning to greet the customer, she was a bit surprised to see Bonnie entering the store. Normally, the late mornings were a busy time in her father's office, with the phone ringing continually and stacks of paperwork from Hadley for Bonnie to get done before the day was finished.

"Hi, sissy! What are you doing here in town? Aren't you supposed to be at work?"

Bonnie greeted her with a hug and a kiss on the cheek. "Dad has spent so much time at the ranch yard here lately, he's staying in his office to get caught up on things. He said he'd handle things for me."

Beatrice eyed her sister. "And you're using your time off to do some shopping?"

"A *little* shopping, maybe. I'm mostly here to have a twin talk with you."

A *twin talk* was what the sisters called a serious conversation about something important to both of them. Beatrice wasn't sure what Bonnie had on her mind, but if it had anything to do with Kipp and her making a fool of herself over him, she could do without the lecture.

Turning to a stack of new merchandise she'd laid out on a nearby table, she picked up a tiered skirt and fastened the waist to a hanger. "We were both home last night—why didn't you talk with me then?"

"Because I thought I could reason with you better if we were away from the ranch and the presence of our parents."

Beatrice frowned at her. "Reason with me? What have I done?"

Bonnie rolled her blue eyes. "Nothing. That's just it. You're not doing one darned thing to get your life back on track."

She hung the skirt on a circle rack. "I didn't know it was off track," she said in the most casual voice she could muster.

Bonnie groaned. "You know, I always told you that you were wasting your time taking drama classes in high school, and I was right. You can't act worth a damn."

It wasn't often that Bonnie used a curse word, and the fact that she used one now caught Beatrice's attention. "Are you angry with me about something? If I said anything—"

"Yes, I'm angry with you! I—"

Bonnie paused in midsentence as the bell over the door rang and two customers entered the boutique.

Leaving her sister, Beatrice made her way over to the two women to ask if they needed help finding anything. When the pair assured her they were merely browsing, Beatrice went back to where Bonnie was waiting.

"Okay, get on with whatever you have to say, sis. I'm busy. And I would appreciate you making this twin talk a quick one."

"All right, be sarcastic. At least you're showing a little life. This past couple of weeks since you've returned from Idaho, you've been just a step above comatose. And I'm getting tired of your pitiful behavior. Tired of seeing you moping around miserable—with your heart breaking!"

Turning her back to her sister, Beatrice blinked back the moisture filling her eyes. "This is not the time or the place for such a conversation! Couldn't you at least wait until I got home from work?"

"No. I'm not waiting another minute. If necessary, I'll go tell your boss you need to take off early—that you're ill. Which would hardly be a lie! You're definitely sick. In the heart and the head."

"Look, Bonnie, go ahead and say 'I told you so.' Remind me of the day before I left for Idaho with Kipp when you warned me not to fall for the guy. I thought you were overdoing the big-sister act. But I should've listened to you. Now I realize I was a fool with the common sense of a child."

Bonnie's arm came around Beatrice's shoulders and gave her an encouraging squeeze. "Oh, Bea. I'm hardly an expert about these things. You've had a ton of boyfriends and I've had a handful, which ought to tell you how far

I get with men. But this time with you—I don't think you were wrong to fall in love with Kipp. Where you're wrong, sissy, is not going back to Idaho and making it crystal clear to him how you feel. And you need to tell him that you don't intend to let him go—ever!"

Beatrice could feel her jaw dropping as she stared at her sister. "Are you serious? What good would that do? Kipp has it firmly in his head that I wouldn't be happy there—with him."

Bonnie turned Beatrice just enough to allow them to look directly at each other. "*Would* you be happy there? And don't give me a flip answer. I want the truth."

Suddenly tears were making it impossible to see her sister's face. "Oh, Bonnie—of course I would miss my life here. And I'd miss you the very most. But Kipp is the man I love. I'd be happy wherever he is. Someday—when you find a man you love—you'll know what I mean."

Bonnie's expression was full of empathy and love as she gave Beatrice a brief hug. "Someday I hope I find what you have, Bea. Real love isn't easy to come by. That's why you can't stand by and lose him over pride or stubbornness. I want you to pack your bags and head back to Idaho."

Beatrice looked at her with hope and wonder. "Do you really think I might change his mind? So much of his reasoning is mixed up with the past—I just don't know how to fight that, Bonnie."

"It's up to you to pull him out of all that muck he's been living with and show him the future."

Bonnie was right. She couldn't give up on Kipp. No matter what he said. No matter how much he tried to send her away, she was going to stand her ground and make him understand that her love for him would never change or die.

She grabbed both of Bonnie's hands and gave them a hard squeeze. "You're right, sissy. I have to go. Just as soon as Dahlia can arrange for someone to work in my place. Will you help me pack most of my things? Because this time I'm going to stay."

Laughing, Bonnie gave her another hug. "Except for visits, of course!"

"Yes. Plenty of visits," Beatrice promised, while in her heart she prayed that once she arrived on the Rising Starr, Kipp wouldn't turn her away.

Three days later, Kipp was staying late at the barn to bottle-feed a baby calf when Warren entered the small holding pen. The four men had been working hard all day hauling feed to several small herds located over the mountain on the south side of the ranch. Now the hour was growing late and he and Warren were still trying to finish up the last of the barn chores before they quit for the night.

"She's coming along, Kipp. Getting worn out with the bottle-feeding?"

At the sound of the foreman's voice, Kipp looked away from the red-and-white calf nursing the bottle he was holding to see Warren standing over by the gate, pulling on his jacket. Tall with dark hair, he was somewhere in his late forties, which made him several years younger than Andrea. He had a stocky build and a wide, plain face, and most of the time he didn't say much. At least, not to him or Ben and Zach. And when he did say something, it was usually just to go over what needed to be done around the ranch.

Like he saw Andrea, Kipp had often viewed the man as the enemy. After all, he and Andrea had an affair going even before his father had died. But in the past few days, something had caused him to take another look at the man. Kipp found himself wondering if, like him, Warren had simply been drawn in by the love of a woman.

His gaze fell back to the tiny heifer. "I don't mind feeding her. It's good to see her getting stronger every day. And her mama should be over her mastitis in a few days and be able to feed her naturally."

"Yeah. The vet is coming out tomorrow to take a look at the bull's infected horn. While he's here on the ranch, I'll have him check the cow."

"She's looking much better. But I'll feel better about her if the vet checks her."

Warren buttoned his jacket, then stuffed his hands in his pockets. "Well, I'm off to the house. I hope you plan to go home after you finish with the calf. You've been looking peaked."

If Kipp's misery was showing so much that even the foreman had noticed, he must look like hell.

"Yeah. I'll shut the barn down and head out soon," Kipp told him.

Warren left the building, and while Kipp finished feeding the baby calf, he thought again about the foreman's remark. Other than what Andrea might have told him, Warren didn't know about Kipp's close connection to Beatrice. Other than the fact that she'd stayed at Kipp's house during the heavy snowstorm. Ben and Zach didn't know, either, although both of them had made subtle remarks to the fact that he hadn't been acting like himself.

Hell, Kipp wasn't himself at all. Ever since she'd driven

away that dark morning, he'd turned into someone he didn't recognize. The house was cold and empty without her. And surprisingly, it wasn't the bedroom where her memory haunted him the most. No, it was the kitchen. Each time he entered the room, he could see her standing at the cookstove or working at the cabinet counter with the cats at her feet. He could hear her saying how she loved the room and how she wanted a poinsettia to set in the middle of the table.

Yesterday, when he'd gone into Burley to pick up a few supplies, he'd seen a live poinsettia in the grocery store, and on a foolish whim, he brought it home and placed it on the table. For her.

But buying her a Christmas flower yesterday was too little, too late, Kipp. Besides, she needed more than a flower. She needed you. She needed your love. And you refused to give it to her.

Cursing at the tormenting voice in his head, he looked down to see the calf had drained the bottle and was butting the nipple for more.

"No. That's all for now, little one." He gently stroked the calf's face and down its sides before he nudged it over to the corner of the pen where a nice bed of straw would keep it warm and cozy through the night.

With the calf settled, he left the pen and walked over to collect his jacket where he'd hung it on a nail on the wall. He was pulling the garment on when his hand connected with the paper he'd stuffed deep into the pocket. It was a letter he'd gotten from Clementine this morning, and even though he'd already read it, he decided to pull it out and read it again.

Thank God living back in civilization hadn't changed her that much, he thought. Getting her handwritten letters in the mail was so much nicer than a few abbreviated sentences of a text message.

He opened the letter and picked up reading the second paragraph.

> *...I could go on and on about Quint and the sheep and living on Stone Creek. It's a whole new world for me, Kipp. And for the first time in years, I'm truly happy.*
>
> *Hadley is helping Quint find a contractor to start building the new sheep barn and we hope for it to be finished by this spring and shearing time. My biggest news is that we've decided to get married on Valentine's Day. The ceremony will be on the ranch and not all that big if we can keep Claire and Hadley from adding to the guest list. I really wish you could be here for my wedding, Kipp. It would mean so much to me to have my brother join in on our happiness. I've not mentioned it to Mom yet. And your guess is as good as mine as to whether she cares enough to make the trip. But either way, I'll send her an invitation. Whatever she decides to do will be okay with me. After all, Kipp, I've learned that I had to find my own inner peace before I could be good for Quint, or anyone else. I figure it's the same for Mom.*
>
> *Everyone here is doing fine. Beatrice seems to be especially down since she returned from her trip. But Quint seems to think it struck his sister pretty hard to find the grandmother she never knew in a state of dementia. I know it had to be*

tough on her. I think Hadley wishes he'd never sent her on the trip, but how was he to know?

Hunter is coming home next week and bringing all his rodeo stock with him. I can't wait to look it over. Especially the saddle broncs. Maybe he'll let me try to ride one. Ha ha! I'm kidding, but I doubt it would buck any harder than some of the colts I've started.

The weather here has finally cleared and...

The sound of a horse softly nickering had him lifting his head and he glanced around to see Zach's mare gazing wistfully down the barn to where his two geldings were stalled. The interruption reminded him it was getting late.

He quickly folded the letter and was stuffing it back in his pocket when his cell phone rang. His first instinct was to let the call go to voice mail. But fearing it might be something important, he pulled the phone from his shirt pocket to glance at the name on the caller ID.

Nuttah! What could be going on with her?

He punched the accept button and jammed the phone to his ear. "Hello, Nuttah. What are you doing still up at this hour?"

She laughed. "You think I'm so old that I go to bed as soon as it gets dark out? I'm getting ready to go out dancing. What are you doing?"

"Nothing that crazy," he told her. "I was about to leave the barn to go home."

"Oh. Well, I won't keep you long. Fred will be here to pick me up in a few minutes. I just had to call because— you've been on my mind these past few days. I'm worried about you."

Damn. "Has Clem been talking to you about me?"

"No. I haven't talked to Clem since she called me on New Year's Day. Why? Is something wrong with her?"

He walked over and took a seat on an overturned feed bucket. "No. She's doing great."

"Uh-huh. My feeling was right. It's you that hasn't been doing so good."

Closing his eyes, he bit back a groan. Nuttah and her feelings. Beatrice and her feelings. The two women scared him. Mostly because they both had the uncanny ability to see inside him.

"I've been okay, Nuttah. You know how busy things are on the ranch at this time of year. We're working overtime."

She paused, then said, "Clem told me you went to Coeur d'Alene with her fiancé's sister. This sorrow you're feeling wouldn't have anything to do with her, would it?"

"Sorrow? Hell, Nuttah. Do I sound like I'm in mourning or something?"

"Don't try to fool me, Kipp. In my heart you will always be my son. And I saw you in a vision yesterday. You were gaunt and weak and your eyes were black with tears. A shiny crow came down from the sky and landed on your shoulder. The bird tried to talk to you, to advise you, but you wouldn't listen."

"Oh, Nuttah, you take those visions of yours too literally. Anyway, I don't go around talking to crows. Why would I listen to one?"

She snorted. "Yes, why would you? That has always been your trouble, Kipp. You won't listen to anyone or anything. The earth is talking to you. The animals and birds are speaking to you. Even the sun and the moon and the stars have something to say. You need to open your heart and listen to them. Then you'll understand these feelings that are tormenting you."

Nuttah had always been a mystical and spiritual soul. Because she'd been a second mother to him and he loved her, he would never mock her for any reason. Besides, he'd never known her to be wrong about anything.

"How do you know I'm tormented?"

"How do I know a bear lives in the woods or a bison roams the plains? I just know. Has Andrea been giving you problems?"

"Oddly enough, Nuttah, Andrea has been—decent. More so than she's been in years. No, I'm not worried about Andrea. At least, not right now. This is— Oh hell, you know you're right. You're always right. I am miserable, Nuttah. And it is about the trip to Coeur d'Alene. I was with Beatrice for several days and she ended up being snowed in with me here on the ranch. While she was here we—you could say we got—close."

"And you fell in love with her," Nuttah said knowingly.

"Yes."

"Did she fall in love with you?"

Kipp squeezed his eyes shut and swiped a hand over his face. "I think so. She didn't say it in words, but she was trying to tell me in so many other ways. And I— like you just said—I wouldn't listen. I guess I shut her out like I did the crow in your vision."

"Hmm. I knew the vision meant something. Now I understand."

Kipp dropped his hand and stared out at the deep shadows filling the interior of the barn. "What's there to understand, Nuttah? I sent her away. I told her it wouldn't work. Now I'm miserable without her."

"Why wouldn't it work? Is she too soft to live your kind of life?"

Soft? Oh yes, she was soft inside and out. She was giving and loving and everything he could ever want. But there was a toughness to her that he wouldn't initially have guessed she possessed, and when she'd stood there telling him what a coward he was, it struck him that she wasn't just a pretty girl with fashionable clothes and a yen for adventure. She'd been raised a ranch girl. She had grit. The kind she would need to live in these Idaho mountains. But would she be willing to? Now that he'd hurt her and sent her away?

"She's not soft or weak. But, Nuttah, what do I have to give her? To keep her and make her happy? You know how things turned out for Dad. I couldn't live through that kind of drama and pain."

"Oh, my son, if you'd only listened to the crow, he would've told you. Your love is what she wants and needs. Not what money can buy."

Beatrice had tried to tell him that very thing. But he'd wanted to dismiss her argument. He'd not wanted to believe that he and he alone would be enough for a woman like her. But now, after all these days of misery, he had to believe in himself.

"Beatrice doesn't know how I feel about her. I wasn't brave enough to tell her. I thought—it would be best all around if she didn't know."

Nuttah sighed. "Kipp, you've tried so hard not to be like your father that along the way you forgot to be yourself."

He didn't know how Nuttah did it, but she always managed to put her finger right on the sore spot.

Heaving out a heavy breath, he said, "Beatrice accused

me of living in the past and she was right. I've been traveling a long, lonely road, Nuttah. And I didn't think it could get any worse until I traveled all those miles with Bea."

"You've not finished your journey, Kipp. You have to travel down to Utah. Love is too precious to lose. Tell this young woman what's in your heart. If she really cares, she'll want to be with you—no matter what."

Kipp wiped his face again, and this time when he stared into the shadows, he wasn't seeing everything he'd lost in the past. This time he was seeing the future with Beatrice at his side. And suddenly everything in his heart and mind righted itself.

"Nuttah, if you see that crow again, tell him for me that from now on, I'll listen."

There was a short pause, and then she said, "Travel safely, my boy. Good night."

She ended the call, and for the first time in days, Kipp left the barn with a spring in his step.

The bedroom the twins had shared all their lives looked as if a storm had blown through it. Duffel bags, suitcases and a few cardboard boxes were piled on the bed and the floor. Garments were strewn across both double beds, with some hanging halfway out of a dresser drawer.

Bonnie strained to push down the lid of a rolling suitcase and zip it shut. "Bea, this is a mountain of stuff! I'm not sure the back seat of your truck will hold all of this."

"You're forgetting there's a bed cover on the back of the truck. I can put most of these bags there and close it to keep everything nice and dry."

"Well, as long as you keep the lid safely locked. When you stop during the trip, you don't want your bags lifted while you're visiting the restroom or getting coffee."

"You sound like Flint," she said with a wry chuckle. "Always giving safety advice."

Bonnie walked over to where Beatrice was tossing makeup into a small travel bag.

"It's good to hear you laugh again, sissy. I was beginning to wonder if you'd lost all your sense of humor."

"I was beginning to wonder myself," she told her sister. "But now that I've decided to go to Idaho and confront Kipp, I'm getting my spunk back. Thanks to you, Bonnie, for jerking me out of the pity party I was throwing for myself."

"Thank Mom, too. Yesterday, she gave you one of the strongest scoldings I've ever heard her give to any of us about facing your problems head-on."

"I needed her scolding. It helped me put some steel back into my backbone."

Bonnie said, "I have to be honest, Bea. As much as I want you to be happy with Kipp in Idaho, it's going to be awfully hard not to have you here with me."

Beatrice swallowed as a lump in her throat threatened to choke her. "We'll talk every day and visit often. I promise." Dropping the makeup bag, she reached over and squeezed her sister's hand. "You know, Bonnie, we'll always be twins. Nothing will ever change that. But we also have to be ourselves, too. And I guess that time has come for our paths to go in different directions."

She was giving Bonnie a kiss on the cheek when a knock sounded on the bedroom door. Both women looked around to see their father poking his head around the door.

"Come in if you're brave enough, Dad," Bonnie said.

He chuckled. "I don't want to risk an injury. I'm here to tell Bea a young man is here to see her."

Beatrice threw back her head and groaned with frustration. The last thing she needed tonight was an old boyfriend making a pest of himself. "Whoever it is—tell him I'm too sick to come down. I have a cracking headache."

"Uh—I think you'd better tell him yourself, Bea."

"Dad, I—" The rest of her complaint was forgotten as the door swung wide and Kipp stepped into the room.

Beatrice stared in stunned fascination as he began to walk toward her, while Bonnie rushed out of the room and discreetly closed the door behind her.

"Kipp! What are you doing here?"

He gestured to the pile of bags and cases on the bed. "What are you doing? Running out on me?"

She opened her mouth to speak, but discovered she'd suddenly gone mute. It wasn't until she pressed a hand to her throat and swallowed that she was able to utter the words she needed to say. "I was planning to—run *to* you. Didn't Dad tell you?"

He closed the last steps between them, and Beatrice desperately wanted to throw herself against his chest, to hold him close and sob out the misery she'd gone through since she'd left the Rising Starr. But she couldn't do that. Not without knowing where they stood.

"The only thing Hadley told me was that you were planning to take another trip. From the looks of these bags, you're planning on a long one."

Her chest was aching. Not only to hold him, but to say all the things she'd been carrying in her heart. "I'm planning on a lifetime—however long that might be."

He reached for her hand and tears spilled from her eyes as he drew the back of it to his cheek. "I drove all this way to tell you I was wrong—about us. Wrong to send you away. I love you, Bea. It seems like I've always loved you. But I've been running scared. Afraid that I could never make you happy. That I'd be like Dad. He couldn't hold on to Mom, even though he tried in his own way. And Andrea—only God knows what actually went on between them. But these past days I've come to realize that I'm not my father. And you're not like those women. You're Bea. The woman I love. And will always love. I want to move on to the future with you. If you'll have me."

Suddenly she was laughing with pure joy and she flung her arms around his neck and held him with all her might. "That's the longest speech I've ever heard out of you."

He chuckled. "I had a few hundred miles to practice it. How did I do?"

She captured his face between her hands and looked into his eyes. "I love you with all my heart, Kipp. We're going to have a wonderful life together. Full of kids and joys. Trials and tribulations, and everything else that life throws at us."

He sealed her promise with a long, hungry kiss. Then, lifting his head, he smiled at her. "Do you think your father will approve of me taking his daughter back to Idaho and marrying her?"

"I should probably tell you that only yesterday Dad confessed something to me. He hatched up the idea to send the two of us together on the trip to Coeur d'Alene because he thought we were perfect for each other."

Her soft laugh was full of joy. "Go figure. My father is a matchmaker."

An astonished expression stole over his face and then he chuckled. "I'd better watch my step around him. The man is crafty."

She placed another kiss on his lips, then reached for his hand. "Come on. I think we should go let him know that his matchmaking worked."

"Yes. And to thank him for giving us the chance to fall in love."

Epilogue

With a warm breeze barely ruffling the leaves and a bright blue sky over the mountains, the June day on the Rising Starr Ranch couldn't have been more perfect for Beatrice and Kipp's wedding. A few minutes earlier, on the front lawn of the main house, beneath an arch twined with greenery and white roses, they had repeated their marriage vows and exchanged gold bands. When the minister proclaimed them man and wife, the seated guests had all clapped with happy approval, including Kipp and Clementine's mother, who'd surprised him by making the trip over from Boise to attend the wedding. And in spite of Nuttah's suspicious dislike of Andrea, Nuttah had still driven from Shelley to be with Beatrice and Kipp on their special day.

As for the other guests, the Hollisters were all there in their best Western attire, along with Blake Hollister, the manager of Three Rivers Ranch. He and his wife and children had been visiting Stone Creek and looking over the two families' partnered cattle when Hadley had convinced them to attend the wedding.

But the unexpected pleasure of having the Arizona Hollisters as part of the wedding guest list was not the most surprising thing to have happened. Beatrice and Kipp had been a bit stunned when Andrea had invited them to hold the ceremony and reception at the big house. She'd even insisted on helping with the preparations, including footing some of the cost with Claire and Hadley.

Now, with everyone gathered beneath the huge tent where the reception was being held, champagne was flowing, wedding cake was being consumed and live music was being played by a four-piece band. After Kipp and Beatrice had taken the first waltz around the portable floor, several couples had joined them until the open space was filled with dancers.

With his arm wound tightly around her waist and her hand in his, Beatrice felt as if she were drifting on a cloud instead of polished parquet.

She said, "This is wonderful to see so many of our family and friends here today. And they all seem to be enjoying themselves."

He glanced over at Clementine and Quint, who'd joined in on the dance. "Seeing my sister so happy and knowing that most of these people are now my family—it's almost surreal, Bea. I never thought I'd see all this on the Rising Starr and especially not at *my* wedding party. I still don't know what to think about Andrea. I can't figure out why she'd want to do this for me—us."

Beatrice pressed her cheek against his. "I'm very glad that you accepted her offer, Kipp. I think it will go a long way in healing the hurt that's gone on in your family for so long. I know you're still skeptical about her. And I can't blame you for feeling that way. But so far Flint's secret investigation has found nothing amiss with the autopsy or the will."

At the moment, Warren and Andrea were seated at a table with Beatrice's parents and appeared to be having a friendly conversation. To see the four of them together gave her hope that the old wounds of the past could eventually heal.

"For years she was cold and distant," Kipp said thoughtfully. "But I guess I'd be that way, too, toward anyone who accused me of murder. And I— Since I have you in my life, Bea, I've been trying to look at all sides of the situation. Maybe Andrea isn't guilty of anything—except marrying the wrong man."

She squeezed his hand. "I'm glad you said that, my darling. And I'm especially glad I can say that I've married the *right* man."

Easing his head back, he grinned at her, and her heart skipped a tiny beat. He would always be the most handsome and masculine man she'd ever seen, and she knew that no matter how old they grew to be, he would always make her pulse quicken with desire. She could only hope that Bonnie would find a man who'd give her this much joy.

"This is our wedding day. You have to say things like that to me," he told her. "And if I haven't told you twenty times already how gorgeous you look, I'm saying it again. Did you design your wedding gown, Mrs. Starr?"

Laughing at his nonsense, she glanced down at the floor-length satin dress overlaid with lace. Seed pearls edged the plunging V neckline and the pointed hems of the long, tight sleeves. The dress was very traditional, but that was the kind of marriage she wanted with Kipp. The same as her parents' marriage had been for the past forty-plus years.

"You know I didn't. I've been too busy with my new

job and *you*," she answered with a playful pinch to his arm. "But if Bonnie ever finds her right man, she might let me design hers."

Since she'd moved in with Kipp back in January, she'd taken a position as a manager of a boutique in Burley, and so far she was loving the job and making a new life in Idaho. Kipp often reminded her that he didn't want her to give up her dreams of designing just because of him. But she'd assured him that her biggest dreams were designing babies with him. Later on, after their children were on their way to being grown, she'd think about putting her degree to work.

"She'll find her man," Kipp said. "What one twin does the other has to do, too. Right?"

Beatrice laughed. "Right."

They circled the floor one more time before Kipp ushered her over to the refreshment table where Jack and Vanessa were filling their glasses with champagne.

"You'll have to excuse Van if she sounds a little tipsy," Jack joked. "Now that she's had the baby and can drink alcohol again, she's gone wild on me. I can't keep her away from the champagne."

Laughing, Vanessa playfully gouged a finger in her husband's ribs. "Sure, Jack. Tell them the truth. This is my first glass," she said, then winked at Beatrice and Kipp. "But it might not be my last."

"Good," Kipp told her. "We want everybody to enjoy the party."

Beatrice glanced around for Jack and Vanessa's three-month-old son. When she didn't see him in anyone's arms, she asked, "Where is little Jackson Hadley Hollister?"

"Aunt Bonnie took little Jack inside the house. He was getting sleepy," Vanessa told her. Then, lifting her glass, she slanted her husband a teasing look. "That's why I'm taking advantage of the moment."

Since Vanessa had become extremely busy being a mother, along with her teaching job in Beaver, she'd handed over the family-tree search to Bonnie. And recently, with a little undercover help from Rube and Walt, the twins at the Neighbors' Place, where Scarlett resided, the family had learned Scarlett and her late second husband had two daughters named Debra and Ruthann. So far, however, Bonnie hadn't been able to locate either woman.

"Are you two leaving on your honeymoon as soon as the reception is over?" Jack asked.

Kipp and Beatrice exchanged knowing smiles.

"No," Kipp told him. "But we're going as soon as spring roundup is over."

"We plan to drive back up to Coeur d'Alene for our honeymoon," Beatrice informed her brother and sister-in-law.

Vanessa's jaw dropped. "Surely not to see Scarlett?"

Beatrice nodded, then gazed lovingly at Kipp. "Yes. To see her and our twin friends. And enjoy the beautiful sights in the area. The little city holds a special place in our hearts."

Vanessa raised her brows, then chuckled. "I think I understand."

"Well, I see something I *don't* understand." Jack's eyes narrowed as he stared toward the opposite end of the tent. "Who is that woman with Hunter? I didn't see her earlier."

Beatrice looked around at the tall redhead walking at her brother's side. "I can tell you one thing. It isn't Willow!"

Kipp followed Beatrice's gaze. "You mean his ex-wife? The one he never got over?"

"Right," Jack muttered.

"Well, it looks like you all could have it wrong," Kipp quipped. "He just might be over her."

Laughing now, Beatrice leaned over and kissed her husband's cheek. "Why, Kipp, you're turning into a regular romantic."

"With a wife like you, what else could I be?"

Grinning, his eyes met hers, and in that moment Beatrice sent up a silent prayer of thanks for the two feet of snow that had fallen on New Year's Eve.

* * * * *

#3039 TAKING THE LONG WAY HOME
Bravo Family Ties • by Christine Rimmer

After one perfect night with younger rancher Jason Bravo, widowed librarian Piper Wallace is pregnant with his child. Co-parenting is a given. But Jason will do anything—even accompany her on a road trip to meet her newly discovered biological father—to prove he's playing for keeps!

#3040 SNOWED IN WITH A STRANGER
Match Made in Haven • by Brenda Harlen

Party planner Finley Gilmore loves an adventure, but being snowbound with Professor Lachlan Kellett takes *tempted by a handsome stranger* to a whole new level! Their chemistry could melt a glacier. But when Lachlan's past resurfaces, will Finlay be the one iced out?

#3041 A FATHER'S REDEMPTION
The Tuttle Sisters of Coho Cove • by Sabrina York

Working with developer Ben Sherrod should have turned Celeste Tuttle's dream project into a nightmare. Except the single father is witty and brilliant and so much more attractive than she remembered from high school. Could her childhood nemesis be Prince Charming in disguise?

#3042 MATZAH BALL BLUES
Holidays, Heart and Chutzpah • by Jennifer Wilck

Entertainment attorney Jared Leiman will do anything to be the guardian his orphaned niece needs. Even reunite with Caroline Weiss, his high school ex, to organize his hometown's Passover ball with the Jewish Community Center. Sparks fly...but he'll need a little matzah magic to win her over.